# FALSE ALARM

# FALSE ALARM

## VERONICA HELEY

**W❂RLDWIDE**®

TORONTO • NEW YORK • LONDON
AMSTERDAM • PARIS • SYDNEY • HAMBURG
STOCKHOLM • ATHENS • TOKYO • MILAN
MADRID • WARSAW • BUDAPEST • AUCKLAND

Recycling programs
for this product may
not exist in your area.

False Alarm

A Worldwide Mystery/March 2019

First published by Severn House Publishers, Ltd.

ISBN-13: 978-1-335-45532-1

**Printed in U.S.A.**

# FALSE ALARM

FALSE ALARM

# ONE

BEA ABBOT RAN a domestic agency which did not, repeat *not*, deal with murder…until, that is, she became involved in the affair of Lady Ossett's divorce.

*Wednesday late afternoon*

MAGGIE YELLED, 'My mother is a cow!'

Bea didn't bother to lift her eyes from her computer. 'What you mean is that she's a selfish, conniving woman who has done her best to ruin your life.'

'That's what I said. My mother is a cow! I could scream!'

Bea Abbot blinked. She'd never met Lady Ossett, but understood from Maggie that her mother was a shallow, pretty, fashionable woman who demanded lots of attention.

Bea said, 'Well; scream, then.'

Maggie was a tall, well-built girl. She opened her mouth and yelled. Her lungs were healthy, her range impressive. She made, as they say, the welkin ring.

Bea didn't cover her ears, but she was thankful that the agency had closed for the day and her staff long since departed, or she might have had people banging on her office door, demanding to know who was being murdered.

'Want to tell me about it?'

'No,' said Maggie. 'I'm going to scream and scream till I make myself sick!'

'How about breaking a plate or two? That's supposed to do the trick equally well.'

'Why not? The mood I'm in...' Dressed in jeans, low boots and a violently patterned sweatshirt, Maggie set off for the stairs.

Bea was over thirty years older, and she was wearing a slim pencil skirt and high heels. Nevertheless, she reached the first-floor kitchen just in time to see Maggie pulling the dishwasher open. 'Not those plates, Maggie. We've still got a complete set. What about the ones we keep for the cat? Top cupboard by the back door.'

Maggie screeched, but abandoned the dishwasher. She found a couple of mismatched plates in the cupboard and lifted one high above her head. 'I would like to—'

'Not that one, Maggie,' said Bea. 'You know Winston prefers it. Isn't there something more suitable in the saucepan cupboard?'

'What?' Maggie hesitated, then put the plate down. 'You're trying to get me to be reasonable. Well, it won't work. And don't tell me I should talk it over with my beloved boyfriend because he is an idiot. He thinks I should love and obey my mother—'

'That's because he's never met her,' said Bea.

'True,' said Maggie, and broke into a harsh laugh. She repeated the word, 'True.' Still laughing, she pounded the worktop with her fists. Closed her eyes. Put her head down on her arms, still laughing. Crying.

Bea pushed Maggie on to a high stool and put her arms about her. 'There, there. There, there.'

Presently, Maggie murmured, 'My mother is a cow.'

'I know. She is a selfish, conniving bitch.'

Maggie sniffed. 'I've never heard you use that word before.'

'Not even when that new girl in the office lost our

address list? Not even when the server went down last week?'

Maggie reached blindly for a box of tissues and blew her nose. Bea put the kettle on. Quiet descended; except that this new kettle was rather noisy. Bea didn't like noise and wondered if she should offer the kettle to Maggie to throw down the stairs into the courtyard below. Its destruction would be spectacular.

Only, it was now five o'clock on a dark winter's afternoon, and if you did drop anything from the balcony you probably wouldn't see the result. Also, they didn't have a spare kettle, so perhaps she'd better just make them some tea. Strong, with sugar. And see if there were any biscuits in the tin. Bea pushed a mug of tea at Maggie and sat down beside her.

Maggie had coloured her short-cropped hair purple to match her eyeshadow this week, but tears had smudged her mascara so that she looked like a panda. 'I could emigrate. There are still countries in the world where extradition treaties don't work, aren't there?'

'Mm. Would you want to live in one of those places?'

Maggie shook her head. 'There's no help for it. I'm doomed.'

'Tell me about it.'

Maggie reached for the box of tissues again and blew her nose. Thoroughly. 'There's nothing anyone can do. I've got to go back home to look after my mother.'

Bad news. Years of being denigrated by her mother, followed by a disastrous marriage and divorce, had left Maggie without any sense of self-worth.

Bea remembered how shy and socially inept the girl had been when she'd first drifted into the agency. 'I seem to remember that didn't work too well before.'

'You think I don't know it? Listen; I had an appointment at number twenty-seven this morning, right? The client wasn't happy with the toilet the plumber had installed, said it wasn't the one she'd chosen. The plumber said the client needed an optician not a plumber, so I arranged to meet them both at eleven to thrash it out.'

Maggie was making a name for herself as a project manager for building alterations. She could juggle half a dozen workmen on two sites and never let a tile fall to the ground…but she couldn't cope with Lady Ossett.

'Just as I reached the client's house, there was a phone call from my mother. She was crying. She wanted me to go round there straight away, that very minute. She said it was desperately important.' She blew her nose again. 'I should have known better.'

Bea pushed the tin of biscuits closer. 'Feed your face.'

Maggie took a biscuit. 'I hailed a taxi. I rang the client and the plumber to explain that there was an emergency. I suggested we meet later. They were both furious. The client had been going to give me another, bigger job if I'd managed to solve the problem with the plumber, but as it is… Anyway, I got up to my mother's and, wouldn't you know, she was on the phone to a friend, complaining about the noise from somebody's decorator or builder below, and could only spare the time to ask me to make her some tea and a sandwich. When I did, she said I'd used the wrong tea, and why wasn't there any lemon in it, and couldn't I cut the bread thinner?

'She went from one phone call to the other, rearranging a bridge party or a drinks party or something. She had me dashing around the flat, picking things up for her, and when I said I had to leave, she said she'd been putting a brave front on for my benefit, but I must realize she was in pieces and it would be too, too selfish of me not to help her when she was in such distress.' Maggie took another biscuit. 'It turns out my stepfather has left her.'

Bea counted on her fingers. 'Is he her third?'

'Fourth. Lucas. I liked him well enough, though I thought he was a fool to tie himself up with her, but… men see what they want to see, don't they? A pretty face, blonde hair, a good figure, lots of caresses and baby-blue eyes? They don't see the shrewd mind behind the blue eyes. Well, actually, I think Lucas did. She seemed to amuse him. She's an excellent hostess and she loved being Lady Muck and living in the penthouse. I thought it might last. But he's gone.'

'She wanted reassurance from you that she was still lovable?'

'She wanted me to fetch her best black from the cleaners. She had tickets for the theatre and wanted to wear that particular dress. Oh, and she wanted an escort for the evening, and why hadn't I learned to drive yet, it was extremely thoughtless of me not to realize she was going to need someone to keep her company, though not with that make-up that makes you look like a clown, and why you wear that stupid top, I do not know, because it doesn't give you anything in the way of a shape, dear, which you really could do with, take my word for it, and no wonder your husband decided he could do better, because honestly, dear, you don't even try, do you?' Silence. 'I'm going to emigrate.'

'Mm. Why has Lucas left her?'

A shrug. 'He says someone tried to murder him and it's not safe for him to live there until the culprit's been dealt with. She thinks he suspects her.'

'What!'

'Yes. My mouth dropped open, too. I mean, she wouldn't. No point. There was a prenup. Lucas is no fool. She'd been married and divorced three times before, so he made sure she couldn't claim anything from him if she decided to get rid of him, too. She has nothing to gain by trying to kill him, and a great deal to lose…though I suppose she could still go on calling herself Lady Ossett if he did divorce her. Or would she lose the title as well as the penthouse apartment?'

'I'm not sure. What actually happened?'

'Someone tied a wire across the top step of the staircase so that he'd trip over it and take a header. Which he did, apparently. He had his mobile phone on him and phoned for help. He ended up in hospital with a broken arm and bruises, and lucky to get away with that. He could easily have been killed. I understand he has numerous enemies in the world of business. Maybe he's right, and he is in danger if he stays at the flat. I did wonder if he'd arranged the accident himself, looking for an excuse to leave her. But no; I don't think he'd do that.'

'Not his style?'

'Definitely not. A quiet man, if you know what I mean, but decisive. If he'd decided to leave her anyway, he'd have said so and walked out. Which is what he did. Go, I mean. From the hospital he went to the flat his firm keeps for visiting businessmen at his office. He sent his personal assistant to pack up his belongings.'

'He's filed for divorce?'

'Not yet, but I imagine he will. She'll lose her apartment, which she probably loves more than she ever loved any of her husbands, including my own dear father, who she discarded twenty years ago, and well out of it, I say.'

'Has Lucas called in the police?'

Maggie shook her head. 'She says not. Actually, I wish he would. There have been a couple of other incidents in the block, and I did wonder…but she brushed my concerns aside when I asked about them.' A gesture of resignation. 'She wants—no, expects—me to go back to live with her. To keep her company. To act as a daughter should when her mother is in such distress.'

'To be her slave.'

'Yes.' Maggie's shoulders sank. 'I *can't* leave her in such distress. She is distressed, you know. This is the first time one of her husbands has walked out on her, rather than the other way around. In a funny sort of way I think she really did care for Lucas, and all this froth and fury—it's covering it up.' She squared her shoulders. 'I know I'll be letting you down as well. Do you think you can find someone else to move into my flat upstairs?'

'No,' said Bea, meaning it. 'This is your home. I know I'm not your birth mother, but you are like a daughter to me and nothing changes that. It's your flat for as long as you want it, and it's your office downstairs.'

'Yes, but—'

'Think about it, Maggie. You've built up your own business, you have an excellent reputation as a project manager, you get things done on time and under budget. Your order book is full for the next six months. You employ a part-time secretary and accountant. People rely on you to perform miracles in their houses, and your staff rely on you to pay their wages. You can't throw all that away.'

'I have to.'

'Your mother,' said Bea, indignation rising, 'is a cow!'

Maggie sketched a smile. 'Yes. She's a conniving, selfish woman, who had reduced me to a quivering wreck before you rescued me and gave me a home and a job and showed me I didn't have to spend the rest of my life apologizing for my existence. But, she is my mother.'

Bea wasn't going to give up without a fight. 'She'll ditch you again, as soon as she's captured another husband. That's what happened before, wasn't it? As soon as she laid eyes on number three—can't remember his name, the one before Lucas—she wanted you out of the way and pushed you into a marriage with a total shit who was on the rebound from a failed love affair. And when that no-good creature ditched you and she thought you'd have to return home to live, she got you a job here in the agency—'

'At which I was no good at all.'

'No, but you soon found what you *were* good at, and you've got a delightful, faithful boyfriend and a new circle of friends and I don't think you should throw all that away just because she's had a spat with her latest husband.'

'I know. But I can't refuse her.' Maggie's eyes flicked to and fro. 'She expects me tomorrow morning. I'm trying to think who can take over the jobs I've got in hand.'

'Maggie, this won't do. You aren't thinking straight.'

'She's frightened and all alone.'

'With a dozen intimate friends to call upon.'

'It's not the same.'

Bea knew it wasn't. She cast her mind back over what Maggie had said. 'Lucas says there was an attempt to kill him. Was there? Did you see the string stretched across the staircase yourself?'

'No. It had gone by the time I got there.'

'Did he imagine it? Did he fall down the stairs because he'd got drunk?'

A brief smile. 'Lucas doesn't get drunk. If he says there was a nylon string or a wire across the stairs, then there was.'

'Did your mother see it herself?'

'No, she'd gone out early to a drinks party, and when she got back he'd been taken to the hospital… As a neighbour was only too pleased to tell her.'

'What neighbour? Doesn't your mother live in a penthouse?'

A shrug. 'He phoned someone else in the building, I suppose, or he wouldn't have been able to get the front door open to let the ambulance men in.'

'Your mother didn't see any sign of a booby trap? I wonder…'

Maggie stared at Bea. 'What are you getting at?'

'You said there'd been other "incidents". What were they?'

'Nothing important. Youthful mischief. Some vandalism, putting stuff through letter boxes, that sort of thing. Oh, and the old lady on the ground floor had a heart attack and died, but you can't count that, can you?'

'Yet these "incidents" were enough to make Lucas flee for his life when he himself fell victim to some kind of "prank". If that is what it was. And your mother is frightened.'

'She can't really be frightened. No, she's putting it on to make me feel sorry for her. She can't stand being on her own.'

'You said she collects men as other people might collect beer mats.'

'She needs reassurance that she's not old and ugly.'

'Which you are now supposed to give her? Come off it, Maggie. At least get Lucas's side of the story before you wreck your career.'

Maggie's mouth set in an obstinate line. 'I promised I'd move back in tomorrow morning.'

Bea hit her forehead. 'At least let me try to explain

to her that you can't jettison your career without giving proper notice to everyone concerned. She ought to be able to understand that.'

Maggie huffed, meaning she didn't think her mother would see her daughter's career as being of any importance.

Bea improvised. 'Look, I could find her someone to babysit her, someone she could play bridge with; perhaps someone who could chauffeur her around?'

'The archangel Gabriel?'

'No, no. She might try to seduce him.'

That got a laugh, even if it was only a weak one.

Bea cast around for ideas. 'What about a toy boy? Someone to flatter and amuse her?'

'The agency doesn't have any toy boys on their books.'

'True. Regretfully. But it might be one answer to the problem.'

Maggie took a deep breath. Frowned. Let the breath out slowly.

'Yes?' said Bea.

'Suppose… Do you think you could persuade her to go on a cruise or something?'

Bea said, 'That's a good idea. She'd have to go out and buy some new outfits, which would divert her mind wonderfully.'

'She would need someone with her to approve of everything she bought and carry her purchases, get her taxis and stuff.'

'We do have people like that on our books. "The Last Resort", I call them. Older women with the patience of Job and calculators for brains to keep track of their expenses. Shall we try that?'

Maggie lunged at Bea and gave her a bear hug which left the older women feeling that she'd been assaulted.

'Bless you!' Having neatly passed the buck to Bea, Maggie got out her mobile phone. 'I'm going to give that plumber hell!'

BEA TOOK HERSELF off down the stairs and into her office, wondering if she hadn't promised to do more than she could easily perform. Her computer was still running; she'd left the lights on and the curtains open.

She turned off all the lights except for the one on her desk, so that she could stand by the window and look out over the paved courtyard in the dark. Oblongs of light fell across the stone flags from the kitchen on the floor above, picking out the huge stone pots which Maggie had filled with wallflowers, bulbs and ivies.

Bea looked across and up…up through the naked branches of the big sycamore tree at the end of the garden to the spire of the church at the bottom of the road… and beyond that to the twinkle of the odd star…or were those the lights of a plane going in to land at Heathrow airport?

Peace and quiet descended. Standing in the semi-dark by the windows, she was neither in the busy world of the agency and her extended family, nor in the shadows of the garden outside.

*Dear Lord above, what have I got myself into now? I know…at least I think I know that you'd want me to help Maggie, but…*

*I am not the right person to deal with a selfish, conniving little screw-head like Lady Ossett. I just don't have the patience. I'd want to tell her to pull herself together or slap her or… I mean, tact is required here, don't you think? And is that my strong point? Well, not without an effort, no.*

*All right, I know I'm not supposed to despise Maggie's*

*mother, however difficult she may be. If Maggie's right
and the woman is frightened, then I should be trying to
help her, not thwart her desire to have her daughter at
home with her.*

*Except that...if she really is frightened...*

*I don't understand what's going on here. All I know is
that I am not the right person to deal with Lady Ossett.*

*All right, all right. You've dumped it on my plate, and I
suppose I have to deal with it. But not without complaining. I am allowed to complain, right?*

*I mean, I'm no saint, am I?*

Having argued herself into a better frame of mind,
Bea pulled the curtains to and turned on the overhead
lights. Her computer was still humming. She brought
up the document she'd been studying when Maggie had
burst in upon her, and sighed.

Another problem that she didn't know how to solve.
Should she sign a contract to have a binding relationship
with another firm or not? She must decide soon. They
were pressing her for a decision, and it made sense in
so many ways to link her agency with them. And yet...
and yet.

She saved the document and shut down her computer
for the night.

Her landline rang. A glance at the clock showed her
it was the right time for Oliver—her adopted son—to
ring. He often did so on a Friday before he went out for
the evening. Oliver was at university studying something
wildly academic and non-understandable in the field of
higher mathematics, so perhaps he'd have some words of
wisdom for her in the matter of the contract.

Oliver was on another tack altogether. 'What's this
about Maggie's mother wanting her back home? I told
her that's ridiculous, she'll be on tranquillizers within a

week and then what good will she be to man or beast? You've got to stop her.'

'You've heard, then.'

'Heard? I was just about to go out when she rang, hardly making any sense, saying that if you don't think of something to rescue her, she's going to do her duty if it kills her, which it probably will—'

'Agreed.'

'Can't you talk some sense into her, Mother Hen?'

The use of her nickname made her smile. Wryly. 'Have you tried, Oliver?'

'She wouldn't listen. Look, term's nearly over. I could come back early if you like. Maggie thinks you shouldn't be left on your own.'

'Absurd!'

'Yes, but what about the end of year party? You won't be able to do it without her.'

Bea bit her lip. She hadn't forgotten it exactly, but it hadn't been high on her list of priorities. It had been Maggie's idea to celebrate the launch of her business as a registered company, Bea's sixty-second birthday and the signing of the contract with Holland and Butcher. Maggie had wanted it to be a splendiferous event in the annals of Kensington, with entertainment and champagne flowing regardless of cost. Bea wouldn't have dreamed of holding such a big 'do' if Maggie hadn't suggested it. And in any case, she wasn't at all sure she wanted to plunge into a relationship with H & B… Or not without giving it a lot more thought, anyway.

'I want to stop Maggie committing suicide as well. Any ideas?' she said.

'Just one. I gather Lady O enjoys an extravagant lifestyle. You could hint that Maggie might become a drain on her finances, that she might even be sued, if she doesn't complete her current contracts. And if she's not earning, then who would have to pay her debts?'

'A really underhand suggestion. Not worthy of the fine, upstanding, down-sitting young man that you're supposed to be. I shall adopt it with pleasure.'

'Good.' Silence. 'Maggie said her mother was frightened because Lucas fell down some stairs. Is that right?'

'Isn't it enough that she fears losing her husband, her comfortable way of life, and her home?'

'You know her sort better than I, but I don't like the sound of Lucas's fall down the stairs. There really is no cause for alarm, is there?'

# TWO

*Thursday morning*

BEA PAID OFF the taxi and looked up—and up—at the block of flats in which Lady Ossett lived. It was built of cream coloured London brick and had rounded corners, giving the impression of a ship about to sail. Not as tall a block as some. Not a skyscraper. Six or seven floors only? Nineteen twenties, probably. Substantial, not to say solid-looking. Windows shining, paint glistening. Well-maintained. Pricey.

A single 'For Sale' notice from a national agency advertised a three-bedroom apartment. Not 'flat'. 'Apartment'. Appealing to buyers with money to burn?

Glazed porch at an angle over two steps led up to wide, glass doors.

A speakerphone entry system. 'Lady Ossett? Bea Abbot here.'

A tinny voice, 'Who?'

'Bea Abbot. Your daughter Maggie asked me to call on you to explain—'

'She's late. Has something happened to her?'

'She gave me a message for you.'

Pause. 'Take the lift to the top, and then the stairs.'

Click. The front door opened and Bea entered the hall, which was lined with pale wood panelling, with bands of a darker wood in horizontal stripes. The floor was tiled in a geometric pattern; black, white, fawn. The ceiling lights must be original; fluted, understated elegance. Everything was design conscious. Perhaps too much so?

Directly inside the hall there was a rank of numbered letter-boxes, one for each flat. To left and right were doors leading to ground-floor apartments, while straight ahead there was a lift with a staircase winding around it. Up… and down. Down to a basement? A garage? The lift doors were panelled in the same light wood as the rest of the hall and embellished with marquetry panels.

Bea summoned the lift and rode it to the top. She got out and looked around. Here were doors to two more flats plus an arrow advising visitors to take the stairs one more flight up to the penthouse.

Why didn't the lift go up to the penthouse? Had it been added to the building at a later date? Or perhaps the original occupant had not wished to be disturbed by the almost noiseless whine of the machinery?

Bea took the stairs up until she reached a small landing. The stairs were uncarpeted, of polished wood. The banisters were of the same light wood. More geometric patterns. No expense had been spared, had it?

Bea scrutinized the newel posts at the head of the stairs. Feeling somewhat silly she produced the small magnifying glass she carried in her handbag for those occasions on which she'd forgotten her reading glasses, and… Yes, if you looked hard, you could see where a tack or a nail or something with a sharp point had been driven into the wood of the newel post and later removed. The hole was still there; and yes, there was another on the opposite side of the staircase. At ankle height. If you had a vivid imagination, you might think someone could have tied a nylon thread or perhaps a thin wire to one nail, stretched it across the stairs and tied the end to the other nail. In poor light someone might not notice and take a nasty tumble down…how many steps before the flight turned in a different direction?

Bea counted them. Eight. And then you'd come up against the wall. Or if you were very unlucky, you might continue headlong down the next flight as well. It was very quiet up here, well above the other flats. If he hadn't had his mobile phone on him, Sir Lucas might have had to stagger down the stairs by himself until he could thump on another occupant's door and summon assistance. He had indeed been lucky to get away with a broken arm and bruises.

Someone had come along afterwards to remove the thread and pull the nails out of the woodwork. Bingo. Nothing left to see, except two tiny tack holes.

Bea took a photograph of both holes on her camera and, standard practice kicking into action, checked to see that the evidence had been recorded and saved.

There was only one door at penthouse level. Beside it was a wrought-iron table holding a pot with an orchid in it. Bea checked. The flower was artificial but could pass for real. A stained-glass window offered a view of a busy street many floors below.

Bea put her magnifying glass away and rang the door-bell.

A vision in peaches and cream opened the door. 'Mrs Abbot? I've been looking forward to meeting you so much, though not, of course, under such difficult circumstances. Is my daughter ill? I have been out of my mind with worry about her. Do put me out of my misery.'

Gush, gush, thought Bea. But found herself smiling, for Lady Ossett was quite charming, looking hardly a day older than her twenty-something daughter. Petite and sweet.

And, Bea reminded herself, lethal. Remember, '*My mother is a cow!*'

'Maggie's quite well but couldn't come this morning. She asked me to make her apologies.'

'Oh no! Oh, this is terrible. I was relying on her to... But please, do come in.' With a gust of teasing, expensive perfume, the vision ushered Bea into a spacious, cream-carpeted hall with archways leading off in different directions. Bea noted a telephone table, carved oak chair and a number of doors, one of which the vision opened to reveal a clothes cupboard with lots of space at one side. Had the gap been caused by the removal of Lucas's clothes?

A vacuum cleaner whined somewhere nearby. A cleaner at work?

'My dear, ugly duckling of a daughter! She is the light of my life but I do worry about her, as I am sure you must do, having taken her under your wing, quite too charitable of you considering all the trouble she causes. Do hang your coat in here; my! How tall you are! I can never reach that peg, but my dear husband insists that...'

Here she applied a tiny handkerchief to the corner of her eyes. There was a huge diamond on her ring finger, and the hankie was lace-edged. Bea smoothed out a smile. Diamonds and lace; typical.

Lady Ossett led the way into one of the most stunning living rooms Bea had ever seen. It was huge, filled with light from windows on two sides, adding to the impression the building gave of being a luxury liner at sea. The room was furnished in a mixture of art deco and modern taste, with glass and steel and cream leather on areas of silk carpet in pastel colours. Very *Homes & Gardens*.

Had Lady O furnished it herself? Possibly. If so, then she was a very clever woman and not an ordinary cow.

Or perhaps she'd employed a top designer to create a fitting background for her beauty?

There were modern lithos between fluted uplighters on the walls, and one striking portrait above a long settee. Everything was dust-free, vacuumed and polished.

Through French windows at the far end of the room, Bea glimpsed a prettily arranged terrace garden, decorated with huge pots, containing palms, and a water feature. The garden furniture had, very sensibly, been hooded for the winter. The view of the London skyline was amazing, even on this gloomy day. Central heating ticked.

Lady O waved Bea to a low-slung chair and seated herself behind a glass-topped coffee table, on which reposed today's paper and a lacquered, Chinese style tray holding a small cafetière and a gold-rimmed cup and saucer. One cup only. A silver bowl held lumps of sugar, with a pair of tongs laid on top.

Sugar tongs? When had Bea last seen those in use? Amazing!

'Coffee?' The offer was made in perfunctory fashion and was not meant to be accepted.

Bea declined.

The vision said, 'It really is too bad of Maggie to let me down like this. I shall give her such a scold when I see her! So, tell me; why the delay?'

'I'm afraid work intervened. The client threatened to sue if Maggie didn't complete the job she was doing for him.'

Lady Ossett looked as if she couldn't make up her mind whether to be annoyed or indulgent. Indulgence won, by a narrow margin. 'Oh dear. The scrapes that child gets herself into. However much is it going to cost me to get her out of this one, I wonder!'

Bea said, 'Tens of thousands, I should think.'

'Mm?' The teeniest of frowns disturbed the bland forehead. Botox? Undoubtedly. Lady O lifted her cup to her lips. 'She does so exaggerate. Helping a neighbour out with some housework or typing up a bill or two; that doesn't sound very important to me. Surely you can find someone else in the agency to take on her jobs?'

Bea took a deep breath. Had Maggie never made it clear to her mother exactly what work she was doing? Or had she tried, and her mother not listened? The latter, most likely. Time to disabuse the little lady of her delusions. 'A good project manager is worth her weight, and Maggie has a raft of contracts to fulfil.'

Lady O repeated the word, soundlessly. 'Project…?'

Bea put the boot in. 'You could do far worse than employ her professionally if ever you wanted to change the layout here, or put in another bathroom, or whatever.'

The cup in Lady O's hand rattled as she replaced it on its saucer. 'Maggie is working as a…? My Maggie?'

'Your ugly duckling is quite some businesswoman. I must congratulate you. She rents an office from me nowadays and has had to take on a part-time accountant and a secretary to help her keep the books straight. You know how particular the tax man can be if the accounts are not well kept.'

The wide blue eyes lost their focus. The finely-chiselled nose took on a pinched look. The make-up was too good to allow her to go pale, but the cords stood out on her neck as the lady took in what Bea had said.

'You mean that she's refusing to help me in my hour of need?'

Bea tried to work out what was happening to Lady O. Was she truly in shock? Did she really have cause for alarm? 'She can't abandon her contracted jobs without risking some nasty court cases. She did wonder if she could pass the work on to another firm, but—'

Lady O stood up in one abrupt movement. Ungraceful, even. 'Excuse me for a moment. I must have a word with my cleaner. You'll have some coffee, won't you?'

Had she forgotten that Bea had declined coffee?

Lady Ossett left the room by an inner door. The whine of the vacuum cleaner increased, and then stopped.

*So the lady really is afraid. Maggie said she was, but I didn't believe it. Whatever is going on here?*

Bea looked around her. Next to the lacquered tray on the table, an iPhone sat on top of today's *Times*, open and folded to a crossword which had been more than half completed in a fine blue biro. Beneath that was a paper whose colour gave away its title: the *Financial Times*. Perhaps Lucas had placed an order for these papers, and Lady O hadn't yet got round to cancelling it? What would her own reading be? *Vogue*? *Hello!* magazine? The *Daily Mail*?

Restless, Bea stood and went to look out of the nearest window. Stunning view. Nearby an escritoire was open, supporting a netbook with Skype up and running, ready for use. And a letter from a stockbroker. She wasn't prying, exactly. The letterhead was easy to read from where she stood. She checked who the letter was addressed to. Was it Sir Lucas? No. It was Lady Ossett.

Did Lady O study the markets? Hm. Perhaps she wasn't quite as naive about money matters as her daughter had indicated. Also on the escritoire was yesterday's copy of the *Times*, again folded to reveal the crossword puzzle. Completed in the same blue biro. Bea bent over for a closer look. It wasn't one of those crosswords which you could polish off while you boiled an egg. It was one of the fiendish ones which Bea had never been able to cope with, although her dear departed husband had managed it most days.

Surely Lady Ossett hadn't the brain for crossword puzzles, had she? These must have been completed by Sir Lucas. Uh oh. It was today's crossword puzzle in the paper on the coffee table, filled in with the same blue biro as yesterday's, while Sir Lucas had been gone two days. So, if Lady Ossett had filled them in, then…rethink, Bea!

While she was still on her feet Bea walked over to inspect the fine modern portrait which hung over the largest of the settees. A spotlight had been trained upon it to underline its importance. A name came into her head. Lucian Freud.

The subject was a businessman. Lucas? If that picture were by Freud, it must be worth a fortune. She peered at it. Yes, definitely. Freud.

There was no other evidence of a man's presence in the room.

Books? None in sight…except for a couple of library books which were, unexpectedly, from P.D. James and the latest winner of the Man Booker prize. There wasn't a Mills & Boon romance or a copy of *Hello!* magazine in sight.

A superb leather handbag squatted on the floor by Lady O's chair. It lay open, disclosing the usual contents…and a pair of men's sunglasses. Not a woman's. Too large, too heavy, and totally unlike anything Lady O would wear.

Bea seated herself again as Lady O returned, bearing a second coffee cup and saucer. All traces of distress had been erased. She was even smiling. She reseated herself, poured out a cup of coffee for Bea and handed it to her. 'No cream, I imagine. We older women have to watch our figures, don't we?'

Bea produced a polite smile. It was interesting that

Lady O should put herself in the same age group as Bea, who was in her early sixties. Flattering, even, for the vision herself could hardly be more than mid-forties. She'd been born with an excellent bone structure and a mop of fair hair which only needed a little help from her hairdresser to retain its champagne colour. There was no sign of a facelift, though incipient lines had been erased with Botox. Her eyelashes had been dyed, her teeth whitened and her nails extended by experts. Her figure was delightful. A pocket Venus, no less.

Money played a part here, of course. Bea could make a guess at where Lady O had bought the fine wool dress and four-inch heels she was wearing because she'd seen—and considered buying—both in Harvey Nicholls in Knightsbridge.

The coffee was excellent.

'You hinted,' said Lady O, with a sweet smile, 'that my daughter might be able to turn her work over to someone else...?'

Bea set her empty cup down. 'It would be difficult and perhaps have unpleasant consequences. Do you not have a friend who could keep you company for a while?'

Lady O lowered her eyelids and tried to look confused. 'You must think me very selfish, but my daughter's letting me down like this...you can't possibly understand... and Lucas deserting me...though I really find it hard to have to beg, I must ask you to help Maggie reorganize her work schedule so that she may return home. I really do need looking after now that—'

'Perhaps I could find you an assistant, a social secretary to keep you company? I believe you give bridge parties. How about employing someone to arrange a charity bridge event for you? I could find someone to live in, if you wish.'

A hesitation. 'That might… But how much would it cost, and when could they start?'

A telephone shrilled. A landline.

'Yes?' Lady O picked up the receiver and listened with an almost frown on her face. Then she smiled. 'Lovely to hear from you. No, I can't make it this afternoon, I'm afraid. I'm having one of my little bridge parties here. Perhaps you might care to join us? A few friends, some of whom you will know and…yes, yes. That's good. I look forward to seeing you.' She put the phone down with a pleased air. 'An old friend, visiting London for a few days.'

'Which means you won't need Maggie this afternoon?'

'Well, perhaps not.'

'You already have another man in your life?'

'What? You mean…?' This time her neck flushed. 'How dare you?'

'That wasn't your toy boy on the phone? Yet you have a pair of men's sunglasses in your handbag.'

'How dare you! Those are my husband's, left behind by mistake.' Her face set like stone, Lady O marched to the door and held it open for Bea. 'I must ask you to leave, now!'

Bea was annoyed with herself. How could she have been so stupid? She'd made a serious error of judgement and alienated Lady O. And it was Maggie who would suffer from it. 'I apologize. I'll leave you my card, in case you change your mind.'

Lady O lifted Bea's coat down from the cupboard—having no difficulty in reaching the peg now, Bea noticed—and held it out to her. 'I do not feel you are a fit person to have any contact with my daughter. I must insist she returns home at once!'

Bea collected her coat and walked out of the flat in silence. She'd visited Lady O to plead Maggie's case, made one of the biggest boobs of her career, insulted the client and only made matters worse for her protégée. She took the stairs down one floor and summoned the lift.

Well, if there were no toy boy—and Bea accepted Lady O's denial—then the lady was being very forgiving in keeping her husband's sunglasses in her handbag, close to hand. Meaning to return them to him?

Perhaps Lady O was hoping for a reconciliation? It was all a bit of a puzzle. And talking of puzzles, what of the half completed crossword in today's *Times*?

Maggie was a bright lass, but not academic. Was it possible that Lady O's helpless, little-me persona was a front, and behind it was the sharp brain of someone who read the *Financial Times* and did brain teasers in her spare time?

Bea wondered if, despite Lady O's denial, there was another suitor lurking in the background, waiting to move into the vacant position. It was understandable that Lady O wouldn't wish it to be known that she'd taken another man into her bed the moment her husband had left. That wouldn't go down well in a divorce court, would it?

Another thing; if Lucas really had walked out on her and sent his PA to remove his belongings, why had he left that valuable portrait behind?

Bea smiled, imagining a scene in which the PA tried to take the picture, while Lady O stood in front of it, defying her to remove it over her dead body. Perhaps the picture had been given to Lady O and she was entitled to hang on to it?

Well, if that was the case, he'd probably have to go to law to get it. It was the type of dispute which people did go to law about, and it would probably cost more in legal fees to sort out than the picture was worth.

Another niggle. A big one. Lady O had been anxious to get her daughter back because she was afraid…but afraid of what, exactly?

Bea got into the lift and pressed the button for the ground floor. The lift whispered its way down, stopping without a tremor to allow a red-headed woman in a fur coat to get in. A fake fur? Yes, but an expensive one. Ditto the hair colour. The woman didn't look at Bea, but stood with her back turned to her as the lift resumed its way towards the ground floor.

Bea mentally raised her eyebrows, determined to use the opportunity to learn more about the lady she'd just visited. 'Forgive me; do you know a Lady Ossett? I was given this address for her, but I've been up and down in the lift, trying to find her flat without any luck.'

The woman didn't even turn round to look at Bea. Didn't answer.

The lift stopped at the ground floor and the woman got out, still without acknowledging Bea's presence. She stalked off on slender legs and ankles. A well-preserved fifty? She wore mid-ankle, well-fitting boots with a stiletto heel. Enormous handbag which screamed Prada. Fine leather gloves. Mahogany red hair, dyed. And slightly too vivid make-up.

Bea, ruffled, wondered if she were someone's mistress. Fur coat sashayed out of the front door into the street and walked away.

Bea stood on the pavement, watching the woman disappear. What now? She'd failed in spectacular fashion in her errand. She got out her mobile phone.

'Maggie? Lucky to catch you. Your mother is probably going to get on the phone to you in a minute to say that—'

'She has, but I decided not to take her calls till you

got back. Did you persuade her to get someone else in to look after her?'

'She's a difficult woman.'

'Tell me about it.'

'She's desperate to have you back but    '

'You're not going to give in to her, are you? I thought you were on my side.'

'No, but I've got a couple of questions for you. What newspapers does she read?'

'High-powered stuff. Way above my head. She plays the stock markets, would you believe. Can't make head nor tail of them myself.'

So Maggie had, without meaning to, misled Bea about Lady O's level of intelligence? 'Right. Does she own the Lucian Freud, or does he?'

'It was a wedding gift from her to him. It's his.'

'Has she got another string to her bow at the moment? Someone who could do the crossword in the *Times* with her?'

'No. She does it herself. Lucas helped her, sometimes, over breakfast.'

'Could she still be seeing him for breakfast?'

'I don't see how. He's left her and cleared out all his stuff.'

'Except for the picture.'

'So? I don't get it.'

'Neither do I. I think I'd better pay a call on your step-father. Where can I find him?'

# THREE

*Thursday at noon*

BEA PAUSED OUTSIDE a glass-clad skyscraper and looked up and even further up. Up a good few more storeys than the building in which Lady O lived. Twenty more, or perhaps even thirty?

Bea didn't often visit the financial heart of the City and was impressed. Also depressed by the sheer weightiness of the buildings around her. They might have been built on the footings of businesses in medieval London with crooked alleyways inching them apart, but there was nothing ancient about these glittering towers.

The imposing stairs leading to the entrance of Sir Lucas's building were made of polished, grey granite blocks. A half-landing supported a monumental piece of art, in the shape of…she couldn't make out what it was supposed to represent, but it had undoubtedly been hideously expensive.

The building itself was named 'Vicori House'. Bea seemed to remember from her school days that '*Vici*' was Latin for 'I conquered'. Was this a variation on the conqueror's theme? Had someone inserted 'or'—or 'org', perhaps?—to remind the public that the corporation was a multinational business in a big way? No; it wouldn't be 'org' or people would think of corgis, which was definitely not the way one was supposed to think of this organization.

According to the engraving on a free-standing block of granite just outside the revolving doors, Vicori Corporation was supreme in the fields of plastics, energy, the media and pharmaceuticals. They probably also produced plaster of Paris, pop stars, soap powders and pizzas. What was there to stop them?

She wondered whether there would be a floor of office space for each company in the trading empire. This was the headquarters of the corporation, but their various factories would be located anywhere from Asia to South America.

As she'd traipsed around the building to reach the entrance, Bea had glimpsed an open plan floor in which hundreds of youngish men and women concentrated on individual computer screens. The building reminded her of a beehive. How many workers were employed, and did they like their jobs? Were they well paid?

Bea shuddered. She'd never had to work like an ant in an anthill as these people did, and she was grateful that she would never have to do so.

She'd telephoned ahead for an appointment with Sir Lucas and to her surprise had been granted one immediately, so she squared her shoulders and marched through the revolving doors into the huge, well-lit foyer.

A large water sculpture dominated an expanse of marble floor, while black-clad blondes and large security men directed the flow of visitors in and out of ranks of lifts. On a board nearby there was a montage of photographs of the VIPs in the various companies which made up the Vicori Corporation. Bea thought they looked interchangeable; smooth, well-groomed, and well-off. Including the women.

Bea announced herself at the desk, was signed in,

given a tag to wear and directed towards the very end lift; the one that went straight to the twenty-eighth floor.

Twenty-eight floors. She hadn't been far out in her estimate.

Sir Lucas was a big bug. Not exactly Queen Bee… Bees didn't have kings, did they? Did ants? How little she knew about such things.

A secretary or minder or personal assistant—an earnest-looking youngish man wearing the turban of a Sikh—met her at the lift and led her through a hushed, deep-carpeted hallway into a sunny office with a fine view of the river.

Had the sun really come out, then? No, it hadn't. But the room was full of light and there was a sunburst of a tapestry spread across one wall. This was quite some office; a desk with no computer or paperwork on it, a group of armchairs and settees set around a coffee table by the far window and not a filing cabinet in sight. Well, everybody wanted a paperless office nowadays, didn't they… Which was fine till there was a power cut or the computer developed a mind of its own.

A large, comfortable-looking man sketched an attempt to rise from a giant leather chair behind the desk, but only made it so far before collapsing back into it. One arm was in a cast, currently supported in a sling. There were barely-healed abrasions on his forehead and cheek, not to mention a spectacular black eye. Speaking of eyes, his were an icy blue, contradicting the easy-going, not to say soft lines of his face. She began to understand how he'd come to be CEO of this giant corporation.

'Welcome,' he said, smiling. 'I wasn't sure whether it would be you or Maggie coming to demand satisfaction from me.'

Bea started to laugh as most of the pieces of the jigsaw

fell into place in her mind. Not all of them. But at least she now understood he harboured no ill feelings towards his wife. 'Maggie's working, and I've just left Lady Ossett—as I'm sure you know.'

'Of course.' That day's *Times* was on the table in front of him, turned to the Crossword, which had been completed in a broad-nibbed black pen. Beside it was the latest in computerized tablets.

She indicated the paper. 'Did the two of you manage to finish the crossword separately this morning, or did you do it by phone?'

'She got four down, which had eluded me. I have a meeting with our lawyers at two and was about to have a light lunch. Will you join me?'

'Delighted.' Bea shucked off her coat, which was whisked away by the PA even before she seated herself opposite Lucas.

He said, 'You accused my wife of having a toy boy.' Did his mouth twitch with amusement?

'I apologized. I misread her completely.'

'Hah!' He barked out a laugh. 'You understand why I had to leave?'

'Someone tied wire or thread across the top stair, with intent to harm or frighten either you or your wife. There have been previous incidents of petty vandalism in the flats which neither you nor your wife considered to be of any importance. This time you were caught in the trap, took it seriously and did the sensible thing by removing yourself from the danger zone. After all, you have a multibillion-pound business to run.'

He nodded. The Sikh returned with a youngish woman in a black trouser suit, pushing a hostess trolley. On a table at the far end of the room they laid out a tureen of soup, some bread rolls, a range of open sandwiches cut into bite-sized pieces, a plate of cheeses, some fruit and bottles of sparkling mineral water.

A better lunch than Bea would have had at home.

Lucas gestured for Bea to precede him to the table and informed his staff that they'd wait upon themselves. The Sikh and the woman in black left the room as noiselessly as they'd arrived.

Bea seated herself and served them both to soup. 'I suppose it was only natural that you should think it an attempt on your life.'

'Wouldn't you?'

'You've probably been looking at your executives to see who might want you disabled, dead, or otherwise removed from power.'

He nodded again, sipping soup. 'I set my head of security on to it. There are several candidates, including a man I dismissed a while ago. I don't want it generally known that someone has made an attempt on my life because it will affect the share price of our corporation and we have a shareholders' meeting coming up soon. I hope to keep the police out of it until we can produce some evidence against the person I have in mind.'

'You are fond of your wife, who is in many ways a perfect foil for you—'

'Indeed. We complement one another. We usually finish the crossword between us, over breakfast. She only has to look at an anagram for the answer to leap into her mind. Would you be so kind as to cut up a bread roll for me? And pass the salt? My wife prefers her food rather more bland than I… Ah, thank you.'

'Yet you didn't think it a good idea to whisk her away with you to safety?'

'She'll be perfectly safe now I'm out of the picture.'

Bea treated him to an old-fashioned look. 'She doesn't share your confidence, and I'm not sure that I do, either.'

'She has no need to fear anything now I've gone.' He seemed to believe it.

Bea told herself to check his background. Did he, perhaps, have another woman in mind? 'It must be a comfort to her that you've left your portrait behind, which you wouldn't have done if you'd really abandoned her. Or would you? Your departure has left her in an exposed position.'

'That was not my intention.' He seemed to make up his mind to be frank. 'To tell the truth, I think she's over-reacted. I suggested we move into the Dorchester for the time being. I said that we could make the excuse that we need the penthouse redecorated. She refused to leave, became almost hysterical. She'll calm down in a few days, I'm sure.' He pushed his empty soup plate aside and reached for the open sandwiches. 'Do help yourself.'

Bea considered that when people say they're going to tell the truth about something, it usually means they're going to lie. So who was lying in this instance? Sir Lucas, or Lady O? She said, 'I know fear when I see it. She's afraid.'

He shook his head. 'She has no need. I am well guarded here.' He frowned, undecided whether to choose smoked salmon or Stilton.

'For a clever man, you are being…obtuse. She's afraid because she's not at all sure the booby trap was meant for you. The other incidents—'

'Kids playing around. Would you pour me some mineral water?'

'The other incidents have escalated into violence. You were fortunate not to have suffered more serious injuries.'

'It hasn't affected my brain.'

'No talk of concussion?' asked Bea, with a sweet expression.

Did he flush? Yes. He tore a bunch of grapes apart. Seedless grapes, of course. There should have been some scissors with them. Or didn't his staff see the need for such refinement?

'She's afraid of being left alone in the flat,' said Bea, 'and that's why she wants Maggie back.'

Lucas met her stare. 'I did say that if she didn't want to go to the Dorchester, she could always move in here with me, but she refused.'

'Of course she did. Not her scene, and you know it. But she shouldn't be left on her own.'

A gentle, iron-hard smile. 'She is in no danger. I did warn her, by the way, that Maggie might not be available.'

'Lady Ossett has a good line in emotional blackmail. Last night Maggie was prepared to throw up everything to return to her mother's side.'

'Ah. Until you intervened?'

'I pay you the compliment of knowing what sort of work Maggie does, and why she can't easily lay it down.'

'You've given her a good start in business; her own office and staff.'

Bea paused with the last of a smoked salmon titbit on the way to her mouth. 'You've been making enquiries about me?'

'Naturally. My wife has always been worried about the girl, and I heard all about the problem daughter from the moment I came on the scene. Maggie's disastrous marriage! And then a non-job at your agency—where I suppose she must sorely have tried your patience—and finally the move into project management which has turned out well, for which I must thank you. Yes, of course I've kept an eye on her and on you. May I congratulate you on the way you've developed what was once a very small concern? I believe you're now considering a merger with another firm?'

Bea was disturbed to find he knew so much about her. 'No doubt you'd advise against it?'

A gentle smile. He was pleased to have riled her. 'I wouldn't dream of offering advice—unless you asked for it.'

Bea gritted her teeth. She would not ask. Definitely not. She helped herself to some mineral water and wondered if coffee would arrive soon. 'Meantime, your wife needs someone to hold her hand until this business of the vandalism—or whatever it is—can be sorted out. I understand why you don't wish to go to the police for the moment, and I'm glad you've taken on board the reason why Maggie can't drop everything to be with her mother. So what are the alternatives? If Lady Ossett doesn't wish to leave her home, may I suggest a paid companion, someone who plays bridge and knows where all the best shops are? Or maybe you could send her on a cruise or a shopping trip to New York?'

His eyes became diamond points. 'You persist in thinking the problem lies in the building?'

'Yes.' Bea got out her phone, accessed the pictures she'd taken of the tack holes in the staircase, and handed it over to him. 'Evidence of malice aforethought, don't you think? Consider this; it would be difficult if not impossible for an outsider to gain access to the building in order to booby trap your stairs.'

He rose with some difficulty to take the phone over to the window to get a closer look. Standing with his back to her, he said, 'Access to the building?' He sounded as if he were thinking of something else. 'Well, it can be done. You wait till someone enters the building legitimately and follow them in.' He shut up her mobile phone and returned it to her with a social, unmeaning smile.

'This prankster knew where you lived in the building? There are no names on the letter boxes in the foyer, only numbers. How did this person know where you lived, unless one of the tenants told them? Surely you ought to turn your head of security loose on the flats, rather than on your ambitious executives? How do you think any one of them could have accessed the building if they hadn't had an accomplice inside?'

'How much do you charge?'

'What?' She recoiled. 'I don't—'

'That's not what I heard.'

'Who from?'

'A mutual friend.' Another of his gentle-seeming smiles. 'A man I know who has a formidable range of contacts.'

Bea was taken aback. Did he mean that he was acquainted with her old friend CJ Cambridge, who was something hush-hush in one of the ministries, and who certainly knew a great many people? True; CJ had known Bea for years and had taken an interest in her young protégé, Oliver. Would CJ have talked to Lucas without warning Bea that he had done so? Surely not.

Lucas was removing himself from the table, glancing at his watch. His PA and the girl in black had returned and busied themselves removing all evidence of lunch.

'Mrs Abbot, I have a meeting in five minutes. Suppose you ask your toy boy to move in with—'

'What! I have no—!'

'What's sauce for the goose is sauce for the gander. I've been keeping an eye on your clever young man— what's his name?—Oliver. I'm always interested in talented mathematicians. He's due to come down from university for the holidays soon, isn't he? My wife will teach him how to play bridge and show him off to all her friends. He won't object to being thought a toy boy, will he?'

'Strongly, I should think.'

'Then we must soothe him with some sort of pourboire. Perhaps he'd like to go round our IT department, discuss what openings there might be here for him. Also, I'd be happy to pay him a consultant's fee if he can discover who's been helping someone to put me in the morgue.'

Bea opened her mouth to object and closed it again. There was too much going on, in too short a space of time.

As to his suggestion about drawing Oliver into his net, she didn't like it at all but didn't know how to counter it. He was one powerful man, and she had a sneaking suspicion he was a lot brighter than her. This suggestion would let Maggie off the hook, but...

She said, knowing she sounded weak and hating herself for it, 'I'll ask him but I can't promise anything.'

'Thank you, my dear.' He lifted her hand to his lips, air-kissing it. Now where had he learned that? With a wide smile, he produced a memory stick and pressed it on her. 'I think you'll find all you need on this.'

His PA was holding out Bea's coat. The interview was over. She had a cold feeling at the back of her neck. She'd been outgunned, outmanoeuvred and outsmarted. She'd made a crass mistake earlier on by suggesting that Lady O had a toy boy, and she'd apologized to Lady O for it. Sir Lewis had used the same tactic on her and not apologized at all.

An idea struggled into the forefront of her mind. He'd carefully researched his wife's family circumstances, so he'd have researched the background of the people who dwelt in the block of flats in which he'd made his home... wouldn't he? Which meant that he knew everything about everybody who lived there.

The PA was holding the door open for Bea to leave, but she hesitated. 'What about the redhead in the fur coat?'

He was amused. 'Ms Carmela Lessbury. Flat number seven. Visiting hours by arrangement. Do you really suspect her?'

'In your shoes, I would. What about the others?'

'I leave it to you to discover who might wish me harm.' He nodded to his PA, and Bea found herself gently urged out of the room. The door gently, soundlessly, finally closed behind her. A blonde personal assistant was waiting in the foyer to usher Bea into the lift. She wondered how he summoned members of his staff when he needed them. Perhaps everything said in his office was recorded and listened to by one of his security team?

A large man was lurking at the elevators. He was not in uniform but his hefty build and blank gaze screamed 'Security'. He wouldn't be the head of security, of course. A minion, merely. There were probably spy cameras everywhere, recording every movement made on the top floor. On other floors, too?

Bea shivered. She wouldn't like to live like that. It occurred to her that Lewis lived like one of the Roman emperors, always aware of plots and counterplots against him, knowing that ambitious executives were watching and waiting for him to show a moment of weakness so that they could clamber over his dead body to take his place. Power brought its own problems, didn't it?

Once outside in the street she debated whether to hail a taxi or to take the tube. Traffic was gridlocked so she opted to walk to the nearest Underground station, accessing CJ on her mobile phone as she walked along.

Luckily he was able to take the phone call, which wasn't always the case since he was often tied up in court, or in chambers. It occurred to her that if he'd lived in Tudor times, he'd probably have been a member of the Star Chamber, the equivalent of today's MI5 or whatever they called it nowadays.

'CJ? Bea here. I've just had the most extraordinary meeting with Sir Lucas Ossett, who claims to know you well.'

'Hrrmph. In a manner of speaking, yes. We move in the same circles.'

'Has he been asking for information about me?'

'Not exactly. He was concerned about his stepdaughter, and I was happy to inform him she had found an appropriate home with you.'

'When was this?'

'Some time ago. It was only natural that he be concerned. It does him credit, don't you think?'

'I suppose so. Well, he wouldn't have wanted Maggie under foot when he married her mother.'

'Would you?'

'No, probably not. Oliver had only just left school when he and Maggie came to live with me, but Sir Lucas has informed me that he knows the boy is doing well at university, so he must have been keeping himself up to date about us. Has he applied to you recently for information? Within the last week, say?'

'It is information in the common domain.'

'Within the last two days?'

'Mm. It is possible.'

'And you told him I'd investigated a murder for you in the past?'

'I wasn't as specific as that, no. He seemed to be very knowledgeable, has many contacts, I assure you that I—'

'I don't like him.'

'Really?' CJ almost purred. 'Now, that might be unfortunate.'

She exhaled. 'I didn't know I was going to say that, but it's true; I don't. You owe him something?'

'No, no. But there are wheels within wheels—'

'He wants me to discover who's been trying to encompass his death. Do you have any idea what that would entail? There is no way I can infiltrate the Praetorian Guard, which is set up solely to guard the Emperor at his headquarters. And if he thinks he can get Oliver to do so… Surely you wouldn't want to put Oliver's life in danger?'

'Of course not.' Annoyed. 'But Oliver's perfectly capable of identifying the culprit in the flats if he can get access to his or her computer.'

'He'd need a search warrant for that.'

'Mm…possibly not. Surely none of the tenants would wish to obstruct Sir Lucas if he wishes to have a sight of what is on their computers?'

'That's some pressure! Almost, blackmail. "Please, sir; can I look at your private papers to see if there's anything there which might incriminate you?"'

'Now you're overreacting.'

'I don't think so. By the way, Lady Ossett is terrified of being left alone.'

'Is she, now? That's interesting. And gives you a perfect excuse to delve into the doings of the other tenants.'

'Using Oliver as bait? I'm not convinced that I should or could—'

'It would be a pity if Sir Lucas were to lose the confidence of the markets at this particular time. He has the ear of some very important people.'

Bea pulled a face. 'Got a member of Parliament or two in his pocket, eh? I don't think I want to know.'

'Oblige me by obliging him, Bea. There's a certain bill coming up in Parliament next session which we would like to have passed without too much comment.'

She gritted her teeth. 'Give me one good reason why—'

'Will you join me for supper one evening soon? I've heard of a rather pleasant restaurant not far away and would be glad of your opinion—and your company, of course.'

'Grrr.' She shut the phone off with a click and took the steps down to the Underground station.

# FOUR

*Thursday afternoon*

BEA WAS STILL fizzing with rage when she turned into the road in which she lived...and halted in mid-stride.

Her important member of parliament son's car was parked outside her house. Of course she was delighted to see him. It gave her a lift of the heart to think he'd come to visit her...followed by a downturn of spirits when she remembered that he didn't usually call on her unless he wanted something.

She picked up her pace. Perhaps there was something amiss with her adorable grandson, whom she could never see often enough? But no, she'd have heard if that was the case. Anyway, Parliament had broken up for the winter recess and his mother had taken him up to her parents' house where he'd be spoiled rotten, the little love. Bea had handed her Christmas presents over to them last week before they left.

Max had said he was staying on this week for some urgent parliamentary business. All Max's business was of the utmost, if not national, importance...according to Max. But surely he'd said he was going up north to join his family this weekend?

Perhaps he was bringing Bea an extra present?

Don't get your hopes up, girl. He'd have asked his wife to send a hamper over as usual, and it wouldn't even be from Harrods. He wanted something.

As she got out her front door key, Bea looked up at the big sash windows of her living room, half expecting to see him standing there, waiting for her, as he used to do in the years after her first husband had left them and she'd had to struggle to bring Max up on her own. What a nice boy he'd been! He'd promised that when he grew up she would never have to go out to work again, that he'd take care of everything for her.

Ah well. Their fortunes had changed for the better when she went to work for her dear Hamilton at the agency, because he'd married her and adopted Max. When Hamilton had succumbed to cancer, there'd still been no need for Max to provide for her since she then had the agency to run. Max had got into parliament and married into a politically minded and influential family, so he now moved in different circles.

There'd be no clingy, tearful small boy looking out for her today. Instead, he met her in the hallway.

Once upon a time he'd been described as tall, dark and handsome, but good living and insufficient exercise was padding out his figure and blurring the lines of his face. 'Where have you been?' Checking his watch. 'I have a meeting in twenty minutes.'

She found herself apologizing. 'Sorry. Something came up. Have you time for a coffee?' She dumped her handbag in the kitchen—no sign of Maggie, of course—and put the kettle on.

'No. Oh, maybe.' A frown. Banished by a smile. 'I called round to see how you were getting on with the contract for Holland and Butcher. I understand you haven't signed it yet, and I thought you might need some help with it.'

Bea gritted her teeth. Why did her son persist in thinking a woman would be unable to read a contract? Was it only his mother whom he treated like this? Surely he didn't talk down to all women in this way?

'I am looking at it very carefully, yes. Did you say you had time for a coffee?'

'And a slice of cake, if you have one.'

'You can have a biscuit. I haven't done any baking this week. Too busy.'

His expression indicated displeasure. What! Couldn't she even spare the time to bake a cake in case he might call in and feel peckish? After all, what else did she have to do with her time?

'Too busy to sign the contract? Isn't it to your advantage as an employment agency to tie up with a renowned training establishment for domestic staff? What are you holding out for?'

She sighed. Made a cafetière of coffee, found him a mug, sugar and milk. 'They want me to become a director of their firm, and in return they'd like to propose someone from their board of directors to become a director of this agency. I'd prefer a looser arrangement. They could recommend their graduates to us, and we would try to find them suitable jobs. I see no need for a contract.'

'They want closer ties. They want—no, they need— you to be more involved with their day-to-day business, to oversee and improve their training methods. You have a good manageress here, so why not oblige them by going over there a couple of days a week? You'd be sure then of getting the right sort of person for the agency.'

He gulped coffee, reached for the biscuit tin. 'In return, they could appoint someone to advise you on the, well, larger issues, marketing strategy, perhaps some advertising slots in television.'

She narrowed her eyes. How did he know so much? Had he been discussing her agency with them? And if so, why? She prevaricated. 'I'll have to think about it. Marketing, advertising; aren't we doing well enough as it is? Television slots? They're not really my scene. And there's something in the small print that's been nagging at me.'

An indulgent smile for a woman verging on her second childhood. 'Show me what it is, and I'll explain it to you.'

'Why are you so interested?'

'I don't like to see you throw away a good business proposition.' A lie. He must be involved in some way. Oh dear. Had he been bribed to get the contract signed? What a nasty thought. But it clung to the back of her mind.

She said, fearing he wouldn't understand, 'Apart from anything else, I'm not at all sure I want to work with that firm. I accept that Mr Holland was responsible for building the business up in the past, but I don't believe he has a firm enough hand on the tiller nowadays. He's getting on in years. He allowed his previous managing director to run the business into the ground and only sacked him when he turned out to be a scoundrel of the first water. I know he's appointed a new MD, but it's a question of trust. What if bad habits were to creep in again? Would Mr Holland notice? Or do anything about it, if he did?'

'That wouldn't happen because you'd be around to see that it didn't.'

'I'm not the keeper of their conscience, Max.' She tried to smile. 'It's almost as if they want me to join their board and be responsible for what happens to them.'

An uneasy silence. Was that really what was at the back of their minds? Was this contract the thin end of the wedge? Did they want her on their board with a view, eventually, to a full-scale merger? Mr Holland must now be knocking seventy, was perhaps getting tired of running the business. Did he, perhaps, want to sell out to her? Would that be feasible?

Well, it might be. But where would she get the money from to buy them out, and could she see herself running a training college as well as the agency?

It would be a huge step up in the world, but did she want that sort of responsibility? No doubt the bank would… No, no. She'd be in debt for ever.

And yet.

The prospect dazzled and intimidated in equal proportions.

Max drained the last of his coffee. 'They want your expertise and are prepared to pay for it, that's all. Now, I must be going. I really only dropped in to give you a couple of names for the guest list for your party. And don't forget to invite Mr Holland and the other directors.' He laid one of his cards on the table and wrote on the back of it.

Ah, the party which Maggie was hoping to hold in the New Year. Bea could see her wish for it to be a small, intimate affair for friends and family disappearing. 'Max, it's not going to be a business "do". I don't want it tied to the contract.'

'You're not backing out of negotiations at this late stage, are you?'

'Backing out?' The feeling strengthened that he must have got involved in some way. But how? And why? Money? But… Oh dear. Try a delaying tactic. 'I rather thought I'd ask CJ to have a look at the contract. See what he advises.'

'That's the ticket.' Yet he was half-hearted in his farewell hug. 'Ring me if you find there's a problem, right?'

She saw him off.

All was quiet in the house. Maggie still hadn't got back yet, which Bea hoped meant that her argument with the plumber had been resolved.

She went down the stairs to the agency. All was quietly busy there. The new manageress was a treasure, clients were returning time and again, there were very few outstanding bills, and in the run-up to the Christmas holidays the agency's services were required more and more often.

Bea flicked through the messages left in a sheaf on her desk and on her answerphone and dealt with the ones that couldn't wait.

It was urgent that she speak to Oliver. She had a horrid feeling that CJ was going to push Oliver into the arms of the Vicori Corporation to serve his own ends, and she did not want that to happen. He was too young to realize that all that glitters is not gold, and that big corporations crunch up and digest promising young mathematicians before breakfast every day.

She must get to him first.

Oliver wasn't answering his phone. She left a message.

Next, Maggie...who answered her phone in a bright, don't-bother-me-now voice. 'Oh, it's you? I'm a bit tied up, but I did pop round to see my mother before I came on here...' Her voice faded as she spoke to someone in the room with her. 'Yes, everything's just fine, but... Just a minute. I promise I'll be with you in a minute.' And came back again. 'My mother's got a bridge party this afternoon. I said I'd pop in again to see her this evening, but I'll come home for supper before then.'

Bea said, 'Yes, but—'

Maggie switched off.

Bea found the memory stick which Lucas had pressed upon her and inserted it into her computer. There was just one document on it, giving the names, addresses and phone numbers of the tenants in the building. There was a garage in the basement, then a semi-basement flat occupied by a caretaker-cum-handyman. There were two more flats on each of six floors…and then the penthouse, which was the only dwelling at the top. No details were given for the occupants of the penthouse.

Bea thought about that, and she thought about Lucas and his…hubris? Was that the right word? Something lurked at the back of her mind about the skewed perception of the world that immense power gave to people at the top.

Power corrupts and absolute power corrupts absolutely?

Was Lucas corrupt?

Was CJ being corrupted by some political 'necessity' to get a certain bill through parliament?

It gave her a headache to think about it.

She scrolled down through the names on the document and one of them rang a faint bell. No, she couldn't think where or how. Possibly a client, from way back?

Another thought. She accessed the Land Registry details and discovered that, yes, Lucas owned the freehold of the building. Well, he would, wouldn't he? With his wealth he could afford to buy the property, which would no doubt appreciate in value as time went on. Neat.

Bea tried Maggie again; but the girl didn't pick up. She tried Oliver; likewise.

She worked on agency matters till her manageress came in to say that they were shutting up for the night and was there anything…? Bea switched her mind to everyday matters and dealt with one or two queries that had cropped up. Nothing of earth-shattering importance; not like Maggie's problem.

Peace and quiet descended. Bea turned off her computer, checked that every door and window was locked and went up the stairs to draw the curtains in the living room…and to see what she could throw together for supper in the kitchen. Still no Maggie? She was usually home by now.

Her landline rang. Maggie. 'Sorry, so sorry. Got held up I'm at my mother's and she's a bit weepy, so I said I'd stay the night, if that's all right with you?'

'Yes, of course,' said Bea, thinking that Lady O had managed to have people around for her bridge party that afternoon, and now had her daughter for the night.

'Tarra, then,' said Maggie and clicked off.

There was a stir in the hall. The front door opened and a man shouted, 'Hallo?'

Oliver? But…what…?

Bea scurried out to find him unloading his belongings from a hired car. 'My dear boy!'

He gave her a quick hug and waved the driver off.

'Don't we have to pay him?' said Bea.

'All paid for.' He threw off his car coat and laughed down at her.

Since when had he grown so tall that he looked down on her? He'd been a slender youth, but now he was filling out. Oliver was growing up fast. He was doing well at university, and she had a horrid feeling that he was growing away from her.

'I'll take my stuff up later. Meanwhile, I've time for a cuppa.' He made a beeline for the kitchen and put the kettle on.

She followed, thinking unpleasant thoughts. 'CJ has been on the phone to you? He arranged a car to bring you home?'

'He said you needed me to sort something out at the Vicori Corporation. He says that if I play my cards right, they'll take me on the strength. The opportunities… The sky's the limit! I can hardly believe I'm being offered…

I'd never have dreamed, so soon! And it's all thanks to CJ.' He was beaming.

She was not amused. *Take this slowly, Bea.* 'Dear Oliver, why didn't you ring me? Maggie's staying at her mother's overnight to keep her calm, and I'm not sure we've anything much in the freezer for supper.'

'Not to worry. CJ suggested I go round there for a bite to eat so that he can fill me in on what's been happening. He'll give me a bed for the night and take me over to Lady Ossett's for breakfast. I'll keep her sweet tomorrow morning while Maggie goes off to work. Then I go into Vicori House in the afternoon. I'm to shadow the chief suspect as he goes about his work, something complicated in the business of buying energy from the Middle East. I'll soon get the hang of it. Isn't it exciting!'

The kettle shrilled. Hands on automatic, she made a cafetière of coffee. 'Did CJ tell you exactly why he wants to help Sir Lucas?'

'Yes, yes. He's known him a long time. Something to do with the European Court of Justice, he didn't give me the details.' He looked at his watch. 'I've only time for a quick cup of tea. Said I wouldn't be late.'

He wanted tea, not coffee. Was there enough water left in the kettle to make him a cup of tea? There wasn't. Fill kettle. Keep calm. 'CJ didn't tell you Lucas has to be kept sweet, in order to push some bill or other through in the next session of parliament?'

'Yes, yes. He said you didn't like him. Honestly, Mother Hen…' His nickname for her slipped out, but without its usual fondness.

'He told you that I didn't like him?' She stared at Oliver. Stared inside herself. 'I can't justify my dislike.' She shrugged, trying to minimize the damage her words had done. 'First impressions. No doubt when I get to know him better…'

'It's not like you to be so hasty.' He grinned at her; the superior smug smile of someone who knows much better than a woman old enough to be his mother—or even, in this case, his grandmother.

'No, it's not.' The kettle boiled, and she poured water over a tea bag in his favourite mug. 'I can't explain it.'

'I can.' He gave her a quick hug, at the same time removing the mug from her hands. 'I take it with lemon now, no milk. Have we got any lemons?'

She got one out of the fridge for him.

He said, smiling, sharing a splendid secret with her, 'You've been everything to me since you picked me out of the gutter. You've fed me and scolded me and taught me everything you know. You've sent me to university and been better than a mother to me. Now that I'm grown up and moving into the great wide world, now that other people are beginning to take an interest in my career, I do understand that you can't help feeling, well, left behind.'

She stared at him. Was there any truth in what he said? Could she be that self-centred that she didn't want anyone else to help him climb the ladder of success?

No, surely not. She looked deep into herself and grimaced. Perhaps there was an element of that in her stand against Lucas? But her main objection remained; she neither liked nor trusted the man.

Had CJ insinuated these doubts about Bea's position into Oliver's head? If so, how very, very clever of him, because Bea didn't know how to counter them.

She must, however, try.

'Look at it from my point of view, Oliver. You've been doing marvellously well at university. You are only in

your second year, but already they're asking you to take
on research in this and that. If you leave now—'

'Opportunities like this don't come along every day.
Most people would give their eye teeth for a chance to
join Vicori, and I'm not letting anything stand in my
way. You don't really want me to refuse him, do you?'
He could use charm as others used butter.

'A man like Lucas doesn't think as you or I do. He
uses people, rewarding and discarding them at will. I
suspect that if he finds out—*when* he finds out—which
of his executives is seeking to supplant him, there'll be
a bloodbath—'

An amused smile. 'Now you're going too far.'

She wasn't getting through to him. She tried again.
'Oh, it will be a sanitized affair. A convenient accident,
or a depression leading to suicide. I'm sure no one will be
more sorry than he to lose a valued member of his team.'

'Ridiculous!' He put his arm around her to give her
a hug and gulped down the rest of his tea. 'You won't
mind if I leave most of my stuff in the hall for tonight,
will you? I'll only need my overnight bag for now. Is it
all right if I borrow the car?'

'Sorry. No. I need it.' She didn't. She felt a pang of
contrition at having lied to him, but she was too annoyed
with him to let him have it. Besides, if he took it now to
meet up with CJ for supper, he'd take it over to Lady O's
tomorrow and then on into the City. And where would
he park it? Was he going to be given a parking slot at
Vicori House?

No, it was her car, and she needed it. Probably. What
she really meant was that she was cross with him and
didn't want to lend him her car.

He glanced at his watch. 'I'll walk round there then;
it's probably the quickest. See you at the weekend, right?'

She made one last effort. 'Before you go; I may be quite wrong about Lucas—I hope I am for your sake—but he can afford the very best lawyers and you can't. If he asked you to sign something, anything, would you get CJ to vet it first?'

'Oh, really!'

'I'm serious. Also, I think his office is bugged, probably so that he doesn't need to take notes of any conferences he has there, so—'

'You're way off the planet!'

'Keep your eyes open, that's all I ask. And keep your eyes open at Lady O's. Remember there's a killer about!'

He wasn't listening. He was off, and she was left to think how badly she'd handled the interview. For instance, would it really matter that she didn't like Lucas if he was prepared to further Oliver's career? Working for a man didn't mean you had to like him. Loads of people didn't have a choice in the matter of their boss; he existed, and they toed the line or else.

But she could imagine a scenario in which Oliver was demoted for some reason or other and ended up at the bottom of the anthill, staring at a computer in a prescribed space...rather like a battery hen. Feed, sleep, produce. Die.

She shuddered. Decided she didn't want to drink any of the coffee she'd made, put Oliver's mug in the dishwasher and rummaged in the freezer for a frozen meal. Cauliflower cheese. It would have to do. Microwave it. Tidy the kitchen while it cooked. Eat it at the counter. Fend off their big, black, hairy cat. 'Winston! No!'

Winston gave her a fat grin and lifted one paw in a begging movement. He was as full of charm as Oliver.

She fed Winston and removed herself to the living room, which ran from front to back of the house. Large sash windows at the front overlooked the street, while at the back a pair of French windows let out on to a cast-iron balcony with a spiral staircase leading down to the courtyard. Because of the slope on which the house was built, the agency occupied semi-basement rooms at the front of the house while her office at the back led straight out on to the garden.

She checked that all the windows were locked and the curtains tightly drawn against the damp, chill night. There was an almost full moon over the spire of the church.

She was restless. Eventually, she sat down at the table by the windows at the back of the living room and took out her patience cards. Her dear husband Hamilton had been accustomed to sit there of an evening, his hands moving the cards around while he pondered this and that…or prayed in silence.

Now his portrait looked down on her. Round-faced, wise…she missed him so much. He seemed to be saying, 'Patience.'

She threw the pack of cards down, halfway through laying out a game.

Patience. Ugh. Not her scene.

But necessary, perhaps? If she couldn't alter what was happening…?

There wasn't anything she could do about it, was there?

Hm. Well. Perhaps there was, though it was a long shot and probably wouldn't get her anywhere.

Why bother, then?

Because even if it didn't get her anywhere, at least she'd have done everything she could to avert what seemed to her to be a looming catastrophe.

She went back down the stairs and into her office.

Switched her computer on. She'd saved the information on the memory stick in a document. Accessed it. Now... where was that name she thought she recognized?

Mm. Mm. No? No. Ah, there!

She ran the names through the agency's client list. No, the name she thought she'd remembered didn't match. She nearly gave up. This was the sort of thing which Oliver excelled at. There was, however, one name which stood out on Sir Lucas's list because of its plethora of initials. L.A.M. Emerson. Reading 'lame'. But not at the right address.

Bea stared at the screen, wondering. People did move. They moved into a better address when their husbands got promotion. They downsized when grown-up children left home or their spouse decamped or they lost their jobs or whatever. They kept their phone numbers if they could.

It was five years since the agency had supplied Mrs Emerson with a chef and silver service waitresses for a party of twelve at an address in Knightsbridge. A party of twelve indicated a spacious dining-room which was a luxury in today's terms. A far cry from the two or three bedroom apartment in Lucas's building. Perhaps the husband had died since that memorable party. Would she still have the same telephone number? Bea returned to the list supplied by Sir Lucas. No, the phone number was different.

Bea's hand hovered over the telephone and withdrew. What could she possibly say to Mrs Emerson, even supposing it was the same woman?

*Dear Mrs Emerson. Can you give me the low-down on Lady O? You aren't acquainted with her? Oh dear. Sorry to have troubled you.*

Think again. She dialled. 'Is that Mrs Emerson? This

is Mrs Abbot here, of the Abbot Agency. You may remember using our services some years ago?'

'Indeed, yes. Our golden wedding celebration.' The cracked voice of an older woman.

Relief! It was the same woman.

'Happy days, long gone. But...?' Mystified.

'I'm so sorry to trouble you, but I had occasion to visit Lady Ossett today and noticed a For Sale board outside the flats. As it happens we have a client who has asked us to keep an eye out for a place in your area...' It was quite true that they were occasionally asked to do this for a client now and then, but such queries were always passed on to a reputable estate agency. 'I thought it might suit him very well, only I was disturbed by some hints that Lady Ossett dropped about vandalism...?'

'Far be it from me to discourage your client from considering the purchase of a flat in our building, although I must warn you that considerable redecoration will be needed, as nothing has been done to the ground floor apartment since the occupant, who was an old lady who'd lived there for ever, died. As for the other, I understand it will need considerable refurbishment. The tenant has gone completely to pieces since his partner—if that's what they call them nowadays—walked out on him. I'm not sure that that one is officially up for sale yet, but since the man's lost his job, perhaps it will come on the market soon as well.'

Bea made notes. One flat was for sale because some-one had died, and the tenant of the other one had got the sack so would also have to sell.

'They will both need updating, if that's what they call it nowadays, which, as I said to my dear friend Carrie, Mrs Kempton, who lives above me, means that they will tear out a perfectly good bathroom and kitchen, cover every surface in black marble, put in a wet room instead of a shower, not to mention a false ceiling and dotting it with those tiny lights that you can't get at to replace when they burn out.'

'I know they can be difficult—'

'Difficult? If my husband were only alive, God bless him, he'd have dealt with them in next to no time. As it is—'

'I sympathize. I found all that side of things hard after my own dear husband died.'

'Ah. You understand, then.'

Bea took a deep breath. 'May I come round to see you some time, Mrs Emerson? Perhaps you could introduce me to Mrs Kempton, too. And maybe the man whose flat is up for sale? What number is that flat, by the way?'

'He's opposite Carrie, at number eleven.'

'So she's below Ms Lessbury, is that right?' said Bea, making notes.

'No, indeed.' A definite coolness. 'Ms Lessbury is at number seven, but I doubt if you'd find her disengaged from teatime onwards, if you understand my French.'

Bea grinned. So Ms Lessbury was known to be a lady of afternoon appointments, was she? 'Well, if the apartments are in reasonably good condition, and we can discount the unfortunate happenings which Lady Ossett told me about, then my client might well be interested in having a look.'

'Hm. I wouldn't take much notice of what Lady Ossett says!' Scorn in the voice? Lady O was no fan of Mrs Emerson's? Or vice versa? 'Well, shall we say ten thirty tomorrow morning? I don't sleep well nowadays and it takes me a while to face the day, so Mrs Kempton usually joins me for a coffee mid-morning.'

'Thank you, Mrs Emerson. Ten thirty would be splendid.'

Bea put the phone down and started to make a chart of who lived where in the flats and what sort of person they might be. She told herself that it was too soon to generalize, but a picture was emerging of a number of single men and women each occupying a two or three bedroom flat. Bea told herself there was nothing unusual about that, but for some reason she had a sense of disquiet about the situation.

After a lot of thought, she rang CJ to take him up on his offer of supper. Well, why not? At least she could talk through her reservations about Holland and Butcher with him—and avoid the subject of Sir Lucas and his near encounter with death.

# FIVE

*Friday morning*

MRS EMERSON AND her friend Mrs Kempton were a double act.

Two elderly ladies with comfortable figures in woolly sweaters, unfashionably long grey skirts and support hose. Trainers with Velcro fastenings. They had no-nonsense short-cut grey hair; no make-up except for a colourless lipsalve; no nail varnish. One had a heavy gold locket on a chain round her neck, the other had a marcasite brooch pinned to her sweater. Their wedding rings could no longer be eased over thickened knuckles.

They took Bea's long black coat and hung it up in an old-fashioned wardrobe in the hallway; no fitted cupboards here. Everything in the flat was from an earlier age. You could call it Out of Date, or you could call it Date-less. There was even a hallstand with a mirror above and a lead-lined receptacle for a variety of sticks and umbrellas below.

In the sitting room, the furniture was slightly shabby but solid, most of it pre-war. With some reupholstering it would be good for another decade. The temperature in the room was warm, the windows hermetically sealed against draughts. Airless.

Mrs Emerson was called Lucy, and Mrs Kempton was Carrie-short-for-Caroline. Bea couldn't distinguish between the two, but perhaps that didn't matter since they spoke and thought as one. Perhaps they'd been friends from childhood?

Bea said, 'You mentioned a flat on the ground floor that's up for sale—'

'Probate hasn't been granted yet, but the word is that Sir Lucas will buy up the remainder of the lease. But the one opposite me—'

'We must warn you it's not in good decorative condition because the removal people seemed to be there every other month. Tenants on short-term contracts, you know. Management level, moved around the world at a moment's notice. Carrie even said she wondered if a curse had been put upon it, though of course we don't believe in that sort of thing, do we? The people before last, such a pleasant couple, were posted to Manchester at short notice and had to sublet in a hurry—'

'It's not that we pry, of course—'

'But we couldn't help noticing, when we called on the new tenant, as of course we always do—'

'To warn him about the end dryer in the basement which has never been satisfactory, and tell him about the caretaker who also does the cleaning but you have to speak *very* nicely to him because he takes offence at the slightest opportunity—'

'And of course about keeping the noise down—'

Bea sat back and listened as coffee was poured into fine bone china cups and a plate of home-made short-bread biscuits was passed around. Carrie had a mole on her left cheek. Lucy had the larger bust. Or perhaps it was the other way round?

'So you see,' they chorused, grey and brown eyes sparkling with what Bea could only think of as innocent malice, 'he was warned.'

They both nodded.

'More coffee?' asked their hostess. So she must be Lucy Emerson and the mother and grandmother of the children and young people in the silver-framed photographs lying around; two weddings, a christening and a degree ceremony.

'I'd love some more coffee,' said Bea. 'As you probably know, Lady Ossett's daughter lodges with me, so when I was asked to look out for a flat locally, I called round to see her, and she hinted…or perhaps you don't know about it? Am I right in thinking that Sir Lucas is taking a break from his marriage?'

Both nodded, heavy chins wobbling. 'We hope it's not going to come to that, but—'

'We did wonder, we did indeed. She says it's only temporary, but of course we know how such things happen. I do feel so sorry for her.'

The other bridled. 'She never troubled herself to invite us for a cosy cup of tea in all the time we've lived here, but now her husband's done a runner, she's ringing up and suggesting we might like to spend the day with her.'

Her friend was more forgiving. 'Well, dear; I expect her husband kept her busy. She must feel lost without him.'

The other tossed her head; she really did. 'Making use of us. I declined for us, of course. We attend her bridge afternoons—'

'It's very kind of her to invite us, but they're playing for rather high stakes now which I did mention to her, in passing, but she doesn't quite understand how it is for us, with the service charges seeming to rise every month—'

'And we really do worry about how long we can stay on here. I was only able to get a short lease when I moved in, and it runs out in eighteen months which is all very worrying as I can't possibly afford to renew on the terms he's asking—'

'Fortunately, mine has some years to go now. So we're thinking of dropping out. Of the bridge parties, I mean.'

Their dropping out wouldn't be anything to do with the sharpness of their brains. They were as bright as buttons but wouldn't wish to run into debt. Living on reduced pensions, with prices rising all round, the future did indeed look grim.

Bea prompted them. 'You know about Sir Lucas's fall?'

A slight frown from Mrs Emerson. Lucy. 'Oh, that. The landing light was out, or he hadn't put it on and missed his step. What a fuss! When my grandson broke his leg playing rugby, he walked around on it for two days before his mother made him go to the hospital and have it seen to. Young people nowadays have no stamina.'

Carrie lent forward, happy to gossip. 'I heard him bellowing even above the wireless, would you believe. I almost didn't go out to see what was the matter because I knew the people above me were away because they asked me to rescue their post and put it through their door—'

'Lucky you did though, dear. Might earn you brownie points with His Lordship.' A sarcastic tone. It seemed that Lucy was the one less likely to forgive and forget.

Carrie Kempton might be the less dominant personality, but she was no doormat. 'I was never a Brownie or a Girl Guide like you, dear. I was evacuated during the war to Wales and never had the opportunity. Sir Lucas would have been all right, anyway. He was on the phone to the ambulance men by the time I got to him.'

'But it was you who had to put yourself out by going downstairs to let the ambulance men in.'

Carrie gave a weak smile. 'I suppose he was right to

be frightened. He'd cut his head, and there was a lot of blood. The caretaker was *very* upset about that.'

Lucy announced, 'I don't object to blood. When I was a nurse…'

Carrie nodded. 'Yes, dear. And I've done first aid in my time.'

'Not the same.'

A ripple of annoyance. So the two women didn't think as one all the time? Bea put down her empty cup. 'So, Sir Lucas's fall was an accident. What about the other incidents that Lady Ossett referred to?'

A pinching of lips. A sly exchange of glances.

'We…ll,' said Lucy, in grudging tones. 'We don't wish to cast aspersions—'

'We do feel sorry for him, in a way. But he did bring it all on himself, and as he's leaving anyway and he really does need to sell the flat, then perhaps we ought…'

Another exchange of glances. A nod each.

Lucy prepared to Tell All. 'You can tell your friend that whatever happened, it's all in the past. It's true we have had one or two little problems—'

Carrie was enjoying this. 'But nothing to take to the police. I mean, it was annoying when cards for call girls were left in the mail boxes in the foyer, can you believe it? It meant nuisance calls for some of us, which was—'

'Irritating, of course. But not serious. No, dear. That wasn't the start of it, and you know it.' To Bea, 'It all started when someone keyed Sir Lucas's car.'

'I think it started even before that,' said Carrie, not to be outdone. 'We've lived here for years and nothing untoward ever happened, except for the usual comings and goings and we were used to those. But when someone you've known for ever dies unexpectedly, well, it's a shock.'

'Natural causes, dear.' Lucy swept her friend's words aside. 'Natural causes. But there was nothing natural about the damage to Sir Lucas's car, was there? Even though it was understandable.'

'You see,' said Carrie, drawing her chair even closer to Bea, 'we knew who was responsible, and really we couldn't blame him. Or at least, not very much, and we don't want him to get into any more trouble.'

Bea looked a question.

Carrie looked around as if to check for eavesdroppers—she really was enjoying this, wasn't she?—and dropped her voice. 'It was Tariq, of course. He lives opposite me in number eleven. He moved in when the last couple went up north. It was a sublet through someone at the firm they both worked for. I don't know exactly where his people came from originally—Tariq, I mean—but he was born here, and he's ever so polite, helping us up the stairs with our shopping when the lift is out of commission, and although he did have lots of parties at the weekend it wasn't so bad in the cold weather because we didn't have the windows open at night. It's true that Lady Ossett did complain about the noise a couple of times, and he did keep it down for quite a while. But then...' She hesitated, glancing across at Lucy for permission to proceed.

Lucy nodded in magisterial fashion. 'A delicate matter. Of course we'd rather have seen him marry a nice young British girl, but you have to be broad-minded these days, don't you, and if hadn't been for the noise... You see, he invited a friend to move in with him to share the costs, and he was black as... Well, much blacker than... Really, really black. Though I know it shouldn't make a difference, but his taste in music was...well, like all on one note—'

'It's called "rap", dear.'

'I don't care what it's called. It was very loud indeed. Lady Ossett complained again, and I can't say I blame her.'

'He was a really nice young man,' said Carrie, with the mildest of rebukes to her friend in her voice. 'We understood that they were serious about one another and going to have a special ceremony, some sort of lifetime commitment, and of course they invited us to attend because… well, just because.'

'Because we've always behaved politely to him,' said Lucy. 'We declined, of course. They said to come to the party afterwards, and we didn't really want to, all that spicy food doesn't agree with us, but we said we'd love to drop in later and we bought a couple of pot plants to give them from Marks and Spencer's.'

'Only, the music was so terribly loud that night. They left their door open, you see—'

'And their guests kept coming up the stairs and using the lift and shouting and I said to Carrie—we were watching television together in here that evening as we sometimes do, particularly when it's a good thriller which we both like and it's so much more cosy watching with someone, isn't it? And my television is bigger than hers. Anyway, the noise was so loud, and the visitors were all very young, from all over the place, if you take my meaning, that I said to Carrie that I didn't think his idea of a party was quite our cup of tea and we could take the plants in later in the week. And she agreed.'

Carrie nodded. 'But after our programme finished it got noisier and noisier. When I went back upstairs it seemed as if the whole building was shaking, and I wondered if there'd be more complaints, which there had been before only this was much worse. I took a herbal sleeping pill but it didn't seem to work and I was tossing and turning… I even thought of going across to complain myself but of course I didn't and I thought they'd get tired and stop but then I woke up with a start at just after four o'clock. Someone was banging on the door and I thought at first it was my door, but it wasn't. It was theirs. So I got up and opened my door a crack to see.'

Lucy's turn. 'It woke me up, too. It was the Noise people. They had been round to warn Tariq earlier that evening but he'd not taken any notice, so they went in and confiscated all his lovely music equipment and people were screaming and…well, it was quite something. That was the start of it all, if you ask me.'

Carrie said, 'Tariq's friend, or husband or whatever, left that weekend, which says something about his commitment to the relationship, doesn't it? It was his music equipment that was taken away, you see. Perhaps he loved his stereo more than he loved Tariq? And then we heard Tariq was being let go from his job. Under the terms of his sublet, he's got to find a new tenant or he'll be in debt for ever.'

Lucy nodded at a fine azalea on the window-sill. 'We kept the plants, naturally. As my mother said, plunge the root ball in water to cover, once a week, and spray the leaves. Keeps them going a treat, even with central heating; though of course I don't keep mine turned up too high because I have to think of the fuel bills, don't I?'

'Mine died,' said Carrie. 'I've never been any good with house plants.'

Bea tried to gather her wits. 'You think Tariq was responsible for the vandalism?'

'We didn't think so, at first. But we wondered, didn't we, Carrie? Who it might be. When it was just the cards for the call girls, we thought it might be someone who objected to the goings on in a certain flat… Well, no names, no pack drill…'

Bea mentally filled in the gap with the name of Carmela Lessbury.

'Lucy thought it might be our caretaker because he disapproves of what he calls "those nasty goings on". Then one of Sir Lucas's cars was vandalized, not the Rolls of course, but the sporty one, and we knew the caretaker wouldn't ever have done anything to it because he worships those cars. Spends hours cleaning and waxing and polishing them. No, he wouldn't harm those cars. But Tariq, now. It was Them Upstairs who brought in the Noise people and confiscated his music equipment, you see, and that caused the break-up of his marriage or whatever you like to call it—'

'Careful, dear. Don't let the Thought Police hear you being so un-PC. But it's quite true. Sir Lucas was the one who complained—'

'No, no. It was Lady Ossett. But we know it was really him who got her to do the complaining, and I'm sure she was very sorry about having to do so.'

'And Tariq was let go from his job with Sir Lucas's firm the week after.'

They both nodded.

'What happened to Sir Lucas's car?' said Bea, trying to keep up.

'I think they call it "keying",' said Carrie. 'You take your keys and scrape the paintwork. And the hood had been cut with a knife. It's a what-do-you-call-it? A convertible. Very expensive, I'm told. I don't keep a car nowadays.'

'I know nothing about cars,' said Lucy, grandly. 'Sir Lucas kept his in the sub-basement. You won't have seen the entrance to the garage, perhaps? It's round the back.

You have to pay extra for a bay down there. Tariq has
had to sell his car already.'

'Sub-basement?' said Bea.

'The lift goes right down to it. The basement level
is partly at ground floor level at the back, but not at the
front. Mr Pancko has his flat there, and his cleaning cupboards and workshop. There's also the washing and dry-
ing machines for the whole complex, only we don't use
them because we've got our own up here.'

'His name isn't *Pancko*, dear. It's not Poncho, either.
I can't think exactly what it is, but it's not Pancko. He
comes from Yugoslavia, I think.'

'It's called Croatia nowadays, isn't it? All I know is
that he's not the most obliging of men. No, it wasn't him.
It was Tariq, I'm sorry to say. So he'll be leaving, and
I suppose his flat will be coming on to the market, if
you're interested.'

Carrie lamented, 'It means the decorators will be coming in again. It's never ending in this place. Upstairs,
downstairs. Everywhere. Banging and crashing just when
I want my afternoon nap.'

Bea's mobile shrilled, and she dived into her bag to
rescue it.

Surprise! It was Lady Ossett's sweet tones on the
phone. 'Mrs Abbot, I'm afraid I was a little short with
you yesterday—'

'Not at all,' said Bea, glad that her faux pas about the
toy boy was to be overlooked.

'Such a misunderstanding about my husband's glasses,
which he was going to send someone round for, but I
understand that your protégé Oliver—such a pleasant
young man—will deliver them for me this afternoon.
So I'm wondering, I've been thinking about your offer
of someone simpatico, as you might say, someone who

would fit in with our circle of friends, who might perhaps take pity on me in my hour of need.'

Bea felt the two elderly ladies' gaze on her. Lady Ossett's crystal clear tones could probably be heard throughout the whole flat. 'May I ring you back when I'm free?'

'My nerves are shredded. If you could just give me a tiny ray of hope?'

'Er, yes. Of course. I'm sure I can arrange something but… I'll pop in to see you later, shall I?' Bea cut the call off.

Lucy and Carrie switched their eyes to their coffee cups. Their ears were perfectly formed and set neatly to the sides of their heads, but to Bea's inner eye had at least doubled in size during her telephone call.

Bea produced a social smile. 'A client in trouble. I must get back to her, but in the meantime…'

Half an hour later she left Lucy Emerson's flat, shutting the door firmly behind her. She had a notebook full of scribbles and a burning desire to be out in the fresh air. The air in the flat had seemed short of oxygen. An illusion, of course, born of the two ladies' relentless gossiping. You met this in villages, where the inhabitants were more interested in the number of times a neighbouring man or woman might or might not change their underclothes or claim benefits to which they were not entitled. You met it in built-up areas of towns and cities where people never travelled more than five miles from home. You didn't expect to meet it in a vibrant, capital city like London.

It left a nasty taste in the mouth.

Bea hung over the banister for a while, breathing deeply, knowing that her interview with Lady O was likely to call on all her reserves of patience. Still, if Oliver was going to be at Vicori House that afternoon, someone had got to keep Lady O company. The lift emitted a soft, almost inaudible whine as it passed Bea on its way upwards. She heard the gentle grind of the doors opening, a pause as someone entered, and the doors puffed shut. The lift descended; taking Oliver down to the ground floor?

Prompt on cue, Bea's mobile rang. Lady O.

'I'm on my way.' Bea didn't wait for the lift, but took the stairs.

*Friday noon*

BEA PAUSED ON the landing outside the penthouse to catch her breath. Was she so badly out of condition that a couple of flights of stairs had her puffing and panting? Er, yes. She really must try to take more exercise.

The morning had been cloudy but the sun was trying to break through. A ray shot across the landing. Bea checked to see if it would show up the tack or screw marks which she'd noted on her previous visit.

The hole on the right had disappeared. What? It can't have done. She hunkered down and got out her magnifying glass. No mark.

She checked the opposite side of the staircase. No mark there, either. She sat back on her heels. Thought. Rubbed her finger across where the mark had been and… yes…there was the slightest of irregularities there, as if a spot of paint, or filler, or some other pliable material had been rammed into the hole to make it disappear from sight.

On the opposite side, too. She hadn't imagined the holes, had she?

She got out her mobile phone and checked. No photos of the holes. None.

She drew in her breath. Remembered handing her

phone to Sir Lucas, who had taken it over to the window to inspect the evidence. He'd carried on the conversation for a few minutes with his back to her, before shutting up the phone and returning it to her.

Conclusion; he'd deleted the photographs.

Why had he done that? He'd said he thought he knew who was responsible for his tumble down the stairs, and he'd have needed the photographs in order to prosecute the man, or to persuade him to resign. Whatever. So he wouldn't have destroyed the evidence.

On the other hand, he didn't want outsiders knowing that he was under attack because it might affect the share price of his company. So what had he done? He'd deleted the pictures on Bea's phone so that she couldn't use them in any way, but only after he'd first stored them somewhere for his own use.

He must have used those few minutes when his back was turned to send them on to somebody else for safekeeping and further investigation. To his own phone, perhaps? And only after that had he deleted Bea's photographs.

Bea shook her head. Whatever had she got herself into now? This man outclassed her in every way. Why didn't she just give up and go home?

Well, for one thing, she couldn't abandon Maggie. And for another, Lady Ossett was afraid of something, and that something had not disappeared with her husband's departure.

Bea rang the doorbell and was let into the penthouse suite.

# SIX

*Friday noon*

LADY O WAS dressed in pale blue and white today. As pretty as a picture, except that lines of strain were beginning to show around her artfully made-up blue eyes.

'Oliver left half an hour ago. You've taken your time, I must say.' She turned on her heel and left Bea to hang up her coat for herself.

A certain disarray—today's papers scattered around, a cushion on the floor, a curtain not properly drawn back—indicated that Lady O was no longer on top of her housekeeping. Ah, her cleaner didn't come on Fridays, did she?

'Coffee?' The offer was made in perfunctory fashion and received as such.

'No, thank you.'

Lady O went to the window at the far end and stood there, looking out. She fiddled with the gauzy scarf at her neck.

Bea took a seat by the table, noting that that day's crossword had been completed. Had Oliver helped Lady O with it today? Probably.

'I'm a bag of nerves,' said Lady O. 'I really can't go on like this. You really must find me someone… Maggie has been so unkind, refusing to help me…'

Good for Maggie.

'I asked young Oliver, but he seems to think it wouldn't be exactly… I'm at my wits end.'

Bea recognized desperation when she saw it. 'They don't understand the strain you're under.'

Lady O shot Bea a haunted glance, two parts of surprise to four of hope. 'You know, then? I haven't said anything. I wouldn't. I promised Lucas I wouldn't.'

'He thinks the wire across the stairs was arranged by someone at the corporation with the help of an accomplice who lives in this building—'

'Lucas is convinced Tariq has been helping one of his vice chairmen to incapacitate him in some way, but he won't go public with it and Tariq's still here because he can't find anyone to take the tenancy off him. I told Lucas to end the contract and then he'd be rid of Tariq; but he won't. He's penny wise and pound foolish.'

'You don't agree with your husband on this, do you? You think that Tariq might have been responsible for some of the incidents that have been going on here, but not for the attack on your life.'

Lady O crumpled into a nearby chair, wringing her hands. Yes, she really did wring her hands. Bea watched with interest. She'd never seen anyone actually doing it before.

'How did you guess? Oliver said you were pretty bright.'

It had been a guess, but Bea had noted how various incidents had escalated into attempted murder and added Lady O's almost palpable fear to the mixture.

'Tell me about it.'

Lady O made a helpless gesture with both hands. 'I wasn't absolutely sure at first, but yesterday... As you probably know, we play bridge here on Thursday afternoons from three to five. We chose a Thursday because Lucas has meetings well into the evening on that day, so he's not inconvenienced. My cleaner comes in three mornings a week for a couple of hours, on Mondays, Thursdays and Saturdays. She's Polish, but very good. Only, she does like to air the rooms. She opens the windows even on cold days, particularly in my bedroom. She says my scent gives her asthma.'

Bea went to the nearest window and looked out.

'No, this way. I'll show you.' Lady O led the way back into the hallway and turned through an archway into a long corridor leading off left and right. Of course, the layout would not be the same as for the flats below.

She opened doors on the corridor to the right. 'This is the room where we have our bridge parties.' A large room, full of light, with tables and chairs all set up, ready to go. 'Then at the end here we have Maggie's room, and the spare bedroom, both en suite. Turning back again here we have the utility room, junk room, and then—opposite the bridge room there's the kitchen and the dining room, though we don't use that much. We usually have a table set up in the living room when we're by ourselves, and of course we hire staff if we give a dinner party.'

A bewildering number of rooms. But of course the penthouse covered the area of the whole building, and was therefore twice the size of the flats below.

Lady O continued down the left-hand corridor. 'Another toilet. Here we have Lucas's TV room, his study and his bedroom...and finally the master bedroom, en suite.'

She threw open a door on to a beautiful room done in shades of mushroom and cream with gilt trimmings. Several mirrored doors no doubt concealed extensive clothes closets. The bed was a four-poster with silk curtains held back by gilded cherubs. The carpet was silk, too. It was breathtaking. And yes, the lady's perfume was perhaps a trifle overwhelming.

Lady O led the way to some French windows which,

when opened, would let you out on to the terrace garden, which seemed to run around three sides of the roof space and provided yet another stunning view of the city…and of the sky. The sky at night must seem so close you would want to reach out and touch the stars — if there wasn't too much light pollution, that is.

Lady O opened one of the French windows and stepped out on to the terrace. The chill wind outside caused her to clasp her arms around her body, and she rapidly returned to the warmth.

'My cleaner always opens this window. I've told her time and again, but she will do it. The fire escape is just round the corner. It's on the outside of the building, connecting all the flats via a series of balconies, such an old-fashioned idea, but this block is nearly a hundred years old, so what can you expect?'

'You don't get burglars?'

Almost a smile. 'There's an excellent alarm system—Lucas saw to that—but of course it's turned off when my cleaner is around. No, it's the cat that gave me the most trouble. Professor Jacobsen has—had—a long-haired grey cat…'

Bea mentally accessed the information provided by the two elderly gossips. '…*On the top floor under the penthouse there's the Old Codger, as we call him, and his cat. Jewish. With a twice-a-week housekeeper. The place is full of books. His daughter comes over regular as clockwork to see he changes his clothes, and she keeps the freezer filled though mostly he goes out for meals…*' So that was Professor Jacobsen.

'The cat was called Momi, it did its doodahs in the tubs on my terrace, and left hairs all over the place, perfectly horrible, but my cleaner doted on him, used to bring him titbits, would you believe? So Momi visited me almost every day, no matter how often I shooed him out, and of course the open window was an invitation. At night he'd caterwaul outside my window. I kept an aerosol handy, with water in it. One spray with that, and off he'd go, complaining. It was worse during the day. He used to sneak in, and I'd find him on my pillow, or in my favourite chair...'

She paused, breathing deeply. 'I'm sorry, of course. It was a dreadful thing, and I haven't dared tell Professor Jacobsen. He's been up asking if I'd seen his cat, and of course I said I hadn't. He, the cat, is in a black plastic bag behind the biggest of the tubs outside. I thought of asking Maggie to get rid of the body for me, but she's mad about that cat of yours, isn't she, and I didn't think she'd do it.'

Ah. Now we're getting to the truth. 'The cat's dead?'

Lady O's eyes were wild. She nodded. 'We were well into the bridge party yesterday afternoon when I remembered I hadn't prepared anything for my supper, so I popped across to the kitchen to take a piece of steak out of the freezer and put it under a mesh cage to defrost. When my guests had all gone, I went back to the kitchen and the cat was lying on the floor. Dead. He'd shoved the cage aside and eaten nearly all of the steak.'

'That might not be—'

'To make sure I got the point, there was a tin of rat poison nearby, with the lid off. An old tin. Rusty. There wasn't much left in the tin.' She led the way back through the corridor and into the kitchen. A modern kitchen though not large by today's standards. She pointed to a work surface. 'There. Rat poison. Remains of steak.' She pointed to the floor. 'There. Dead cat. I suppose I should thank Momi for alerting me to the danger. I made Maggie get us takeaways last night, and I'm going to throw away everything I've got in the freezer and the fridge. Who knows what else has been poisoned?'

'You believe it was a warning meant for you?'

Lady O cracked out a laugh. 'Well, it wasn't meant for Lucas, was it? He's gone. And it wasn't a warning. It was pure chance that Momi ate what was intended for me. Someone meant me to die.'

'You don't know who it was?'

Again, she wrung her hands. 'I wish I did, but I don't.'

'What does Lucas think of this?'

'He thinks I'm "a little hysterical". He's so sure he's the target that he can't even consider that I might be the intended victim. He thinks it's all part and parcel of the plot to drive him out of office. He says that if I'd eaten the steak, I might have been made ill, but that it wouldn't have killed me. I wrapped the remains of the steak in cling film, using new rubber gloves which I then threw away, and I sent it to him, asking him to get it analysed, together with the tin labelled "Poison". He turned all patronizing on me, said that if I insisted of course he'd send it to the laboratory in due course, though I must remember that they are terribly busy and—'

She bent over, retching. Made it to the sink. Threw up.

Bea located some kitchen towels and put them at Lady O's elbow.

'Thank you.' Lady O ran the cold tap, dunked a kitchen towel, wiped her mouth, removing her lipstick. She got a glass, poured out and drank some water. 'I apologize. I don't usually give way like this. I can usually take things in my stride. Four husbands, a dysfunctional child, money difficulties… I've always managed to keep smiling. I keep asking myself, who have I offended so much that they want me dead? And what's going to happen next? Do you wonder that I can't bear to be left alone here?'

'You should leave, go to a hotel, stay with a friend.'

'I've thought of it. God knows I've thought of nothing else much these last few days. Lucas doesn't want me to. He's convinced I'm in no real danger. He says he's relying on me to stay here and pretend nothing is happening so as not to upset a volatile share market. He says he's closing in on the man he suspects is behind all this. He says that if I leave it will alert the conspirators, who… But I honestly don't think Tariq is capable of it!'

She rang the cold water tap some more and dabbed at her forehead with a wet kitchen towel, removing even more of her make-up. 'I thought of getting a doctor's certificate to say I'm ill, but Lucas wouldn't believe it.'

Bea looked searchingly at Lady O. Conclusion; the lady was in awe of, if not actually afraid of her husband. 'Don't try to rationalize it, but give me your gut reaction. Who is doing this?'

'I don't know. I DON'T KNOW! Do you think I haven't thought and thought…? I mean, why would anyone want to…? Perhaps Lucas is right and this is all aimed at him and I'm collateral damage. But—'

'Which member of your bridge party would be willing to become an accomplice to your murder? It must have been one of them who brought in the rat poison. Someone who went to the loo, saw the steak laid out in the kitchen and took the opportunity to poison it?'

Closed eyes. Head shaking. 'Someone might have come in from outside. They must have gained access to the building somehow or other and sneaked into the flat while we were all playing bridge.'

Or arrived via the fire escape? Bea started back to the master bedroom, with Lady O at her heels. Bea opened the French windows and a gust of icy wind wrapped around her. She closed the windows. 'Does the fire escape go all the way down to the ground? Could someone from outside have gained access that way?'

'I don't see how they could. All the flats have access to the fire escape, but the bottom two stories are enclosed in a brick wall. When you reach the ground floor you're in a sort of well. There's a door with a bar on it that you push down to get out, and then you're in an alleyway, near the entrance to the garage. You can't get into the building from outside, not even with a key.'

'I don't believe some stranger gatecrashed your party. The odds on their being seen would have been too great. Someone from the bridge party was responsible.'

'That's impossible.' Lady O wiped the back of her hand across her mouth and inspected the result. 'I must look a mess.' She opened a mirrored door into an elaborate en suite with gold taps on everything in sight. She switched on concealed lights and slid back a mirror to reveal a cornucopia of beauty products.

Reaching for a bottle of cleanser, she said over her shoulder, 'You'll want to check the fire escape out for yourself. Take a torch from the first drawer on the right in the kitchen because it can get dark at the bottom of the stairs. Close the French windows behind you to keep the heat in. Tap three times when you come back, so that I can let you in again.'

Bea pulled on her big coat, found a torch in the place indicated, and went out into the wind and rain. Yes, it was now spitting rain. And clouding over. She rounded the corner of the terrace and came to the fire escape. Wrought-iron rungs led to the floor below. She could see through them to the next floor down. The gaps between would ruin the high heels of her boots if she weren't careful. Oh well.

One storey down and she was on a balcony which

served the back doors and wide windows of the two flats directly under the penthouse. On one side there were a couple of wooden garden chairs and a table, which had been folded up and covered with plastic for the winter.

She tried to recall what the twins had said about the occupants on this floor. One side was Professor Jacobsen, whose cat Momi had been too greedy for his own good. No lights showed in the flat on that side. The garden furniture would belong to him.

She could see right into the other flat because some-one had switched on the lights in both the kitchen and the bedroom beyond. A radio played pop music. The decorators were in. Stepladders, an awkward mound of furniture in the middle of the room, covered by dust sheets. Workmen moving to and fro. One window had been cracked; by the workmen? Another had been left open, and the scent of new, oil-based paint drifted out to her. The decorators had dumped some empty tins of paint and bags of rubble outside on the balcony. Tut-tut.

According to Lucy and Carrie, the people who owned that flat had gone off to their second home in France, tak-ing the opportunity to have the decorators in. So far as they knew, that flat was not for sale.

Bea tested the back doors of both flats, noting that Professor Jacobsen's back door had a cat flap at the bot-tom. Neither door budged an inch. She shone her torch upon their locks. No signs of forced entry.

The iron staircase led on down. She caught the high heel of her best boots, wrenched it free. However careful she was, her heels were going to be ruined.

Another balcony, another set of doors. Carrie Kemp-ton on one side. Tariq on the other. Neither flat showed a light. These doors hadn't been touched either, as far as she could see. An untidy heap of cardboard boxes mixed with polystyrene packaging occupied much of the balcony on Tariq's side. A couple of garden chairs and some large pots filled with ivies and polyanthus gave the impression that Carrie Kempton liked to sit outside in good weather.

Down, down, down. Bea caught the heel of her boot again and this time had quite a struggle to get it loose. Bother. Now who was on this floor? Lucy Emerson and… who? She couldn't remember. Mrs Emerson's back door and windows were both dark. There were garden chairs, pots *and* window boxes on her part of the balcony. The pots were filled with winter-flowering pansies, skimmias and ivies. Very pretty. No lights within; she must have gone out for the afternoon?

The other side of the balcony, including the kitchen door, had been shut off with bamboo screens so that no one could look in. Why? Bea tried to remember who lived opposite Lucy. Some words floated back to her… '*A Muslim family; very quiet.*' No lights showed within. It seemed that everyone on that floor was out, too.

Down and down. Bea was getting confused. More garden furniture on either side; one lot was plastic, the other wood. Who lived on that floor? Was it the woman in the fake fur coat? Lucy and Carrie thought she was a call girl, didn't they? They'd said, 'She was a model, they say. Probably christened plain Carmel. Irish. She has men to pay the bills for her, if you get my meaning.'

Bea had nodded. She'd wondered as much, herself. 'She's not on visiting terms with the Ossetts?'

Lucy and Carrie had both laughed, short and hard. 'She comes to the bridge parties, but she's not exactly friendly, if you know what I mean.'

Down and down. Suddenly, she was plunged into darkness as a brick wall rose up around her.

Who was on this floor? She looked into the kitchens on either side. Tidy. Not much used on one side. A bit messy on the other. More garden furniture and what looked like a barbecue, well wrapped up against the winter winds.

Lucy—or perhaps it was Carrie—had said, 'Two couples; yuppies, I think they call them. Out all day. Banking. Advertising. Striped shirts, three-piece suits, fold-up bicycles and the latest laptops or whatever they call them now.'

And the other one had said, in a tone of rebuke, 'Except, of course, for dear Helen, but she wouldn't cause any trouble. She's been rather poorly.'

Poorly or not, Bea considered that Helen's kitchen could do with a good clean.

Bea switched on the torch and descended to the ground floor. She located the exit door, pushed down on the bar and let herself out into an alley which ran along the back of the building. To prevent the door closing behind her, she wedged it open with the torch.

The alleyway was kept clean. Each of the flats had a numbered wheelie bin, and they were lined up in strict order from one to fourteen. Mr Caretaker liked things to be neat, didn't he? Bravo.

Next to the fire escape door was a tunnel sloping down into the sub-basement. The garage entrance? Yes. There was a barrier across the tunnel which would only lift if you inserted a special card into a machine on the wall. Beyond the entrance to the tunnel was a lighted window and a door belonging, presumably, to the den of the disobliging caretaker.

Bea walked along the alley, her heels crunching along the gravel which had been laid on top of the concrete surface. The hum of traffic grew louder as she emerged into a busy thoroughfare. Buses screeched, taxis whirled, children in pushchairs demanded treats, mothers young and old negotiated pavements, youths lounged... Normality.

She retraced her steps to the other end of the alley, which petered out into a narrow space between two blocks of flats.

'What you doing?' Mr Pancko, or Poncho? Narrow eyes and mouth, not much hair and that cut to a stubble, a big frame, well-muscled. 'You, trespass. This private road.'

'You are the caretaker? My name is Mrs Abbot. Lady Ossett gave me permission to check the security at the back of the building, as I have a client interested in buying one of the flats.'

'I, security. You no move. I check.' Menacing.

Bea decided she wouldn't like to cross this man, not least because he was carrying a heavy wrench. She waited, huddling into her coat. The rain was not heavy but it was insidious.

He kept his wrench under his arm while he accessed a slender iPhone. Listened to the person he'd called. Nodded. With reluctance. Turned his phone off. 'OK. You go now. I watch you, right? Security here good. Understand?'

She nodded. She now saw the point of the gravel laid on the concrete. It made the footsteps of anyone who walked along the alley easy to hear. It was indeed good security.

She retrieved her torch and let the exit door clang to behind her. A strong door, made of steel? Yes. She climbed the stairs again. And again. And again. And... She stopped for a breather only twice, which she thought was pretty good. Looking down into the yard, she saw the caretaker watching her progress, with his phone still in his hand. If she'd tried to access any of the flats on the way up, he'd have been after her in no time at all.

She reached the top—wow! Wind and rain together, how delightful! She tapped on Lady O's French windows and almost fell inside. Oh, her heels! She'd have to throw those boots away.

'Satisfied?' Lady O had restored her appearance to its norm and banked down the panic that had overtaken her earlier.

'Your caretaker is quite an ogre, isn't he?'

'He's an excellent watchdog. Mrs Abbot, would you care to join me for a late lunch? I'm about to send out for something. What do you like to eat?'

'Anything. I agree with you about the fire escape. Which means that, whether you like it or not, whoever tampered with your steak must have been a member of the bridge party. I also agree that you may still be in danger. If you won't leave—'

A bitter smile. 'I can't argue with Lucas.'

'Then you must have a bodyguard.'

'Maggie would be perfect, but you say she's unobtainable?'

'Maggie would not be perfect, as you very well know. Oh yes, she'd be easier for you to boss around, but she doesn't have the sort of suspicious mind that's needed to spot anything out of place; a missing light bulb, an improperly addressed package in the post.'

Lady O grimaced. 'You're right, of course. The girl's made great strides. She was always such an ugly duckling, so unresponsive to all my efforts to help her, I hadn't realized that she'd become a swan. Well, not a swan, exactly; we mustn't overstate the case. But—'

'In view of her liking for bright clothing…a peacock?'

Lady O managed to laugh almost naturally. Then sobered. 'Your Oliver, now. He's got the right kind of mind.'

'He helped you complete the crossword today?'

'With his mind on his meeting with Lucas. I could have warned him that my husband eats bright young things for breakfast, but he'll have to find it out for himself. Anyway, even if Lucas didn't want him for his own purposes, Oliver wouldn't do for me. I won't have anyone gossiping about me and a young man.'

It was Bea's turn to smile. 'No toy boys?'

Another laugh, and this time it was natural. 'No toy boys. And no other suitor waiting in the wings. Lucas is more than enough for me. Shall we forget the diet and share a pizza, perhaps?'

Bea nodded. As Lady O rang in her order, Bea wondered exactly how long Lucas intended to leave his wife in limbo. The grounds for his doing so seemed, well, flimsy to Bea. Surely if he loved her, he'd have removed her to a place of safety before now? But then; successful, ambitious men often put their wives second to their work. And if he had another woman in his sights… Oh dear.

How was Oliver getting on at Vicori House? Would Lucas really offer Oliver a job? Would it be right to stand in his way…even supposing that it were possible to do so?

The pizza came. Crispy and tasty. They ate at a table below the Freud portrait.

Bea refused coffee, looking at her watch. 'It's a Friday afternoon, and I have a business to run, so if you will give me a list of who was at your bridge party, I'll be on my way.'

Lady O shivered. 'I'll write it out for you later this afternoon. Do you really have to go so soon?'

'When I get back to the agency, I'll sort out someone to come round to look after you for a while. Meanwhile, there's one person in the building whom I think you can rely on, and that's Professor Jacobsen. He knew his cat was in the habit of visiting you, and he wouldn't have put the animal in danger, would he? Was he a member of your bridge party?'

'He doesn't always come, but he was there this time. He doesn't approve of me. I've heard him refer to me as a "blonde bimbo" as if I were still sixteen and not knocking fifty. Tell the truth, he's the one person in the flats who scares me. He's a scholar of the old school. I know I ought to have gone down and told him when I found Momi, but I was so shaken that I… I put it off. And then I lied when he asked me if I'd seen his cat and now… it's just too difficult. I'll get the caretaker to dispose of the body.'

'No, you won't. You'll invite the Professor to come up here, and you will turn on the charm and confide in him about the terrible strain you're under, and then you'll confess that you found Momi dead, and cry a little, and look up at him, all poor little me, and of course you'll offer to buy him a replacement pedigree cat. Right?'

Lady O looked down at her hands and then up at Bea. 'Must I?'

'You know it's the right thing to do. Presumably he's too old to make your husband jealous, and he's bright enough to act as your bodyguard till we can get a professional in place for you.'

Lady O nodded. 'You're right, of course. But perhaps not today. Maggie said she'd come back this evening and—'

Bea got to her feet. 'You need company this afternoon, and if you play your cards right, you can keep him here till Maggie arrives or I find someone to look after you.' She tucked herself into her coat. 'I'm going downstairs now to knock on his door, and if he's in I'll ask him to call on you straight away. If he's out, I'll put a note under his door, asking him to phone you, and you can invite him up. Lock the door after me, and make sure he identifies himself when he comes.'

She left Lady O crumpling a handkerchief in her fingers, with tears starting out on her cheeks. It made Bea feel a bully, but she had to be cruel to be kind, or she'd be there all day. Now, for the Professor...

# SEVEN

THE AFTERNOON WAS growing dark. Rain still spat at the windows as she made her way down the stairs. The merry sounds of workmen continued to come from flat number twelve but there was neither light nor sound at number thirteen. Correction; there was no number thirteen. Professor Jacobsen had altered his flat number to twelve A.

Bea knocked, and then rang the doorbell.

'Hang on a moment!' A man's voice; tetchy but not cracked with age. A slither of curtain rings as a heavy porte cochère was drawn back. A spyhole was consulted. A key turned in a lock. The door opened a crack. On a chain.

'Professor Jacobsen?'

'What's it to you, young lady?'

Bea almost giggled. It was some years since she'd been called a 'young' lady.

She caught a glimpse of a tall, thin man through the narrow opening. A coxcomb of white hair, shaggy eyebrows over a beaky nose, long upper lip, clean-shaven. Lively, light-grey eyes.

'Bea Abbot, Mrs. Called in by Lady Ossett, who has… who is…'

'What's the bimbo been up to now?' A dismissive tone.

'She's no bimbo, and someone's trying to scare her to death.'

'She probably caught a glimpse of a mouse.'

'A dead *mouse* wouldn't faze her.'

Pause.

The door closed, the chain was taken off, and the door reopened. 'You used the word "dead"?'

'She wonders if you would be so kind as to pay her a visit this afternoon. That is, if you are not otherwise engaged.'

He grunted. Heavy-duty sweater and jeans, both clean. Velcroed trainers, also clean. He was a very clean, old— no, perhaps not quite so old—gentleman. He had the faintly Edwardian look Bea associated with successful private school headmasters. Authority, knowledge and a pragmatic outlook on a less than perfect world.

'I'm busy. More than she is. I compile crossword puzzles for a living.'

'Really? Did you know she has a magic eye for anagrams?'

A hard stare. 'For the tabloids?'

'The *Times*.'

'Ah. You used the word "dead"?'

'Yes. She needs help, and you're the only person in the flats whom she can trust.'

He thought about that. His jaw worked. 'Momi.'

'Yes. Will you help?'

'That husband of hers. There's a rumour that he's left her?'

'I'm really not sure what's going on there.'

'Stupid girl,' he said, shaking his head. Did he mean Lady O or Bea? It was an advance on 'bimbo', anyway. 'Momi,' he said, and his eyes took on a faraway look. Then he nodded. 'What did you say your name was?'

'My card.' She handed one over.

He inspected it and said, 'I'll turn off the computer

and go up there straight away.' He closed the door in her face, and she rang the bell for the lift.

THE LIFT FAILED to arrive. Bea rang the bell again. Perhaps someone was already using it? Yes, she could hear the faint whirr of its machinery. Bea looked at her watch. She really must get back to the office. She considered walking down the stairs. Six flights. Ugh.

The sound of an altercation rose up the well of the staircase. A confusion of voices. Perhaps two people were arguing over who should use the lift next?

Bea started to walk down the stairs. Past the flats of Carrie Kempton and Tariq she went. Down and down. Pause for breath, and down again. The shouting below intensified as she passed the flats for Lucy Emerson and the Muslim family. Surely Lucy would have come out of her flat to see what was happening, if she were at home? She must be out.

'You bastard!' A man's voice. From a couple of storeys down.

A girl, screaming, 'No, no! Get off me!'

Bea raised her eyebrows. Down another flight. The woman in the fake fur coat was standing by the door to the lift. Mahogany red hair, superb high-heeled boots, another huge handbag. Carmela Lessbury, lady of leisure. She took one look at Bea and turned her shoulder.

There was a shriek from the girl below, quickly broken off. Someone being attacked? Mugged? Whatever was going on?

Bea said to Carmela's back, 'Yes, I've been visiting Lady Ossett, and yes, I know something very odd is going on in this building. Who is it in trouble this time?'

Carmela didn't react, so Bea continued down the stairs. The sounds of distress below increased. A man's voice threatened someone…the girl? 'You filthy whore! If I have to choke the truth out of you, I'll—'

'You bastard! Leave her alone!'

Bea hastened her steps. She could hear Carmela descending after her. Also curious, but not willing to get involved?

A man cried out, 'Aaargh!'

Had the girl kicked her attacker where it would hurt most? Good for her.

A heavy door clanged shut. The front door?

So much noise! It was a wonder that the caretaker hadn't turned up to tell them off. Perhaps it would be a good idea to ask why he hadn't done so.

Bea rounded the last corner and almost fell over a young man with a shaved head who was lying, doubled over, on the bottom step. He didn't look particularly clean. T-shirt and jeans, no socks or shoes. Moaning noises.

A similarly disarranged young woman was holding on to the newel post. Dark hair all over the place, livid marks on her arms, a torn T-shirt and jeans. She was wearing boots whose pointed toes had probably managed to connect with the tenderest part of the male and thus ended the fight.

The lift door was closed.

The front door to flat number two was open.

Now who lived in that flat? Lucy had said it was 'Daddy's little girl and her bit on the side'.

Carrie had added, 'Daddy has pots of money but his daughter lacks manners and will probably kill herself with alcohol or drugs before she's thirty.'

Lucy had the last word, as usual. 'She hangs around with a crowd… Not our sort, dear. We don't speak except to say "good morning", but they don't even say "good morning" back. And the language they use is quite shocking!'

As usual, the two ladies had summed up the situation rather well. Bea took out her mobile phone. 'I'll call the police, shall I?'

The girl threw back her hair. She looked to be in her mid-twenties and was angry enough to spit tacks. 'Sod off, whoever you are!'

'No police,' said Carmela, speaking from behind Bea.

'My name,' said Bea, 'is Mrs Abbot. Sir Lucas Ossett has asked me to find out exactly what is going on here. I can see you two young people have been fighting. You have a choice; either I ring the police or you invite me into your flat and tell me what's going on.'

Would the bluff work? She had no right to threaten them with the police, who probably wouldn't interfere in a brawl on private property, anyway.

The young man shuffled to his feet, still bent over, one hand holding his nose and the other on his crotch. 'I'be bleeging.' And bleeding he certainly was.

'Serve you bloody well right,' said the girl. She put two fingers up to Bea. 'You can sod off, you old crone.'

From 'young lady' to 'old crone' in ten minutes. Oh well.

Bea pushed the door to their flat wide and walked in. The layout would be identical with that of Mrs Emerson's flat above, but it was a world apart—not only because it was furnished in the latest modern style with blinds at the windows, chunky black and white furniture and stripped floorboards—but also because it hadn't been visited by a cleaner for some time. Takeaway boxes, newspapers, beer cans and empty bottles were on every surface, and the air was laden with cigarette smoke.

Bea opened windows and found the kitchen. It stank. Ugh. Least said.

Would the bathroom be any better? Marginally. She

took the toilet roll and a glass of cold water back to the living room, where the young man was standing, hands over his nose, swaying, not sure what to do with himself. The girl, meanwhile, had turfed some magazines off an armchair and had thrown herself back on to it, sulky mouth set to fire off another set of expletives.

Carmela was obviously not going to help. She hovered in the shadows by the doorway, cuddling her enormous handbag.

'Sit!' Bea gestured the young man to sit down and, surprisingly, he obeyed her. He put his head forward; she slapped a wodge of wet tissue under his nose and instructed him to hold it there and not move.

'Now,' said Bea. 'How many of these impertinent phone calls have you had?'

The girl gaped. 'What? How did you know?'

'Among other irritating things that have been going on here, I was told that some call girls' cards had been left in letter-boxes. My guess is that someone has not only put cards through your letter box, but has been giving them out with your phone number on them.'

'Dod odley—' started the boy.

'Oh, shut up,' said the girl. 'Silly phone calls I can deal with. But that man who's just gone had somehow managed to get my address. He turned up here wanting Miss Whiplash and wouldn't take "no" for an answer. Connor here tried to throw him out and got more than he bargained for.' She turned her stormy face to Carmela. 'I always thought the call girl cards were intended to embarrass *you*.'

'I thought they were, too,' said Carmela, stroking the soft leather of her handbag with long-nailed fingers. 'I did get a number of phone calls so I got rid of my landline and changed my mobile phone. That stopped it.'

'For you. What about me?'

Bea renewed the wet towels for the boy. 'Aren't you both ex-directory?'

'Yes, of course.'

Carmela nodded, too.

'Then don't you see that the person doing this has to be someone either living in this building, or close to someone who is? How else could they know your phone numbers?'

Carmela was thoughtful. 'There's a list of our land-line phone numbers in the basement for the caretaker to use in emergencies. Anyone who lives here, or visits here, could get hold of it. The caretaker did ask me for my mobile number as well, but I made him promise to keep it under lock and key.'

The girl lifted her fists to the ceiling. 'Why is some-body doing this to us?'

'Why, indeed?' said Bea. 'Why the cards, the nuisance calls, the vandalism? Why was Sir Lucas's car keyed and the cat killed?'

'What!' The girl shot upright.

The boy took the wodge of red tissue from his nose. 'It's stopped bleeding,' he said. 'The car, we knew about. Laughed ourselves sick. That was Tariq, of course. He admitted it the other night when he was pissed.'

'Childish,' said the girl. 'Lady Ossett overreacted. The noise wasn't all that loud.'

Bea said, 'You were at the party?' How odd that the gossips hadn't mentioned that fact. Perhaps they hadn't known? So many lies and half lies…

'Of course we were at the party. Of course Tariq did the car. You said a cat was killed? You don't mean Momi?'

Carmela didn't frown because her forehead had been

Botoxed to prevent such a movement, but she looked as if she'd have liked to have done so. 'Not Professor Jacobsen's Momi? He must be devastated.'

Kill an adult, and no one much cares. Kill a pet, and everyone screams for retribution. Bea nodded. 'Poisoned.'

The girl pushed her hair back with both hands. 'But… Momi used to come down here every evening to cadge for leftovers. Salami was his favourite. Come to think of it, we haven't seen him for oh, two or three nights. When was he here last, Connor?'

'Monday night? Tuesday? No, we had Indian then, didn't we? Momi didn't like Indian and went off in a huff.'

'How does he get in?'

'Cat flap. Installed by the previous people. We're used to him wandering in of an evening. He sticks around for a while and then goes off again. Why would anyone want to poison him?'

'It's escalating, isn't it?' Carmela lifted some dirty jeans from a chair and sat down. This brought her into the light. Bea had a good look at her face for the first time and caught her breath. A figure to die for. A face like a horse; an intelligent horse. A horse that had been slashed by a knife. It wasn't a recent knife wound. Plastic surgery and Botox had alleviated the worst of the effects, but one eyelid was slightly awry.

Bea checked to see if the boy and girl were taken aback by the distortion, but they seemed to take it for granted, so they must have been exposed to it before.

The girl yawned, stretched. 'Yeah, yeah. But I don't see what we can do about it. Sorry about the mess. The cleaner's given us notice.'

Connor wandered over to a misty mirror to check how much blood he'd got on his face. 'You mean that Daddy said if you weren't going to get a job, you could clean the place yourself.'

She kicked out at him, missing by a mile. 'What about you, you lazy so and so? I only let you stay here because I thought you'd pull your weight financially.'

He was aggrieved. 'You know there's no jobs out there for me. I'm worth more than the minimum wage.'

Carmela said, 'Oh, I doubt if anyone would take you on, whatever the job. They expect applicants to be clean and neat, turn up in good time and work a full eight-hour day.'

The girl laughed. 'She's got you sized up, hasn't she, Connor?'

Carmela turned her eyes on the girl, who flushed and said, 'So? Am I also unemployable? Daddy said he'd find me a job in one of his shops, if I wanted. But I don't want.'

'Of course you don't,' said Carmela. 'You'd be on your feet for six hours a day and have to be polite to customers. Besides, you'd miss the booze, wouldn't you? My brother drank himself to death, and I know better than to try to stop someone anyone else from going that way.'

Silence.

Carmela stood up. 'Well, I must be going. Mrs Abbot, would you care to walk with me?'

Bea followed the fake fur out of the fug into the comparatively clear air of the foyer. The lift doors opened, revealing the two elderly ladies dressed for the outdoors. 'Is it safe to come out now?'

'We came down earlier but there was a lot of screaming—'

'She wanted to see what was happening, but I said we should wait awhile—'

'So we went back upstairs till everything was quiet.'

'Yes, it's safe to come out now,' said Carmela, almost

smiling. The two older women fluttered out of the front door, nodding and smiling to Bea as they went.

The caretaker appeared with a mop and bucket, and proceeded to put an 'Out of Order' notice on the lift.

Carmela held the front door open for Bea to pass out before her.

Ah, clean air. Well, clean for London, anyway.

Carmela set off at a good pace. 'Most afternoons after lunch I walk around the block and have a coffee at the Maison Blanc. Care to join me?'

Bea looked at her watch. 'I was due back at the office hours ago, but…yes, I'd love to. I take it that one of your gentlemen friends is that girl's father—and another is Sir Lucas himself? Or perhaps they are one and the same?'

'No, no. Two different men. I've known them both for years. To anticipate your next question; I'm a therapist, not a call girl.'

*And if you believe that*, thought Bea. And then, *Well, it might be true, I suppose.*

Carmela continued, 'This scar on my face was inflicted by a manic depressive patient who stopped taking his medication and went berserk.'

Bea nodded. That explained a lot. 'I thought you might have business ties to Sir Lucas, despite what Lucy and Carrie had to say about you.'

'Terrible gossips, aren't they? Though their hearts are more or less in the right place.'

'And Lady Ossett's heart?'

A frown. 'Do you remember the Carry On film in which Julius Caesar exclaims, "Infamy, infamy; they've all got it in for me"?'

'Vividly. What you mean is that, like Caesar in the film, the fact that Sir Lucas is paranoid doesn't mean someone isn't after his job. I suspect he's already asked

you to find out who may be conspiring with his enemies
to do the dirty deed—'

'I've told him I don't think it's Tariq but he won't listen. He says I'm blinkered, don't want to see the truth.
He's asked you to investigate instead?'

'He's told you about me?'

'Indeed. And about your intelligent young protégée,
whom he's thinking he might offer a job to. Oliver? Is
that his name?'

'Yes. I'm against it.'

Carmela nodded. They rounded the corner into a busy
thoroughfare and turned into a high-class patisserie and
coffee shop.

'You'll join me for coffee and some cake?'

Bea decided to forget her diet for the second time that
day. 'Delighted.'

And a good time was had by one and all.

Eventually, Bea said, 'Can you clear up something
for me? Where would someone display business cards
for call girls around here? And would just any stationers
print them up?'

'The girls' pimps pop them inside the nearest public
telephone boxes every day, to catch the eye of tourists
or…well, anyone with an itch to satisfy. And, yes; any
jobbing printer would turn them out for you.'

'And the ones dumped in your letter boxes at the
flats?'

'Printed locally, yes. I visited a couple of places
which I thought might have produced them. The man-
agers wouldn't confirm that they'd been responsible, but
pointed out that they hadn't broken any law if they had.'

Quite so.

Finally, replete with cake and coffee, Bea accessed her
mobile phone to see if there were any messages on it. Yes.

Two. Maggie to say she'd be returning to her mother's that night, and someone at the agency to say there were a couple of matters which needed to be looked at, but they could wait till the morning. Nothing from Oliver.

'I must go,' said Bea. 'But before I do; I believe Sir Lucas owns the freehold of the building. Does he select his tenants personally?'

'He buys up the leases as they fall in and grants short tenancies to people he likes the look of. Just two of the existing residents have long leases that predate his purchase of the freehold and have refused his offer to buy them out.'

'Professor Jacobsen and one of the gossips?'

'One of them. Can't remember which. The other one bought the remains of a longer lease from someone who was moving away. He owns my flat, of course. He's let a ground floor flat to that silly girl's father, and another up top to the people who've gone abroad and sublet to Tariq. That young man will be out on his ear soon since he's lost his job and can't keep up with the rent.'

'Do you think Tariq keyed Lucas's car?'

'It seems most likely.'

'Lady Ossett believes that this separation from her husband is all a pretence. I'm not so sure, myself. Except, of course, that he's left the Lucian Freud portrait in situ.'

Carmela picked her words with care. 'I suppose that, if he did intend to leave her, the insurance people would have to be consulted before it could be removed.'

'Do you think he's already selected another wife? Someone younger, perhaps?'

A shrug. 'We are talking hypothetically here. I imagine that if he were looking for another wife, he would want someone with her own money.'

'Have you any idea when he intends to inform his current wife that their marriage is over?'

A shrug. 'You go too fast for me. If he were thinking of divorce, then I suppose he might keep up the pretence until he's dealt with the snake in the grass at headquarters.'

Bea leaned back in her chair. 'It's like watching a chess-master at work. A bloodless coup. Only, I think Lady Ossett will probably bleed quite badly.'

Another shrug, dismissing the subject. 'My treat, by the way.' Carmela handed the bill and some notes to a hovering waitress.

Bea gathered herself together. The thought of going back to the agency did not excite, and something was bothering her. She tried to think what it was.

'Carmela, is the lift at the flats often out of service?'

A shrug. 'The caretaker likes to give it a good clean once a week.' A frown. 'Usually early in the morning after the business people have left, and while the rest of us are having breakfast.'

'Do you mind if I come back with you for a moment? The lift shouldn't be out of service at this time of day, should it? Also, I'd like to ask the caretaker why he didn't intervene when an intruder forced himself on the people in the ground floor flat. I thought he was supposed to keep an eye on, well, everything.'

Carmela hissed something between her teeth and picked up her handbag. 'He has Sir Lucas's best interests at heart. I'm sure he can explain…if there's anything to explain, that is.' She led the way out of the cafe and turned up the road. 'This is the quickest way, through the alley at the back of the shops, and then round to the front.'

As Carmela let them into the building, Bea saw that

the 'Out of Order' notice was still on the lift door handle. There was no sign of the caretaker.

Something which looked like a broomstick prevented the door of the lift from closing completely.

Carmela said, 'Yes, that is odd. Shall I raise the caretaker?'

Bea tried to see into the lift. There was no light on inside, and she thought she could see...but couldn't be sure. 'Can we open the door by pressing the call button?'

They tried it. No, it wouldn't open. The power seemed to have been cut off.

Bea said, 'Can we force it? If I pull the door, and you put your weight behind the broom?'

Together they heaved. The door flew open, and though there was no light on inside the lift, they both spotted the body.

'I'll call the police,' said Bea.

Somebody or something plucked the mobile phone out of her grasp. She cried out, and turned to face... The damaged heel of her boot snapped. She stumbled and fell. And lost interest in the proceedings.

# EIGHT

*Friday afternoon*

SOUND RETURNED FIRST.

'...in here, that's right...'

She was being lifted up and deposited...

A face swam into view.

A face which she recognized, but which shouldn't be there. Should it? Would it be stupid to ask, 'Where am I?'

She'd been laid out full length on...what? A settee with bumpy cushions. Not at home. So, 'Where am I?'

She coughed. Cigarette smoke.

The man she recognized said, 'Are you all right?'

'Oliver? What are you doing here?'

'Rescuing you, it seems. I turn my back for five minutes...'

She struggled upright. Her head clanged, and she put her hands to it. 'Oh!'

'You banged your head when you fell. Lie still, and we'll get the paramedics to have a look at you.'

She forced herself to sit upright. The room went fuzzy, and then came into focus. 'I'm all right. I think. Oliver, what are you doing here?'

Another face swam into view. A girl with hair all over the place, wearing a scared expression. 'Are you all right? What a fright you gave us!'

Ah. She was in the dark-haired girl's flat, which was

on the ground floor of a building she'd been visiting. There'd been something about… No, it had gone. 'What happened?'

Another woman's face. Older. Marred but intelligent. Bea knew her, too, didn't she? The woman said, 'The heel snapped off your boot, throwing you off balance. You banged your head as you fell and suffered a momentary blackout. Do you feel sick at all?'

Bea consulted her stomach. She started to shake her head, learned it wasn't a good idea and said, 'No. I'm all right.'

'Well, if you get any odd symptoms, you'd best go straight to hospital.'

Carmela. That was the woman's name. Silly name. Bea tried to think back. Couldn't remember. She had a flashback to… She'd caught a glimpse of something, some dark shape huddled into a dark corner… No, whatever it was, it had gone.

'Let's get you home,' said Oliver. 'Maggie's breaking off work early so she can look after her mother, so I'll get you home and tuck you up in bed. You'll be right as rain in the morning.' He helped her to her feet. She wobbled, one heel off and one heel on, diddle-diddle-dumpling, my son John.

She sat down again. Plump. Tried to take off her boot, but it was laced up tight and her fingers weren't responding to commands. Tried to laugh. 'Can't walk. If you call a taxi, I'll take my boots off and walk to it.'

Carmela snapped on her mobile. 'I'll call you a cab.'

The dark girl said, 'I've got a pair of slippers I've hardly worn. I'll get them for you.'

Oliver knelt to unlace Bea's boots.

Bea held on to her head, which was throbbing. 'Sorry

to cause such a… What a nuisance I'm being. Oh, where's my mobile phone? I thought I—'

The dark girl said, 'You dropped it when you fell. I'm sorry, it smashed to pieces on the tiles.'

Oh, thought Bea. Something's wrong here. I can't quite put my finger on it, but… 'There's a body in the lift.'

'No, no.' Carmela laughed, and the laughter almost convinced. 'Not a body. Honest. The decorators had put bags of rubble into the lift. They're supposed to take them down the fire escape at the back, but of course it's easier for them to put them into the lift. Only, this time they didn't get away with it. The caretaker heard them and cut the power to the lift, leaving a note on the door to say it was out of order while he went up to tell them off. All sorted now.'

'Decorators,' said Bea, remembering. 'Flat number twelve? They're in France at the moment.'

'That's right. Here, put these slippers on. Take my arm. Oliver, you take the other side, and we'll get her home in no time at all.'

As Bea was steered out of the room into the foyer, she caught a glimpse of a boy with a shaved head chewing his fingernails. Connor, that was his name. What was the girl's name? Bea couldn't remember. If she'd ever known it.

The lift door was closed now, the 'Out of Order' notice removed.

Bea's head ached, and her legs seemed not to belong to her body. But there was a taxi waiting and Oliver helping her into it.

Don't let's start an argument now, because you are not up to it, Bea.

Not yet, anyway.

*Friday late afternoon*

HOME AGAIN, SAFE and sound.

Well, not too sound, but safe.

She shivered. Her head ached.

'Paracetamol and bed for you,' said Oliver. 'No argument.'

She wanted to say, but there *was* a body…

She stopped herself just in time, because if Oliver thought there wasn't a body, and the others backed him up then…was she going mad, or the victim of a conspiracy?

She let him take her into the living room and deposit her on the settee. With a sigh she arranged cushions behind her head and winced at the sore spot where she'd hit her head on…whatever. As he drew the curtains against the dusk outside, she said, 'A cup of tea would be wonderful.'

'Coming up.' He glanced at his watch, frowning.

Was he due somewhere else? Was she being a terrible nuisance, falling over and cracking her head like that? And seeing things.

But if she had indeed seen something and the others—three people, count them; Carmela, the girl and Connor—had conspired to hide the fact then…then what? 'Conspiracy' was a big word, wasn't it?

She said, 'I thought you were being shown over the Vicori empire this afternoon.'

'Oh, yes, a quick guided tour. Sir Lucas wants to keep an eye on me, says he's impressed and all that. Did you think he'd offer me a job there and then?'

She had thought just that. So why hadn't he? She attempted a smile. 'Did he send you back to look after Lady Ossett?'

'Mm. She's gone a bit doolally, I'm afraid. He doesn't

want her doing anything silly. I'll get you some tea.' He disappeared, and she half closed her eyes against the light from overhead. If she had the energy she'd get up and switch to side lights. She didn't have the energy.

Oliver set a mug of tea at her side. Had she dozed off for a moment? Perhaps.

'Thanks. Did you actually see me making a fool of myself, falling about like a clown?'

'No, I arrived just in time to see them trying to pick you up off the floor.'

'How alarming for you. And my poor mobile. Did you happen to rescue that, too?'

'I didn't think of it. It was in pieces.'

She sipped tea. Wonderful. Restorative. 'You say Maggie was stopping work early, to look after her mother? She won't be back for supper, then. So what is it that Sir Lucas wants you to do next?'

'Be his eyes and ears. He knows now who's masterminding the attacks on him at work, but he needs some hard evidence linking him to his accomplice at the flats.'

*He's testing you, Oliver. He wants to know if he can get you to provide that evidence. And if, as I suspect, there is no hard evidence, then he'll want you to manufacture it, and in the process—not that that would worry him—he'll mould you into being a creature of his.*

She must tread carefully. 'He's adamant about not handing this over to the police? Not even to CJ?'

'One word of this leaked to the press and millions would be knocked off the share price. He can't risk it.'

'The caretaker at the flats is in his pay already. Presumably Sir Lucas doesn't suspect him.'

'No. He believes it's someone who gets his orders via computer.'

'Ah, so that's why he wants you, you clever boy. Well,

now; that rules out several people in the flats. I've met quite a few of them by now, and I can tell you that some are hardly capable of reading the time off a digital clock, never mind surfing the net. How will you find out who's capable?'

He reddened. 'Sir Lucas owns the flats and, under the terms of the contracts, he can have access to them to check for water leaks, that sort of thing. He's given me a piece of paper which appoints me his representative, and he's told the caretaker to take me round, and introduce me…or I may borrow his keys.'

'And you're going to search every apartment?' She was appalled, but struggled to hide it. 'Well, that's very… ingenious of him.'

He was defiant. 'It's justifiable. It gives me the right to search for and check all their computers.'

'Checking for leaks is not the same thing as checking what a computer might hold. You've no right to do that.'

'Once I'm in, I shall chat them up, and they'll let me see what they've got. If they're innocent, that is.'

'And if they're not? Will you wait till they've gone out and use the caretaker's keys to enter their flats and spy on them? Oliver, you can't be happy about doing that.'

'If that's the only way to trap the man, then of course I'm going to do it.' A defiant look, but Bea felt—hoped— that he was disturbed by what she'd said, even if he wasn't yet able to see the morass into which Sir Lucas was trying to draw him.

Her head ached, and she wanted nothing so much as to take some painkillers and go to bed. 'Dear Oliver, you're going to have to be as wise as a serpent to get to the bottom of this. You'll have to be careful not to point the finger at an innocent person, who might have no defence against such a powerful person as Sir Lucas.'

'Of course I'll be careful.' Tetchy. Not amused. Another glance at his watch.

'Are you so anxious to get cracking? If you leave it till
tomorrow, I can come with you, introduce you around.
Then you won't have to tell any lies to get in.'

'Not lies.' But he ducked his head so she shouldn't
see his face.

She closed her eyes…and the next thing she knew,
someone was stroking her face. Not Oliver.

She opened her eyes. A shock of dark hair, greying at
the temples, bright dark eyes, a long nose, a humorous
twist to the mouth.

'Piers!' She tried to sit upright and fell back. What was
her long-divorced first husband doing here? True, they
were good friends now, but he wasn't exactly the kind to
nurse a sick child, never mind a sick wife, as she knew
from experience. They hadn't been married for a year
before he'd been tom-catting around the neighbourhood,
and though he was now a nationally renowned portrait
painter, he hadn't changed his ways.

Perhaps she was hallucinating again?

He said, 'Oliver called, asked me if I'd look after you
tonight, make sure you haven't got a concussion. I was
intrigued by his story of high jinks in society and can-
celled an evening with a DVD to fly to your side. You're
looking peaky, my love.'

'Feeling it.' She swung her legs to the floor, noting she
was still wearing a pair of incongruous beaded Indian
slippers. They belonged to the dark-haired girl, didn't
they? 'Oliver shouldn't have bothered you. I'll be all right
after a good night's sleep.'

'So you say. Here, let me carry you upstairs.'

She fended him off with a weak laugh. 'Who are you
kidding? You couldn't carry me over the threshold when

we got married, so what chance have you now?' She got to her feet, staggered, and was glad to have his arm around her.

'I have my orders.' He half-carried and half supported her up the stairs. 'Paracetamol and more tea. Put you to bed. Wake you every hour to shine a torch into your eyes, and get an ambulance if you slip into a coma. Oliver also said that if you started rambling about corpses and corruption, I was to take no notice because you'd had a bang on your head.'

He let her collapse on to her bed. Putting his hands on his hips, he asked, 'Do you want me to undress you and put you in the shower?'

'Heaven forbid.' She was half appalled and half... No, she didn't really want him to... No. Of course not. NO. Definitely Not.

There was no denying the fact that age had not withered him, and he was still the most charming, delightful, charismatic...untrustworthy, unfaithful... Oh well.

'I'll manage,' she said, 'if you could shut off all the lights downstairs and find me some painkillers. Kitchen cupboard, first on the right.'

By the time she'd managed to get herself undressed, sort of washed and under the duvet, he was scraping some slopped tea from saucer to cup and handing her some Paracetamol. No fuss. No bother. As to the manner born. He even stroked her cheek as she lay back and closed her eyes.

'I'll dowse the lights and sit in the chair by the window.'

Her head thumped. It would pass. She could hear him rustling newspapers. Tiresome. She wished he wouldn't. It took her back to the days when they'd been married. He'd been earning a pittance, while she nursed Max and tried not to realize she'd married a man who couldn't resist a flirtatious glance from another woman...

She woke with a start. It was one o'clock. She'd gone to sleep without having her nightly dip into her bible or saying her prayers. She reached out for the bible on her bedside table but it was no longer there. She lifted her head from the pillow—ouch—to see that it had slipped to the floor and she couldn't reach it.

*Dear Lord, I'm sorry I haven't been in touch today. Yesterday. I suppose I should thank you for looking after me, and I do. I'll get back to you when I feel better. Promise.*

Someone was snoring, lightly. Piers had fallen asleep in his chair, reading glasses slipped sideways on his nose, the newspaper around his feet.

She was amused. She hadn't known he'd started to wear reading glasses. He wouldn't want her to know that she'd seen them. Dear Piers...

At four she woke again and was aware she'd cried out, just as she'd cried out when her heel had broken and someone had snatched the phone from her hand.

'What is it?' Piers scrambling awake.

She sat upright, breathing hard. Shaking.

He put his arms around her. 'There, there.' His glasses had disappeared.

She cried a little. 'I saw something. A man, bent over, lying on the floor in the lift. But they said it was some bags of decorators' rubble.'

'Bea, if you say you saw a leprechaun, and six other people said it was decorators' rubble, I'd back you.'

She held on to his arm. Her breathing slowed. 'Thank you.'

He released her, patted her shoulder. 'Back to sleep. You can tell me all about it in the morning.'

She lay back, closing her eyes. 'I thought you were supposed to wake me every hour on the hour.'

'I did at first; and let me tell you, I was shocked by your language.'

She yawned, turning on her side. 'Why don't you sleep in the spare room next door?'

'I'm not leaving you. Of course, I could always…' He lifted a corner of the duvet.

She slapped him down. 'No, you don't. We've been divorced far too long for that. Take a duvet and pillows from next door, then.'

Silence. Did he tiptoe away? She slid back into sleep.

*Saturday morning*

A BRIGHT MORNING. Some red streaks in the east, but for the rest, a clear true-blue sky. She threw back the curtains and thanked God for a sound constitution, a hard head, and Piers…who was still asleep, awkwardly awry in his chair. She felt a little wobbly, but nothing that a good breakfast wouldn't restore to normal.

She showered and dressed, by which time he was stirring and checking the shadow on his chin.

Breakfast. Orange juice and cereal. Scrambled eggs. Marmalade on brown toast. Coffee for him; tea for her because coffee might raise her blood pressure and that wouldn't be good for her headache, which wasn't too bad really. She took some more paracetamol and eased it away.

'Want to tell me what's been happening?'

She brought him up to date, starting with Maggie's plea for help with her mother, continuing through her own visit to Vicori House, Oliver's involvement and her visits to the flats.

He was thoughtful. Nodded now and then. 'You don't think Oliver will find the culprit?'

'I think it's more than a simple case of industrial espionage emanating from Vicori House. It seems to me that some of the happenings at the flats can be put down to spiteful mischief, but others are dangerous. I don't say I've got the half of it yet, but I'm getting there, and now—after what happened yesterday—I have a lever to prise out some more of the truth.'

'It's Saturday and I'm at a loose end. Shall we make a list of who lives where and why you think they're implicated in...whatever?'

Together they worked on a chart and found a gaping hole where information about the people in number six ought to be.

'I don't think anyone mentioned the people in that flat. The two old biddies went on a bit about the old lady who died of a heart attack on the ground floor, but that seems to have happened before any of this started. Or...' She frowned. 'Maybe that started it? No, I'm being fanciful. That was a death from natural causes.'

'Who said so?'

'Mm? The biddies. Oh.' She struck her forehead. 'I am so stupid! I lapped up everything they told me but I didn't check any of it. I thought they were just two elderly ladies without an axe to grind, but... Let me get my notes out.' She scrabbled in her handbag for her notebook.

'Now, what they told me—and it needs checking—is that a woman, I think her name was Lavinia, lived on the ground floor. She was in her nineties and never went out. Social services came in twice a day, and the biddies ran errands for her when they could. The place was a tip, apparently. The biddies said they came back from shopping one day and found her on the floor in the entrance hall, dead. They didn't go to the funeral because it was in the local Catholic church and they're Church of England if they're anything, which I rather doubt—that they go to church, I mean.

'Afterwards the caretaker told them that the old lady's grandson was coming round to see what furniture he could sell or give away. Carrie said she didn't think there was much that they'd have wanted, even as a keepsake. In other words, I suppose they'd have liked the chance to look around and pick up any unconsidered trifles. Sir Lucas is thinking of buying the remainder of the lease from the grandson, if he'll sell.'

Piers pointed to flat six. 'You haven't any details for these people?'

'Harvey something. That's all I've got.' Annoyed with herself. 'It might just be an oversight.'

'Or it might be someone they like too much, so they don't want to point a finger in their direction?'

'Possibly, yes. Or it might be someone tied to Sir Lucas's organization. Tariq used to work for him. It seems Sir Lucas owns the building and that he's "vetting" or possibly "approving" of any new lettings. I only hope Oliver isn't getting himself into difficulties by allying himself too closely to Sir Lucas. I don't care for the man.'

'You have to let Oliver make his own choices.'

She sighed. She knew that.

He emptied the last of the coffee into his cup. 'Talking of Max, which we weren't, but we might as well… He came round to see me the other day, saying he needed to explore what business opportunities might open up for him in addition to his work as a member of parliament. He's looking for directorships in this company or that.'

He sent her a sharp look. She didn't react.

'In words of one syllable,' he said, 'he thinks you

would be happy to appoint him as a director of the Abbot Agency, so that he could go on the board of this other company… What's it called, Holland and Butcher? He says they want closer ties and he'd be able to… Don't throw your mug at me! Calm down. It was not my idea.'

'Nor mine,' said Bea, seething. She pressed both hands to the back of her head. 'Oh. Oh! Now I see why he was so keen for me to sign up with them. The idiot! As if I… He's a lovely boy, of course he is, but not the world's greatest brain, and I would never have thought of making him a director of the agency.'

'That's all right, then. I didn't think you'd like the idea, but I did think I should check.'

'He seems to think that… He doesn't see any difficulties, whereas I see nothing but problems everywhere I look.'

'Tell me, slowly and quietly, in words of one syllable, what happened yesterday. Was it an attempt on your life? God forbid.'

'No, I don't think it was that.' She closed her eyes. 'Yesterday. I'd been talking to Lady Ossett. Then I called on the Professor on the floor below her. I asked him to go up and talk to Lady O. Then I rang the bell for the lift. Nothing happened. It's an old lift, but mechanically sound. It doesn't clang and clatter as some of them do. I thought someone must be using it.

'I started down the stairs which wind round the lift shaft. I could hear people shouting down below. Carmela was standing by the lift on her floor, also trying to summon it. I spoke to her. She didn't respond, so I went on down. She followed me. Nearing the bottom of the stairs, I heard more shouting and then the front door bang shut. The young couple from flat number two were in the foyer. They looked as if they'd been in a fight. The boy had a nosebleed.

'The lift doors opened to reveal the two old biddies, who'd been riding up and down, waiting for the disturbance to be over before they departed for their afternoon's walk or whatever. The girl explained that they'd had a visit from a man looking for a Miss Whiplash at that address. She'd told him to go away, he'd insisted, they'd struggled, Connor intervened and got the worst of it. Their visitor had gone by the time I got there.'

'There really was a visitor?'

'Oh yes. I heard him leave. Carmela confirmed she's had much the same problem. As with the other "incidents", the nastiness had escalated. First, call-girl cards with the tenants' private phone numbers on had been put in their letter boxes, and then displayed in a public place, bringing punters into the flats. Carmela invited me to join her for a cup of coffee down the road. As we left the building, the caretaker arrived with some cleaning materials and stuck an "Out of Order" notice on the lift door. Carmela and I talked. She was helpful though always loyal to Sir Lucas.

'It seemed odd to me that the caretaker should clean the lift at that time of day. On our return Carmela and I saw what looked like a broom handle had been placed between the lift doors, preventing them from shutting. There was no light on inside the lift. We assumed, I think correctly, that the power had been cut to the lift. I saw… It was dark inside, but I thought I saw someone's feet on the floor wearing a pair of trainers. I suggested we call the caretaker, but then I thought—or Carmela said—I'm not sure who suggested it, I'll have to think, my head aches—'

'Leave it for now.'

'Carmela and I between us pushed the door open, but it sprang back. Before it closed I saw…' She took a deep breath. 'I saw a young man with dark hair, dressed in a black padded jacket and jeans. Trainers; white with orange laces. He was lying on something, a pile of something, maybe a sports bag. I think it was Tariq, and I think he was dead.'

# NINE

BEA PUT HER hands to her head. 'Did my imagination run away with me?'

'You wouldn't imagine white trainers with orange laces. You saw them all right.'

'Which means that I saw Tariq lying...' She held up both her hands. 'I'm jumping to conclusions again. I've never met Tariq and wouldn't recognize him if I did. I saw *a* young man lying on the floor in the lift, with his back to me. He was half propped up on something between him and the floor. I assumed that he was young because he wasn't thick around the middle. His head was in shadow but he did seem to have dark hair. I didn't see his face. But three people said I saw decorators' rubbish. Why would they lie? Why would they want to cover up a death?'

He shrugged. 'Do you want to hand it over to the police?'

'On what grounds? "Please, sir; I want to report a suspicious death, but I've had a bad bump on the head and three other people say I'm imagining it." I did think of asking CJ about it, but he's on Sir Lucas's side in this, and Sir Lucas doesn't want anything to get out which might affect the share price of his company.'

She cleared the breakfast things away. The sky had turned ice blue. It would be cold outside. It was a Sat-

urday, and there was no real need to go down into the
agency rooms although she often did so.

Maggie hadn't returned home. Nor Oliver. She didn't
like to think of them staying on in the flats. 'There's
something very nasty going on there. Let me tell you
what else I imagined. The moment I saw—whatever—in
the lift, I got out my mobile and said I'd call the police.
Someone reached round from behind me and snatched
the phone out of my hand. I turned to see what was happening, the heel of my boot snapped, I staggered…and
felt a blow to my head before I blacked out. I didn't fall.
I was pushed. Now you can have a good laugh.'

'I'm not laughing. What happened to your phone?'

'I was told it got smashed to pieces on the tiled floor as
I fell. Oliver arrived just as the others were picking me up.
He saw the phone in pieces and didn't think to rescue it.'

'If we accept that all three of them had something
to hide, I can understand them not wanting the police
brought in—'

'Four,' said Bea, homing in on the recollection of the
moment when she'd fallen to the ground. 'Carmela was
by the lift. The dark-haired girl was standing next to her.
The boy Connor was by the door to their flat. None of
them was near enough to snatch my phone. As I turned
I caught a glimpse of someone looming over me. It was
a fleeting impression, but yes, I think someone else had
come into the foyer at that moment.'

'*Four* people conspiring to hide a body?'

For a moment she wondered if Piers had joined the
opposition in refusing to believe her story.

He hadn't. 'Bea, if you go back there… No, make
that *when* you go back there, I'm coming with you. It's
a Saturday, and we should be able to find everyone in.
We'll talk to every single one of them. We'll check and

double-check until we find out what's really going on. If Oliver tries to interfere—'

'If someone in the flats really is using email to liaise with Sir Lucas's enemies, Oliver could find the link, however well hidden. I wondered at first if they would all have computers but, having met some of them, I think probably everyone does, except perhaps for the biddies, and even they might use one occasionally to keep in touch with their friends or order something online.'

'Give me your gut reaction. Who is doing this?'

Her mind see-sawed between various possibilities. Images of all those she'd met went flittering through her head. 'Tariq may have been responsible for... I do think he keyed Sir Lucas's car, but as for the rest of it... I really don't know.'

'Did Lady Ossett try to kill her husband?'

'No. Definitely.'

'Has he left her, or not?'

'Carmela says he has. If he removes the Freud picture soon, then yes, he has. It's possible he's looking for a younger and more beautiful woman to hang on his arm. Lady O doesn't want to believe she's being superseded by someone younger, and she says he's only pretending to leave her, to protect her from his enemies. That's his cover story, too. I don't believe him and I don't believe her. At bottom, I don't think she believes it, either. She's facing a solitary life as a divorcee again. What's more, she's frightened. She thinks someone is out to get her. I don't *want* to believe her, because if it's true, it's going to affect Maggie's future. Unfortunately, I do. The cat died because it ate her supper.'

'Did she kill the cat to persuade Lucas that she's in danger from person or persons unknown?'

Bea stared into the middle distance, testing this hy-

pothesis. It fitted the facts, but didn't convince. 'No, I
don't think so. The poisoning was done by someone who
was at the bridge party that afternoon. I thought at first
that someone might have come up the fire escape from
outside the building, but that's not possible because of
the way it's constructed. Then I thought someone might
have got *out* of his or her flat on to the fire escape and
climbed the stairs to the top…but then you can't get into
the penthouse or into any of the other flats unless someone opens a door for you from the inside. Which means
you could only do it if you had an accomplice.'

'Which is not impossible.'

A gesture of resignation. 'You know something? I
would like to walk away from the whole boiling lot of
them. Let them fight it out among themselves. What do
I care if Tariq has been killed? He probably deserved it.
Well, no… I can't say he deserved it, unless it really was
him who caused his boss to tumble down the stairs, and
even then… No, he didn't deserve to die. But I really do
not see why I should bother my head with them.'

He cheered her on. 'I understand. If it weren't for Maggie and Oliver getting involved, you'd wash your hands
of them.'

'Yes, I would. I am *not* amused. I'm annoyed about my
mobile phone being smashed. It might have got broken
when it fell to the floor, of course. But I suspect it was de-
liberately smashed because it held—or once held—some
rather incriminating evidence, and someone wanted to
make absolutely sure I didn't have it any more.'

She told him about the shots she'd taken of the tiny
nail marks on the staircase. 'Sir Lucas deleted the pictures on my mobile, probably after sending them on to
his own phone.' With her most angelic expression, she
added, 'Which is exactly what I'd done, too, before I met

him. I've fallen into the habit of sending any pictures I take on my phone back to base as a matter of routine, in case I happen to be mugged on the way home, or have an accident. As soon as I'd got the pictures on my camera, I sent them on to my old mobile which is currently sitting in the top drawer of my desk downstairs. Sir Lucas doesn't know that, and he thinks he's got the only hard evidence there is.'

'Bea, I love you.' He gave her a hug and a kiss on her cheekbone. He probably did love her, too. In his own way. Let's call it *affection*, shall we?

*Later on Saturday morning*

BEA RETRIEVED HER old mobile, carefully transferred the information on it to her computer and, with Piers at her side, set for the flats. He looked up at the building and whistled his appreciation. 'Distinctive. Art Deco?'

Bea began to enjoy herself. 'You should know. Now, who should we annoy first? Lady Ossett should be up and about by this time so we'll ask her to let us in.'

Bea rang the intercom but, instead of operating the door lock, Oliver's voice announced that he'd come down to the foyer to let them in. Which he did, all bright-eyed and bushy-tailed.

'Hello! Are you all right now? Lady O's been asking where you'd got to. Maggie's gone out to stock up with food for the weekend, and the Professor is sitting with Her Majesty. They're discussing a new and fiendishly difficult crossword.'

The caretaker was mopping the floor in the foyer.

Oliver nodded to the man and led them over to the lift. 'There's an electrician and some workmen doing something in Lady Ossett's living room, I'm not sure what, so it's a bit crowded. Lady Ossett says we can use Sir Lucas's study if we want to talk.'

Once inside the lift, Oliver pressed the 'Up' button. Bea looked closely at the floor. Was that a bloodstain? No. The place looked pristine. Did it smell of cleaning fluid? Sniff. Yes. And an air freshener? She said, 'Can you smell anything, Piers?'

Oliver shook his head at her. 'Honestly, Mother Hen. You and your imagination. Bodies in the lift, indeed. Whatever next?'

'You've been talking to the people in the ground floor flat?'

'Ms Lessbury was kind enough to fill me in. A great friend of Sir Lucas's. Known him from childhood.'

Bea rolled her eyes, but forbore to comment. 'You think it's all right to leave Lady Ossett with the Professor? You've cleared him of any involvement in the dirty tricks department?'

A satisfied nod. A careless tone of voice. 'I called on him last night and had a look at his computer, nice little job, masses of special apps. He let me play with it for a while. An intelligent man.'

Bea set her teeth at Oliver's patronizing tone. He'd really got above himself, hadn't he?

Oliver said, 'I told Sir Lucas that the Professor's squeaky clean. One less to worry about. Sir Lucas directed me to look up Tariq next, so I saw him last night. Odd little chap. Quite bright in his own way, I suppose. But limited. Ah, here we are at the top.'

Bea missed a step on leaving the lift. What? Oliver had called on Tariq last night? Tariq was alive? Piers pressed Bea's arm, warning her not to show surprise.

Oliver led the way up the stairs, still talking, oblivious to Bea's reaction. 'I had a good look at his computer when Tariq went out this morning, but there's nothing of any importance on it, more's the pity. Sir Lucas will be disappointed, but there it is.'

Bea controlled her voice with an effort. 'What's he like, this Tariq?'

'Oh, you know. Pakistani origin. Born and brought up here, well educated, but got a chip on his shoulder. His family ought to have got him married off ages ago which would have settled him down, but for some reason he doesn't seem to be in contact with them.' He reached out to touch the doorbell of the penthouse.

Bea stopped him. 'Oliver, did you say that you saw Tariq last night?'

'Mm? He wasn't feeling too good, got an upset tummy or something, so he put me off then. But he was OK this morning. He lent me his spare key while he went to the gym so that I could have a look at his computer without him breathing down my neck.'

'He left the building this morning? Perhaps with a sports bag? How did he get past the caretaker?'

'What do you mean? Why on earth shouldn't he go out if he wants to? I told you, I've had a look at his computer and there's nothing suspicious on it. As for the caretaker, I don't understand what you're getting at. A bit of a thug, of course, but he gave me a list of the tenants this morning and said he'd go round with me when he's got a minute, let me into the different flats, introduce me, that sort of thing.'

'Oliver, did you talk to the caretaker down in his flat? Could Tariq have left the building while you were there?'

Oliver reddened. 'Tariq's not a criminal.'

'Some of the other tenants think it was he who keyed Sir Lucas's car. I don't say that he did, but that's what is being said. Plus he's lost his job and seems to be in arrears with his rent. I suspect the caretaker was given orders by Sir Lucas to keep an eye on Tariq and not let him leave the building till he's paid up what he owes.'

'Nonsense. You've got a bee in your bonnet about Sir Lucas. As he says, this is a perfectly straightforward case of commercial espionage and—'

'I doubt if there's been any such thing.'

Oliver's temper was rising. 'It's clear to me that you are jealous of Sir Lucas because he's made a success of his life, and that you resent his interest in me. He warned me this might happen and I didn't believe him, but I can see he's right. You're way out of your depth on this one. Instead of encouraging me to take advantage of this fantastic career opportunity, you've made up your mind that Sir Lucas is a villain, which is—'

Piers said, mildly enough, 'Steady on, Oliver. You forget who you're talking to.'

Oliver was pale with fury. 'I don't know what you think you're doing here, either. I think you'd better leave, both of you.'

Piers put his hand on Bea's arm, but she'd got herself under control. 'Oliver, *you* didn't ask me for help. Lady Ossett did. And, later on, Sir Lucas. I think perhaps there are two separate mysteries here, so suppose you get on with your industrial espionage—or whatever it is—while I deal with the other problems in the building.'

'What problems? What are you talking about?'

'Have you solved the mystery of the cat's death, and of the marks where nails were driven into the side of the stairs?'

'Cat? What cat? And I don't know anything about nails on the stairs.'

Bea reached past him to press the doorbell. 'Exactly.

Let's each of us stick to our own line of enquiry, shall we? Why don't you get on with your search for the rogue computer buff? I expect you can keep Tariq's key because I don't think he'll be coming back. And, for your information, the reason his family's not keen to keep in touch is that he's gay and it's not approved of in their culture.'

The door opened, and Bea marched into the penthouse, followed by Piers who looked amused...only to be brought up short by a procession of workmen coming towards them down the hallway, carrying a large, swaddled package between them.

The Lucian Freud picture? So Sir Lucas had sent for it, after all.

Bea and Piers stood aside to let the workmen pass. Bea hesitated. Ought they to intrude on Lady O at this delicate moment?

Bea had underestimated the lady, who appeared in the doorway to the living room, smiling brightly. 'Come in. How good of you to call. You find me all at sixes and sevens. My dear husband finds he can't be parted from my precious gift to him and has asked for it to be removed to his office, where he is staying at the moment, the dear boy, so inconvenient for him, but there; in such an important job, one has to make sacrifices, don't you think? But what, I ask myself, can I put in place of what has been taken from me?'

She indicated the bare space on the wall. 'Perhaps the Picasso sketch from the spare bedroom? Though it will hardly be big enough to... Oh dear. I'm forgetting my manners. Professor, this is—'

'I've already met Mrs Abbot,' said the Professor, rising from a chair by the far window. He was still casually dressed, but there was a spruceness about him which had been lacking the previous day. His hair had been well brushed, his eyebrows trimmed. A hint of aftershave mingled with Lady O's perfume.

'And this is…?' Lady O raised her eyebrows and fluttered her eyelashes at Piers, who was so accustomed to that sort of attention that he took it for granted.

'My first husband, Piers, the portrait painter,' said Bea.

Piers was modesty itself. 'Not in the same league as…' He indicated the space where the Freud had been. 'Bea and I are just good friends nowadays. I am so sorry to hear of your loss.' He might have been referring to the loss of the picture, or of the husband.

Bea gave him an old-fashioned look before turning back to their hostess. 'We dropped in to see how you were getting on, but I understand Maggie is looking after you this weekend?'

'The dear child,' said Lady O, her thoughts obviously elsewhere. 'I am so fortunate, so well looked after. This afternoon the Professor and I are going to inspect a litter of exceptionally beautiful pedigree kittens to see if he would like to have one to replace dear Momi, after which he has tickets for a perfectly splendid concert at the South Bank this evening. I am so looking forward to that. You'll excuse me for a moment…?' She made a rapid retreat to her bedroom, hankie to eyes.

The Professor, ungainly but purposeful, came towards them. 'Brave little thing, isn't she?' His tone was half mocking and half indulgent. 'Reminds me of my second wife, who passed away two years ago, greatly missed. Lady Ossett will come out smiling in a little while to rearrange the furniture and make an appointment to see her solicitor about the divorce. I'm sure Sir Lucas will be generous in his arrangements, so she ought to come out of this pretty well.'

Bea stifled a giggle. 'It is splendid of her to want to replace your cat, when they're not exactly her favourite animals.'

A grin. 'Nor mine. Momi was a gift from my daughter. We rubbed along well enough, he and I. I do miss him in a way, but remembering to feed him and cleaning out his toilet tray was a bit of a bind.'

'So you're happy to play along with what the lady wants?'

He adopted a melancholy tone, but his eyes were bright with mischief. 'I am a lonely old man now that Momi is no more, and she is a delightful woman, recently deserted by her husband. What harm is there in offering her companionship?'

'In that case,' said Bea, somewhat at a loss, 'perhaps we should be on our way.'

Out they went. Piers lent against the wall on the landing and gave way to laughter. Bea eyed him with disfavour. Eventually, he blew his nose, with gusto. 'The Professor may be on the lookout for a cushy berth and someone to soothe his brow in his declining years, but she's no fool and won't accept him unless it suits her to do so. I don't think he was responsible for setting Sir Lucas tumbling down the stairs, do you?'

'Or for poisoning his own cat. Even if he'd disliked Momi and wanted to get rid of him, he wouldn't have risked someone else eating poisoned meat, but have taken him to the vet to be put down. Which reminds me, Lady O still hasn't given me a list of the guests at her bridge party. We know the Professor and the two biddies were there; I wonder who else?'

'Not Tariq, presumably. It appears he's not dead, either.'

She led the way down the stairs and summoned the lift. 'Let's go and talk to the caretaker about Resurrection Man, shall we?'

THE LIFT WORKED just as it should. The caretaker was still in the foyer, using an industrial polisher to buff up the tiles on the floor. He didn't give them a second look till Bea marched right up to him and said, 'You can turn that off, now. Tariq escaped while you were giving Oliver the list of residents.'

'What!' The big man glowered at Bea but turned off the machine. 'What you mean?'

'You did your best, but you can't be everywhere all the time. Am I right in thinking Sir Lucas told you not to let Tariq leave?'

The big man produced a rag from his pocket and began to dust the top of his machine. Was he going to ignore Bea's question? Finally, 'Sir Lucas, he boss man. Man from his office tell Tariq, "You stay. Not go away." His man say to me, "You watch Tariq." So; I watch.'

'You didn't just watch him. You prevented him from leaving yesterday, didn't you?'

The big man mumbled, 'Tariq stay put till Sir Lucas say he can go.'

'He's innocent…of plotting to kill Sir Lucas, anyway. Oh, believe me; Oliver would have spotted anything dicey on his computer.'

'Then why he try to go?'

'Because he was scared of what a powerful man like Sir Lucas might do to him. Or of what you might do to him, come to think of it. What did you do to him, anyway?'

A shrug. 'Nothing. He try fire escape; I put two wheelie

bins against bottom door. I hear him, bang bang, clang clang, try to get out.' He laughed. 'No go. Back up he go. I laugh. He try again. Three times he try. Same no go.'

Piers was outraged. 'You blocked the exit from the fire escape? That's illegal.'

'Tariq, he stupid. I put my chair out back, with radio on. He think I sit there, on my break. He think it OK to come down in lift. I wait for him, he opens door, he sees me, and back up he goes again! Hah! Then is trouble with visitor. I listen. I watch. No need to interfere.

'When all is quiet, the two ladies come down. They go out. So I think, Mr Tariq he will try again. How to stop him? I put notice on door, turn off electricity. Now he cannot use lift, must walk down. I hear him coming. I wait here in the foyer. Cat and mouse, as you say. Down he come. He runs for the door and woosh! He fall over my mop with his big feet. Bang! His eyes roll round in his head. He sleep. Accident.' He grinned, displaying inadequately brushed teeth.

Bea sighed. 'Let me guess what happened next. You had only meant to scare him into staying put, but now you had an unconscious man on your hands, and you didn't know what to do with him. To gain time, you shoved him back in the lift, leaving your mop handle stuck in the door so he wouldn't die from lack of air, and went to phone Sir Lucas to tell him what had happened, and to ask for instructions. While you were away, I returned with Ms Lessbury, and we tried to force the door open. I spotted Tariq lying in the lift and announced I was calling the police; you panicked, attacked me and destroyed my phone.'

'No police,' he said. 'No phone. Sorry you hurt. Accident.' He bared his horrible teeth in a grin.

'Accident, my foot. Oliver arrived, knowing nothing of what had happened. You asked him to help the youngsters carry me into their flat and explained to Carmela what had happened, knowing she wouldn't want to offend Sir Lucas and would help you cover up what you'd done. With all of us out of the way, you switched the electricity back on, opened the lift door and…hey presto… signs of life.'

'He sick. Vomit. I tell him, "Now you stay put till Sir Lucas come." I take him up in lift and put him into flat. I clean lift, once. I clean it twice. Phoo!'

Bea felt very tired. 'You do realize you've committed grievous bodily harm, among other crimes?'

He grinned. 'He fall over my mop; accident. You come, you interfere, you trip, you fall; accident. I tread on your phone. I big man, tread on small things. All accidents.'

Bea realized that what he meant was that she was a small thing to him, and that he could tread on her with impunity. He probably could get away with it, too. Backed by Sir Lucas, he was beyond the law.

How dare Sir Lucas think he could hold Tariq captive, and search his belongings, and corrupt Oliver, and leave his wife and not be answerable to the laws of the land!

That bang on the head was getting to her. Another headache threatened. She said, 'I feel very tired all of a sudden.'

Piers hustled her out into the fresh air. 'Come on, Bea. I need to make a couple of phone calls.' He walked away, accessing his phone. Bea was annoyed. What! Was Piers abandoning her, too? It was all too much.

Alternative waves of fear and fury shook her. First came fear. Sir Lucas thought he could get away with murder— well, metaphorically, as he probably hadn't actually killed anyone yet, though she thought he was quite capable of doing so.

If she got in his way he could squash her like a fly, and there was nothing she could do about it. No recourse to police or the law. CJ was on his side. Carmela & Co would back up the caretaker's story. If Sir Lucas decided to ruin the Abbot Agency, he could start a rumour that she was suffering from dementia, or was in financial trouble…any old story. People would believe a man in his position. The agency could be torched that very night, without anyone being called to account for it. Oliver could be crippled for life in an 'accident'. Or she could be run over on the way home.

Fury took over. She announced to the neighbourhood, 'No one should be above the law. I won't have it.'

'Quite right, too,' said Piers, returning to take her elbow and steer her down the road. 'There's a little café along here. You look as if you could do with a sit down. Order me a double espresso, will you? And some kind of baguette or sandwich; preferably tuna.'

He pushed open the door of the café and shoved her inside, letting the door swing to behind him as he returned to his phone call. It was the café she'd been to the day before with Carmela. It was full, but a couple were just leaving a table in the window. Bea stalked to it, testing out various expletives in her mind. None of them expressed exactly how she felt about Sir Lucas and his thug, the caretaker.

She was angry with God, too. What did he mean by shoving her into a situation she was not equipped to deal with? She was way out of her depth.

The menu offered soups, quiches and salads, and of course their range of wonderful cakes. She needed carbohydrates. Or, possibly, alcohol? No alcohol licence. A pity. She couldn't remember when she last got drunk, but it seemed an attractive prospect at that moment. She ordered toasted sandwiches for two, fruit juice for herself, and a coffee for Piers, while glaring at a droopy woman who was trying to take the vacant chair opposite.

Hah! If she couldn't get back at Sir Lucas, she could at least prevent anyone else sharing her table.

The thought that she might be overreacting wormed its way into her mind, but she told it to go away. If she wanted to have a tantrum she would do so, so there!

The woman didn't go away, but stood there, looking miserable. There wasn't another chair vacant. Bea softened. It wasn't this woman's fault that Bea was in such a bad temper.

'Look, my friend's outside making a phone call at the moment, but why don't you take the chair I was keeping for him? When he comes, we'll ask the waitress if she can find us another.'

'Thank you.'

Were those tears in her eyes? Goodness gracious.

'I thought I'd be able to manage it easily, but I'm ready to drop.' She was a washed-out blonde. Correction; her hair, though thin, had been freshly coloured, cut and curled at the hairdressers, but the face beneath the hairstyle looked tired and sallow. Almost, ill.

Bea forced a smile. 'He can eat his food standing up if necessary.'

The waitress delivered the food Bea had ordered and said to the newcomer, 'The usual?'

A smile. 'Yes. Thanks.' A regular customer, then? And speaking to Bea, 'I'm grateful.'

Piers loomed above them, grinning, putting his mobile away. 'Room for a little one?' He smiled at the waitress, who responded to him as women always did, and magicked a chair for him from nowhere.

'Well, Piers?' said Bea, biting into her toasted sandwich. 'What was so important?'

'I had a word with a friend in the business, who tells me that Sir Lucas's position is by no means impregnable. He's facing a hostile takeover bid. It could go either way, and if he loses…' He drew his hand across his throat in a cutting motion.

'Excuse me,' said the droopy woman. 'Are you referring to Sir Lucas Ossett?'

Bea stared at the woman. 'Don't tell me; you know him, too?'

# TEN

'OF COURSE,' SAID the droopy woman. 'We live in the same block of flats. May I ask how you know Sir Lucas?'

'He asked me to investigate…' Bea paused, at a loss. What if she were to say that he'd asked her to investigate an attack on his life? Would the woman summon the paramedics from the funny farm? She said, 'Forgive me; my name's Bea Abbot of the Abbot Agency, dealing with all matters domestic. I am acquainted with Lady Ossett because her daughter Maggie lodges with me.'

'A dear girl. She always helps me up the stairs if the lift's out of order, as it was most of yesterday.' She produced a tired smile. 'I had a little operation three weeks ago and I don't seem to be snapping out of it as I should. Eliot said I'd feel better if only I'd stir myself to get my hair done and a facial but I was so tired when I came out from under the drier that I couldn't face waiting around for the beautician, and I thought I'd better have something to eat before going home. I'm sorry; you don't need to hear all this.'

Piers tucked into his sandwich. 'Going to an important "do" tonight?'

'A dinner at the Guildhall. I'm not sure who for. Is it the Rotary Club? I'm a bit stupid about these things. I do try to keep up, but it's true that my memory is not what it was.'

She couldn't be more than forty, but didn't seem to

have much self-confidence. 'It's the anaesthetic,' said Bea. 'Knocks you out for a good month, they say.'

'Yes, but I must make the effort. It's important, for Eliot's sake.' Her quiche and salad arrived. It looked good, but she only pecked at it.

'Eliot works for…?'

The woman grimaced. 'He works in a private bank in the City and it's all terribly hush-hush but he did say something the other day about Sir Lucas being under pressure. It's a hostile takeover, is it? Oh dear. I used to understand all those things, but radiotherapy does rather take it out of you.'

Bea thought, breast cancer. Lumpectomy to remove the tumour, followed by daily visits to the hospital for treatment. Not funny. No wonder the woman was feeling tired and her mind was not the sharp instrument it might once have been.

'So sorry,' said the woman, holding out her hand. 'Helen McIntyre.'

'Piers,' said Bea, indicating that worthy. 'Portrait painter. He's my first husband, long divorced, but we're still good friends.'

'Oh. Are you *that* Piers? You painted the chairman of the board at Eliot's bank, didn't you? We went to see it at the National Portrait Gallery. Eliot was furious because I said his boss looked like the cat who'd been at the cream, which was very silly of me. As if I would know anything about it.' She gave an uncertain smile, inviting them to share Eliot's opinion of her lack of intelligence.

Piers said, 'That was very acute of you. Several people I know have called him a fat cat. Eliot probably has to toe the line by pretending his boss is a saint.'

A faint colour came into Helen's cheeks; she half-smiled and returned to picking at her food. Not much appetite, obviously.

Bea said, 'Do you go to the bridge parties?'

'Yes, though I'm not very good. Eliot says it's important and I can always help with the teas or sit out if there's enough people without me.' She put down her fork, hesitating. 'If you know Maggie well, and... I don't like to gossip but Lucy said something about Sir Lucas leaving his wife?'

Lucy Emerson, one of the biddies, spreading the good news. With relish.

'I've heard that, too,' said Bea. 'Maggie's spending as much time with her mother as she can. I also heard that Sir Lucas might have someone else in mind?'

'Isabella? Something double-barrelled and Spanish. I did wonder, when I saw them at a charity "do" last week, but Eliot said I was imagining things. Stupidly, I nearly passed out and had to take a taxi home by myself, so don't quote me.'

'Isabella?' Piers finished his coffee and beckoned the waitress for another. 'Do you mean the Spanish heiress, grandfather in olive oil, father in shipping? Quite a catch but slippery. She's been engaged or married four or five times, mostly to footballers, if I remember correctly. Do you think Lucas can hold on to her?'

Almost a grin. 'Perhaps they deserve one another.' She put her hand over her mouth. 'Oh dear! I shouldn't have said that.'

'Of course you should, between friends.' Bea patted the pale woman's hand. 'Do you think Lady Ossett suspects?'

'I rather think she does, but I can't say exactly why I think so. Lucy and Carrie are so good to me. One of them comes down almost every day to make me a cuppa and make sure there's food in the fridge—anyway, Carrie says that Lady Ossett doesn't want to see what's happening. Perhaps she knows but doesn't want to know, if you see what I mean. I'm explaining myself badly, I'm afraid. Lucy thinks Lady Ossett may be too old to capture another husband, and that she'll become miserable and depressed. But that's just gossip. You mustn't take it seriously.'

'Lady Ossett is getting on nicely with the Professor at the moment.'

'I thought they disliked one another. He's terribly clever, you know, and really kind. He asks for me to be his partner if I haven't been paired off with anyone else. He says I always know what he's going to bid, and honestly I don't. Or not very often. Sometimes. But the stakes have been getting higher just lately, which makes him swear under his breath, though of course I can hear him. I told Eliot I wanted to drop out for that reason, but he thinks I should continue for a while at least.'

'What do you think about Tariq? Are you bothered by the noise he makes at weekends?'

'Oh, no. Well, only if he leaves his front door open and then the music does tend to echo down the stairs. Eliot doesn't like it when he's working. But I suppose Tariq'll be leaving soon. He got the sack, you know.'

So Helen didn't know Tariq had already departed? Fair enough. 'What about the young people on the ground floor. Do they have parties at weekends?'

'Occasionally, yes, but they're on the other side of the hallway so they don't disturb us so much.'

Piers sipped his fresh cup of coffee. 'What does Eliot say about them?'

Bea gave Piers a sharp look, but Helen didn't hear the sarcasm.

'We don't really know them at all. Lucy says they're a bit of a nuisance and that they probably take drugs; but I really shouldn't say that, because I've not seen anything myself.'

'What about the people in number six?'

Helen smiled. 'Oh, Harvey. A real softie.'

'Lucy—or was it Carrie?—started to say something about him but her friend cut her off. Is there something wrong there?'

Helen was amused. 'No, no. It's just that he's got a bit of an imagination. To hear him talk… He's something of a standing joke. Sometimes he doesn't seem to know the difference between fact and fiction. I suppose all writers are like that.'

Bea looked a query.

Helen almost laughed. 'He writes pulp fiction, and lives out his plots. Thinks he's another James Bond. There's no harm in him. Now, if you don't mind, I think I'd best be on my way. I need my beauty sleep in the afternoons.'

When Helen had left, Bea said, 'What do you think?'

Piers shrugged. 'Eliot sounds like the usual sort of bastard who marries a nice girl and drains all the blood out of her.'

'She doesn't trust her instincts but she's pretty acute, all the same. That remark about Lady Ossett knowing exactly what was going on, but deciding not to know—'

'I'll bet she's right about Isabella and Sir Lucas. I wonder who might be able to fill me in on that?' He got out his mobile and brooded over the address list.

Bea signalled to the waitress for a cup of coffee for herself. Her headache had gone now she'd eaten, and she was feeling much better. So much better, in fact, that she gave in to gluttony and ordered one of their extra special marzipan, cream and chocolate cakes. Wow! Treat!

She tried to think clearly. If Helen were right and Lady Ossett had suspected her husband was about to leave her, then might she have set that trap on the stairs? Well, possibly.

Bea shook her head at herself. A while ago she'd been so sure that Lady O had been innocent, and now…she couldn't make up her mind.

'Hi, there!' Maggie, looking pleased with herself. With Oliver in tow. Several people had left the café, so there were a couple of chairs free. Maggie pulled up one for Oliver, taking Helen's for herself. 'Phew! What a morning! I shopped for food, only to have my mother say she's going out for the rest of the day and the food will keep for tomorrow. I could spit!'

Oliver was looking smug. Hm. Why?

Bea ignored him to speak to Maggie. 'Well, that's your mother all over. Had you plans for tomorrow?'

'I was going out for the day, long walk in the country, pub lunch, you know. But Mother says she may need me and she doesn't think I ought to let my friends monopolize my time, which is a bit of a laugh when she's trying to do just that herself.'

'Excuse me,' said Piers, turning away to talk on his phone.

Oliver's self-satisfaction continued to annoy Bea as she accepted delivery of her cream cake and Maggie ordered coffees for herself and Oliver.

Bea continued to direct her questions to Maggie. 'What do you make of the Professor?'

'He saw I was a bit flustered, having to cart all the shopping up the last flight of stairs. He even came out to help which was nice of him. Usually he looks right through me. He's terribly clever, you see; and I'm not. Well, not in his way, if you see what I mean. I've known him for years, of course. Both his wives were called Margaret, though he called the second one Peggy, and they both died of cancer, poor things. Did you hear about his cat? Wasn't that awful? I'd die if anything happened to our Winston.'

Oliver got tired of waiting for someone to take notice of him and said, 'Congratulate me, guys. I've cracked the case. All tied up with a red ribbon and ready to hand over to Sir Lucas.'

'Really?' Bea was surprised. 'Well, good for you. Who's the rotten apple in the barrel?'

'No one you've talked to. I was suspicious as soon as he was mentioned, but I don't want you to take it hard. You can't be expected to deal with this sort of thing.' Condescending in the extreme.

Piers snapped off his phone and paid attention.

Bea set her teeth. 'Don't keep us in suspense, Oliver. Who is it?'

'Harvey Middleton. Commercial spy. Convicted by the work of his own hands.'

Bea had a sinking feeling. 'Flat six? The writer?'

Oliver was amused. 'You must admit, it's a good cover. I'm keeping him on ice until I can ask Sir Lucas what to do about him. I don't want to tread on anyone's toes at M15 by handing him over for interrogation.'

'Cor!' Maggie was half laughing, but impressed. Puzzled. 'Is Harvey really M15, then? Are you sure? I can hardly believe it.'

Oliver assumed a bland expression. 'We may never know the whole truth. All I can say is that there probably won't be any prosecution, which will please Sir Lucas.'

He smiled at Bea. 'Don't take it hard that I've cracked the case when you couldn't. I'm sure you did your best.'

Bea dabbed at her mouth with her napkin, removing the last trace of cream. Her hand shook. Was he right? He could be…but… She didn't know what to think…except that she wanted to slap the smile off Oliver's face, or push the table into his midriff, or empty her coffee cup over his head. Or all three. 'Dear me,' she said, as lightly as she could. 'Well, congratulations.'

Piers frowned, picking up her mood, but just then he received a call on his mobile and turned away to attend to it.

Bea signalled for the bill and got to her feet, saying, 'Must go. So much to do.'

Piers followed her out into the open air, talking on his phone the while.

Bea seethed with repressed rage. Ready to hit something or somebody. Or herself. She told herself that she ought to have been able to congratulate Oliver, and instead she'd cut him off. Was she angry because he'd succeeded where she'd failed?

Harvey was a commercial spy in league with Sir Lucas's enemies? But Helen had said… Had Oliver got hold of the wrong end of the stick? Was he riding for a fall? Nice lot of mixed metaphors there. Well, she was feeling thoroughly mixed up, so there!

Piers said, 'See you, then,' and shut off his phone. 'Calm down. That young imp thinks he's a proper detective because he's come across an oddity, but if Helen says the man is a bit of a joke, then Harvey's more likely to be a fantasist than a commercial spy. Do you mind if I take a break?' He gestured with his mobile. 'A prospective client is coming to the boil, wants to meet up, and there's a lead on something I'd like to check out for you. I'll ring you tonight, shall I?' He set off for the tube station at a rapid pace, leaving Bea to glare at his back.

She could happily kill Piers, too. A thought; there were still public phone booths at tube stations, weren't there? Mm, yes. But not terribly suitable for what she had in mind. She looked around. Yes, at the corner of the road by the church there were a couple of boxes; not the new blue ones but the older, red, tourist-attraction boxes. Exactly what she'd had in mind. Conveniently close to the flats.

She opened the door of the first one. No advertisements. No cards. Oh. The second, likewise. But…ah, she could see where some had been attached to the windows with double-sided sticky tape. They'd removed the cards—or whatever they were—but there was still a trace of tacky on the glass.

'You're out of luck. The cleaners have just been round,' said a voice from behind her. She looked down to see a tousled young hoodie sitting propped up against the end booth. He was wearing a sweatshirt, jeans and trainers. He had a half-eaten baguette in one hand and an open can of beer in the other. Drunk? Not yet. But doing his best to get there. 'Give us a fiver?'

She shook her head. 'Why would I do that?'

'I wouldn't have thought you were into that sort. Unless…' He leered.

She could feel her face grow hot. 'Looking for someone of the same sex, you mean?'

'Want a card? Yours for a tenner.'

'You said five. Have you got one?'

'Might have. Nice thick card. Useful for cleaning between the teeth.'

Or for chopping cocaine? She tried not to shudder. He wasn't that old, his accent was that of a reasonably well educated lad and his skin wasn't bad. If he were on drugs, he hadn't been on them for long.

He rummaged in his pocket and produced some call-girl cards. Yes, they were about the right size, but were they the ones she was after? The phone booths might be used as an advertising venue for any number of people or services.

He held one up for her to see. 'I only used this one once.' A picture of a young blonde baring her bottom. 'Miss Rumpelstiltskin', followed by a telephone number. 'Yours for a tenner.'

Bea shook her head. 'I'm only interested in one particular card, one that was put up within the last few days. It's got an address on it.'

'Twenty.'

She shook her head and began to walk away.

He sprang to his feet and called after her. 'Go on. You can afford it.'

She stopped, but shook her head. 'Someone has been playing a nasty joke on an innocent friend of mine, printing up some cards with her phone number on them and leaving them in a place where a man using the phone would assume that she was on the game. Which she isn't. It's been quite distressing. I thought if I could only find out who was doing it, I'd give him a piece of my mind.'

'Fifty pounds if I tell you what he looks like?'

'What?'

He shrugged. 'The pimps come round every morning to put up the cards for their girls, straight after the cleaners have been round. No real names and only telephone numbers. The pimps dress like me, casual. Now this guy is a businessman, in a proper suit with a briefcase and all. I see him come down the road every morning and

cross to the tube station. Every evening he comes back
the same way. Works in the City, I reckon.'

'A businessman?' said Bea, wondering how this fitted in.

'He never pays me no mind. Then, it would be about a
fortnight ago now, he stops by the phones on his way to
work in the morning and I think he's forgotten his iPhone.
But no; he darts into the booth, takes some cards out of
his briefcase, sticks them up on the windows and goes
down the tube station. The pimps are livid. He's muscling
in on their territory, see? But he's an amateur; he does it
too early because the cleaners come round and take most
of them. Only a few get into the right hands. And they've
just got telephone numbers on them.'

'You took one yourself. Why?'

He grinned. 'I could see he was an amateur, pimping
his girlfriend or wife, maybe. Respectable gent like that!
Tut! So I thought I'd take one of his cards and maybe in a
little while he'd be good for a fiver to keep quiet about it.'

'Did you try it on him?'

'Thought about it, but I was always busy when he went
by and he was always in a hurry. He didn't put any more
in for a while and I thought maybe it was a one-off. Then
he did it again last Friday and I thought I'd get him for
sure after the weekend.'

'You've got one to show me?'

'Tell you what, make it fifty and I'll give you one of
each. The first card had two phone numbers on it, but
the ones he put up a couple of days ago gave an address.'

Bea held up her handbag, but didn't open it. 'Describe
the man.'

'Money first?'

'You haven't given me anything yet. I need both cards,
and a description.'

'Ginger hair, smarmed down. Fancies himself. City gent. Handmade shoes, dark-grey pinstripe suit. His tie matches his shirt; pink. Leather briefcase big enough to hold his laptop and all.'

The description meant nothing to her. 'Age?'

'Thirty-five, maybe forty. You're not going to cheat me, are you?'

She paid him out thirty pounds and paused. 'The cards?'

He shuffled through the ones in his pocket and handed over two. She gave him the rest of the money, hoping no one would think she was paying him for drugs. The cards were exactly as he'd said. One had two phone numbers on, and the other gave the familiar address of the flats. As she snapped her handbag shut she said, 'I suppose, silly question, you don't want a job, do you?'

He grinned. 'I've got one. Selling the *Big Issue*. I do mornings and evenings, coupla hours a time. Me and my girl, we spell one another.'

'I don't see any magazines.'

'Under the tarp at the back of the booths. I was on my lunch break when you caught me. Want to buy a couple?'

'No, no. You've had enough out of me. But listen: it may not appeal to you, but I run a domestic employment agency—'

He laughed and shook his head.

She sighed, shrugged. 'You should apply to join the police. You've got a good eye, and they'd give you training.'

He laughed again and turned away. No, he wouldn't go for a job with the police. A pity, but he was old enough to make his own decisions in life.

She walked away, wondering what it was that was

jumping around in her handbag. Oh, it was her old mobile. She'd forgotten she'd muted the ring tone.

'Mother? Where are you? I've been trying to get you all morning but nobody seems to know where you are. I tried your mobile, but it says the number is unobtainable, and it was only at the very last minute that I thought of trying your old number—'

'I'm afraid there was an accident with the new—'

'There's no Maggie here, or Oliver, and the girls in the agency rooms haven't seen hide nor hair of you. What on earth are you playing at?'

'Dear Max. Maggie needed some help with something. I've been out all morning but I'm on my way back now. I'll be there in—' she looked at her watch—'ten minutes. Put the kettle on for me?' She clicked the call off, trying at the same time to switch her mind away from the mysterious goings-on at the flats and back to her one and only son and what he might want from her.

Oh. She remembered now. Piers had said Max wanted her to appoint him a director of the agency, which was a bit daft since they weren't a limited company, didn't have any directors and were doing very well without them, thank you. He wanted to be a director for Holland and Butcher as well? Where did that idea come from? Not from her.

So, it must have been suggested by H & B, who seemed very anxious indeed for closer ties between them and the agency. Which was all very well, but she wasn't at all sure she wanted to get into bed with H & B, since…

Her mobile phone rang again, and she answered it as the traffic lights changed colour and she crossed the road.

'Mrs Abbot?' Someone with no time to waste. 'I've been ringing your landline and your mobile but—'

'Sir Lucas?'

'No one seems to know where you are. Young Oliver finally gave me this number—'

'I've been—'

'Well, never mind that now. Your boy has managed to identify the traitor's accomplice but I can't attend to him at the moment; there's meetings going on till late tonight. I want you to get over there and make sure he doesn't leave till my head of security can collect him. I don't want any more slip-ups, as there was with Tariq. I've told the caretaker to be more careful this time, but he may need backup. Understood?'

The phone clicked off.

Bea started to laugh. Sobered up.

Frowned. How dare Sir Lucas think she would jump to obey his every command? Ah, but he was used to people jumping to it when he gave an order, wasn't he? And if Oliver really had discovered who had been conspiring against Lucas, then that was good for Oliver, wasn't it?

But who was it that Oliver had got in his sights? Harvey something? Helen had said he was not to be taken seriously because he was a writer and didn't always distinguish between fact and fiction. She'd said he was a bit of a laugh, a real softie. Or words to that effect.

Perhaps Harvey really was a dastardly mastermind and a blackmailer and thoroughly deserved to be delivered to the tender mercies of Sir Lucas's Head of Security—who sounded as if he'd graduated cum laude from the university of Torture Cells and Brain-washing.

Bea shook her head. No, she would have nothing to do with it. Besides which, Max was waiting for her and Max didn't like to be kept waiting. She got out her front door key and let herself into her house.

# ELEVEN

MAX HAD ACTUALLY put the kettle on. Wonderful! But it had turned itself off because there was no water in it. What else had she expected? She filled the kettle, discovered an unopened pack of chocolate digestive biscuits and made the tea, while Max talked at her. Sincerely, persuasively, deeply.

'So you see, Mother; because the parliamentary boundary changes are going to affect my constituency in an adverse fashion, I need to look ahead, to consider my options within the party and, it goes without saying, to maximize my opportunities to connect more solidly with the very enterprises which drive Britain forward...'

She translated this as: I need to find another source of income, in case I lose my seat at the next election. She made the tea, poured out two mugs, added milk, pushed the biscuit tin towards him. 'You are a very popular, hard-working politician, and loyal to the party. They won't be in any hurry to get rid of you.'

He reddened. 'That's as may be, but I can't rely on... For heavens' sake, Mother; don't be so obtuse. Everyone understands that members of parliament make up their income by serving on the boards of various companies and promoting their interests. It goes without saying that I've been approached by... No names, no pack drill, but I didn't think that associating myself with certain... You understand what I'm saying? But with you, I'm on safe ground.'

Bea's phone rang, or rather shuddered, in her hand-bag again. She took it out and laid it on the table beside her, noting it was a repeat call. 'Sir Lucas Ossett. Again.'

He frowned. 'You'd better answer it, hadn't you?'

'I don't want to speak to him.'

'What? Mother, do you realize what you're saying? You don't refuse to take a call from Sir Lucas.'

Did he mean that *he* wouldn't refuse to take a call from Sir Lucas? 'You know him, then?'

'Well, yes. Of course. Everyone, that is... Our paths have crossed and he's been kind enough to take an interest in... Though I am solidly on his side in this particular—'

'The bill that's coming up in parliament soon?'

'You know about it? It's not supposed to be generally... But I suppose, the connection through his wife and Maggie... You've met him?'

'Impressive. I understand his business empire is under attack.'

'Oh, that.' Dismissive. 'Bound to fail. The banks are solidly behind him.'

'He's calling in favours from all sorts of people?' Like CJ? Like Max?

Another frown. 'He has his fingers in many pies, that's true.'

Bea shivered. She could guess where this was leading. 'In Holland and Butcher, for instance? I heard they were in trouble, financially.' She hadn't heard anything of the kind, but then she wouldn't, would she? And, judging by Max's grimace, it seemed she was right.

Max finished one biscuit and reached for another. 'You know how it is. Old family firm, needs new blood. Out with the old and in with the new, restructure the debt, ally with a sure-fire, gilt-edged partner and hey presto! We sail off into the sunset together.'

'The new blood being the new managing director. I haven't met him yet. Have you?'

'Of course I have. They've asked me to go on their board of directors and I have accepted their offer, as I have the right connections to help them on the next stage of their journey.'

She put her mug down with a snap. 'What connections? And how many days a week are you going to work for them?'

'A few hours a week, only. And the same here at the agency.'

He'd run the agency for a short while before he got into Parliament so he knew the business. Sort of. But he hadn't been wildly successful at it because his mind had been on higher things. She was dismayed. 'What would you do for us?'

He reddened. 'Smooth the path between the two agencies, of course. As a director of both firms, I shall be your troubleshooter with them. And vice versa.'

She collected the empty mugs to put in the dishwasher. 'The Abbot Agency is not a limited company, Max. We have no directors.'

'It's about time that you got yourself organized.'

'The agency is doing well, and it's true that our accountant has said we might consider becoming a limited company, but this is not something I can do in a hurry, or without a lot of thought. What you are suggesting— forgive me if I've misunderstood—is that I put you on the payroll of the agency to solve problems of communication with a firm to which we are not at present allied. And, problems of communication are ones I would normally deal with myself as and when they cropped up.'

'I would be taking some of the load off you.'

'When you got round to it, yes. Dear Max, I hear you complain all the time of the amount of work you need to do on the various committees for the Commons, and then you're up in the constituency almost every weekend and for long periods of time in recess. Would you really be able to find three or four hours a week for us, year in and year out, and the same for Holland and Butcher? Surely you'd drive yourself into the ground?'

He made as if to speak, but she put her hand on his arm to stop him. 'Yes, I know you'd try.'

'There needn't be so much work, and not every week. Sir Lucas said I wouldn't have to do so much. It's just that you'd have my name on your letterhead…'

Ah. At last, the truth. She came across Sir Lucas's slimy trail everywhere. 'You want a sort of virtual, non-working directorship? It might impress some of our clients, I suppose, but let's look at the cost factor. The agency provides a living for me and the girls in the office. It also keeps this house going, but there's not enough fat in the budget for us to take on a part-time, non-working director.'

'Ah, but it will be different when you merge with Holland and Butcher. That's where we're heading, isn't it? Working closely with them, you'll be able to double your turnover because there's no other agency around who can train staff *and* get them into good jobs. You'd wipe out the competition. You'd need bigger offices, of course. I can see you moving into High Street—'

'I'll think about it.' She could hear herself turn sharp.

He looked downcast. Poor lamb, he'd always had eyes bigger than his stomach. When he was a little boy he'd dreamed of conquering the stars, but in those days he'd been prepared to put in the hours of hard graft necessary to get there. It was this very trait which had got him into the House of Commons. Ambition plus hard work plus loyalty paid off.

This development was ambition without the hard work, and she didn't see how it could possibly pay off. She put her arm around him and gave him a hug. 'Dear Max; you are the dearest, sweetest soul, and a fine member of parliament. You are a wonderful husband and a perfectly splendid father. Forgive me for playing the devil's advocate? I want you to succeed in whatever you undertake. I promise to think about it very seriously.'

He softened. 'Don't take too long, right?'

Her phone shuddered again. This time she picked it up, more to bring an end to the conversation with Max than because she wanted to get more orders from Sir Lucas Ossett.

It wasn't Sir Lucas.

It was Maggie, in a state; half laughing, half crying. 'Are you there? Oliver said you were using your old mobile and… Oh, this is so awful, and I don't know why I'm laughing, but… Go away, Oliver!'

Oliver must be hovering nearby. 'Let me!' Oliver's voice came on the phone. 'Look, it's nothing, really. Nothing to get in a state about, and really no need for you to come over.'

Maggie interrupted. Presumably, they were snatching the phone from one to the other. 'Can you come, though? I'm so afraid he's going to get stuck. He's far too fat to get out through the kitchen window.'

Oliver: 'Such a fuss about nothing. I told him Sir Lucas would want to speak to him and he said he had an important engagement somewhere, which I didn't believe, so the caretaker… Well, all right, it was a bit high-handed but—'

'Use your own phone!' That was Maggie, screaming.

Bea said, 'Calm down, both of you. One of you hold the phone between you, and take it in turns to talk. Maggie; you think I ought to come…where? To your mother's flat?'

'Yes. Well, downstairs a bit. Flat six.'

'That's the MI5 bloke?'

Maggie giggled. 'Oh, I know he talks as if he's in the Secret Service, but honestly!'

Oliver, shouting; 'He didn't deny it.'

Bea broke in. 'So what's the problem?'

Oliver said, 'He's got himself locked in.'

Maggie, gritting her teeth. 'Oliver told him to stay put. He said he had to go out. The caretaker lifted Harvey's keys off him and locked him into his own flat, front and back. Now he can't get out. He's raising Cain, crying and shouting for help out of the window. Half the neighbourhood is out there, and some want to call the police.'

Oliver shouted, 'He's only got to wait till the security man comes for him from Head Office.'

Bea put her hand to her forehead. 'Oliver, you can't detain the man against his will! Go and talk to the caretaker. Get him to give the man his keys back.'

Silence.

Maggie said, 'That's the problem. We can't find him.'

A shiver ran up and down Bea's back. She felt behind her for a stool and sat down. '"Can't find him"? As in… he's missing?'

Oliver sounded uneasy for the first time. 'He's not in his flat, or working on the cars, or anywhere in the basement. I expect he's popped out for something. He'll be back in a minute.'

Maggie was scornful. 'It's been over half an hour.'

Bea was thinking hard. 'Have you tried his mobile phone?'

'Yes. No service.'

Not good news. Bea said, 'Look; is the lift working? He's not in that, is he?'

'Why would he be in there?'

'No.' That was Oliver. 'It brought a couple up—'

'Helen and her husband,' said Maggie.

'A few minutes ago, and there's an older lady—'

'Carrie Kempton, stupid!'

'Shut up, Maggie. She's getting out of the lift now. Her partner in crime—'

'Lucy Emerson, idiot!'

'—has stayed outside on the balcony, trying to keep him calm, talking to him through his kitchen window. They can go down the fire escape at the back and—'

Bea said, 'Yes, I know about that.'

Oliver again. 'The old lady, Mrs Emerson, is just saying… Hold on a mo… No, she says no matter how hard he tries, he can't get out through the kitchen window, which isn't surprising, and… Oh, he's hurt himself, is that right? Cut himself? She says the whole street can hear him, and someone's bound to call the police. Maggie; tell her, no police!'

Bea looked at her watch. How long would it take her to get there? 'What about your mother, or the Professor? Could they sort it?'

'They're out.'

'Could Carmela help?' said Bea. 'She's opposite him, isn't she? She could talk to him from their shared balcony.'

'Also out, we think. We've rung her doorbell but—'

'I expect she's got someone with her.' That was Maggie. 'She works in the late afternoons, you know.'

Bea knew. 'Listen; Maggie, Oliver. Are the decorators still working up top? They might have tools—'

Maggie said, 'It's the weekend. They're not working today. Do you think we should break the door down? Hang on a mo. Someone else has come up.'

A babble of voices. A woman's; Helen McIntyre? A tenor; her husband?

Oliver and an alto; Mrs Emerson?

Maggie again, hard breathing. 'It's the youngsters from the ground floor flat. They want to search the building. The caretaker must be in one of the other flats, doing something to…oh, I don't know. The drains or something.' A hysterical giggle. 'I just hope Harvey doesn't bleed to death before they can get him out.'

Bea reached a long arm for her handbag, shrugging on her coat, holding the phone first with one hand and then the other. 'I'm on my way. Have someone ready to let me into the building.'

Her son Max was getting cross, wanting her to resume her conversation with him. 'Mother, we need to talk. It's urgent.'

She switched off her phone, dropped it in her handbag. 'It may be urgent for you, but it's important for them. There's a problem at Sir Lucas's flats, and maybe I can knock some sense into their heads. Can you give me a lift?'

*Saturday afternoon*

MAX DROPPED BEA off outside the flats. Bea was relieved to see there was no sign of the police, the fire brigade, or the Samaritans. No gawking pedestrians, either. The problem so far had been confined to the flats.

A man was waiting at the front door to admit her; not the shaven-headed Connor. Not Oliver. A stranger in his forties, dark-hair receding, pallid skin, sloping shoulders in a designer jumper, bespoke jeans, brogues. An off-duty banker?

He held out his hand. 'Mrs Abbot? Eliot McIntyre. You met my wife earlier. We've been through the whole building, talked to everyone who's in, searched the basement quarters and the garage below, but there's no sign of the caretaker or his keys. Harvey's quiet enough at the moment. We're taking it in turns to be with him. Helen's just taken him up a cup of tea, though I told her she should be resting. Maggie says you can sort it, but I'm only giving it fifteen more minutes before we call the police.'

'Good thinking. Shall we take the lift?'

He stepped into the lift after her. 'I don't see what we can do except break the door down, except that that will get up the nose of the caretaker. I don't know if you've met him, but he's a surly so-and-so employed directly by Sir Lucas, and no one wants to offend him.'

'So I understand. You know this Mr Harvey?'

'Yes, of course. That is, I see him around and about. My wife sees more of him, being at home at the moment. She says he's an amusing neighbour. "Guess what Harvey's up to this week" sort of thing. I'm off early in the morning, back late at night.' He looked at his watch. 'We've got an important date this evening. I hope Helen isn't too knocked up to attend. I told her to take it easy, but...' A shrug.

He wasn't a bully—as Bea had thought—but a caring, slightly fussy husband, worried about his wife.

The third-floor landing was crowded with people. Oliver and Maggie. Lucy Emerson and her buddy Carrie Kempton. The dark-haired girl from the ground floor with her shaven-headed partner.

No Lady Ossett. No Professor. No Carmela.

No Helen McIntyre, who was presumably holding Harvey's hand at the moment.

Every face turned to Bea as she emerged from the lift.

'You have ten minutes to find him,' said Eliot McIntyre, looking at his watch. 'Or I call in the police.'

'Ridiculous,' said Oliver. 'He's only dropped out for a few minutes.'

A babble of different voices, each holding their own opinion.

Bea cut through the noise. 'Who saw the caretaker last?'

Oliver said, 'Well, he locked Harvey in and got into the lift, saying he'd got work to do, even if I hadn't. That was the last I saw of him.'

'Did he go up or down?'

A shrug from Oliver. 'How should I know?'

'Had anybody else asked him to call in?'

'No. Not me.'

'Haven't seen him since...dunno.'

'Not this morning, anyway.'

'What does he usually do on a Saturday?'

A grin or two. 'Watch football on satellite TV. You can always hear his telly out back on a Saturday afternoon because he leaves his window open.'

'Did anyone hear his television this afternoon? No? He told Oliver that he had work to do. Does anyone know what that might have been?'

No. Heads were shaken all round.

Bea looked at Carmela's closed door. No use asking her for help till her client had gone. 'Mrs Emerson, may I go out on to the fire escape from your flat? Perhaps you can show me the way. And Mr McIntyre, would you come, too, please?' He seemed to have the coolest head, and it would be good to have a disinterested witness to what happened next. 'Let's go up and talk to Harvey.'

'Of course, dear; if you think it will do any good.' Lucy Emerson's eyes were bright with excitement. 'I know it's all very dreadful, dear, but there's no denying that dear Harvey can be a bit, well, awkward, and between you and me, it's only a bit of a graze on the back of his hand and he really doesn't need a doctor.'

Eliot ushered the two of them into the lift. 'I must get my wife to go and have a rest, or she'll be no good for anything this evening.' He pressed the button for the next floor.

Mrs Emerson let them into her flat. The air smelled stale. Windows weren't often opened here. She led the way into the kitchen, neat and tidy with some chicken pieces defrosting on the side, ready for cooking that evening. She opened the door on to the balcony and closed it behind them, to keep the heat in.

'We're directly above Harvey's flat now?' said Bea. 'And the other flat on this floor is for the Muslim family who seem to be invisible. Is that right?'

'They're probably in, dear,' said Mrs Emerson, 'but they don't usually come to the door.'

'This way to Harvey's flat,' said Eliot, impatient of delay. He started down the stairs, calling out, 'Helen; it's me. You really ought to be resting. Here's Mrs Abbot to take charge now.'

Mrs Emerson fluttered down the stairs after him, and Bea followed.

'Hello there.' Helen was huddled into a coat which looked too big for her, but there was a little colour in her cheeks. She'd been a pretty woman once and would be so again if the treatment worked. 'Harvey's been telling me how he ran a ship aground in the war.'

Eliot said, 'Humph!' in a quiet voice.

Bea grinned to herself. Harvey wasn't old enough to have served in the Second World War, and she didn't think he'd served in the Falklands either. He'd thrown his kitchen window open and was sitting on a chair on the far side of the sink below it, sipping a cup of tea. He looked to be in his early forties. He had ginger hair in a quiff above a plump, petulant face, unremarkable except for a pair of very bright blue eyes. Harvey was as gay as a flock of parakeets, and if he'd ever been nearer government headquarters than passing through Gloucester in a car, Bea would be very much surprised.

'Ah-ha, the cavalry arrives!' He had a high, light tenor voice. 'I've been hearing all about you, Mrs Abbot, from my neighbours. They say you're a proper little heroine and will get me out of here in next to no time. I shall have to go online and tweet about meeting you.'

No hysteria. Harvey enjoyed being the centre of attention.

Bea smiled because he was smiling. 'Did you get any idea where the caretaker was going when he left you?'

'I'm afraid I threw something of a tantrum when he departed. The shock, you know; he lifted my keys off me, calm as you please, and threw me across the room when I objected. Because I did object, my word I did. There I was, lying half on and half off the sofa, quite at his mercy, and he storms out muttering to himself. That long lad with the black hair that I don't know what he has to do with anything though he said he'd come direct from Sir Lucas Ossett, which I cannot believe, but anyway, he apologized to me very nicely, that I will say, and off they both went, locking my own front door behind them. Naturally, I called them back, and perhaps I did lose my temper and thump the door, but to no avail.'

He took a deep breath. 'So I opened my window at the back here, and I hollered and I hollered for help, and Lucy very kindly came down, and Carrie, too, and Lucy went back up to see if she could raise the caretaker on his mobile phone, but she couldn't. Carrie went back up to look for him, too, and that's when I tried to get out of the kitchen window and gave myself a nasty scratch on the catch, but it's no good thinking I'm the slender little thing I used to be, because those days are long since gone.'

'Would you like another cup of tea?' said Lucy.

'Thank you. I don't mind if I do. And perhaps a little shortbread biscuit? Must keep my strength up. Then Mr McIntyre came up, which I hadn't expected, but then dear Helen is always so concerned about me, and she came up as well, and then there was such a coming and a going, I've quite lost count of the number of people trying to release me from durance vile.'

Lucy took his empty cup and saucer and disappeared up the stairs. Eliot McIntyre looked at his watch. 'Your ten minutes are up, Mrs Abbot. I don't want to keep Helen out here in the cold any longer.'

Bea made up her mind. 'Helen, would you be so good as to check that Harvey doesn't need medical attention for his scratch? Harvey, can you somehow put your arm out of the window so that she can see...?'

While Helen attended to Harvey, Bea swivelled round and, since her head for heights was not wonderful, grasped the balcony railing with both hands before she looked over into the yard below. Nothing. Look to the right. Yes. Oh dear.

Was she going to be sick?

No. Breathe deeply. Stand upright.

Eliot treated her to a disapproving look.

Bea didn't want Helen to look and be upset, too. She

said, 'Mr Eliot, would you care to walk a little way along the balcony with me? Right to the end. We're outside Carmela's flat now, aren't we? I'm not good at heights. Would you look over the balcony and down into the yard for me?'

He looked. Gagged. Coughed. Said, in a strangled voice, 'That's torn it.'

'Don't let Helen look.'

'No.' He ran the back of his hand across his mouth.

Bea steadied herself and had another look. Straight down, past the McIntyre flat and the now empty flat of the old woman who'd died some months before. He'd been a big man, that caretaker. One arm was outflung, and beyond it a mobile phone. Smashed. There was a considerable pool of blood under the body, and beside it, half under the body, there was a large, flattened cardboard box.

A high-pitched cry. A seagull?

'Helen!' Eliot dashed back to his wife's side, pulling her away from the railing. She'd looked because she'd seen them do so. Bea cursed herself. She ought to have sent Helen back inside before she'd tested her suspicions.

Someone would have to go down and check to see if the caretaker were dead or badly injured. Probably her. Who else got all the dirty jobs around here?

# TWELVE

*Saturday evening.*

'So,' SAID BEA, looking at the menu without seeing it, 'I went down to the ground floor and out into the yard and checked. He was quite dead. Cold. I called the police, who called the paramedics, who called the doctor, and they all agreed that it was a tragic accident. No one had liked the man, everyone was suitably shocked and a perfectly splendid time was had by Old Uncle Tom Cobley and all.'

The menu in this new restaurant was huge, and the dishes seemed to combine foods which were not usually eaten together. The evening would be expensive, but at least she didn't have to pay. Her host, that grey man, CJ Cambridge, liked to be among the first to try out a new restaurant, and no doubt this place would live up to his high standards.

CJ beckoned the waiter over. 'You sound as if you need a drink before we eat. Scotch for shock? Gin and something?'

'I have no intention of reeling out of the restaurant in these high heels. I've ruined one pair this weekend already. I'll have one glass of wine with the meal, as usual.' She put the menu down. 'You choose what we should eat. Anything but shellfish for me.'

CJ scanned the menu. 'It's lobster that upsets you, isn't it? We'll play safe with some game, shall we?'

Normally, Bea would have resented his choosing for

her, but tonight she'd had enough of being independent and clear-thinking and saving everyone else's bacon.

'I would like,' she said, 'to wipe today out of my memory banks. It's a Saturday, and it ought to have been a time for recuperation from the day-to-day worries of running a business. I ought to have spent an hour going over the accounts and dealing with any problems that might have arisen in the office. Then I would have gone shopping, or taken a walk in Kensington Gardens, or perhaps even gone to bed with my Kindle this afternoon.'

CJ was amused. 'Instead of which, you kept your head while others were losing theirs, and were ready on time—looking as charming as ever, if I may say so—when I called for you.'

Bea shot him a glance which ought to have skewered him to the wall. 'You think I kept my head because I didn't bring Sir Lucas's name up when the police came? I'm not sure I was right to do so.'

He smiled, the all-powerful alpha male indulging the frail female's quite unnecessary fears. 'Now what possible good could have been achieved by dragging his name into what was clearly, as you say, a tragic accident?'

'Pull the other one. How long had the caretaker worked there? Years. He was as familiar with the fire escape as he was with the lift. Judging by the way he was lying and the shape of the pool of blood beneath him, he'd fallen from one of the balconies on the right-hand side of the building. A higher floor, rather than a lower one.

'It's impossible to access the fire escape from outside the building unless someone inside opens a door to let you in. The same applies to getting into one of the flats from the fire escape. You can't, unless someone lets you in. However, the caretaker had keys to all the flats and could get out on to their balconies at any time by letting

himself in through one of their front doors and leaving
through the kitchen. Are you following me?'

'I am.' Humouring her.

'The police asked which flat, and we all chipped in
to tell them which one it must have been. We worked
from the bottom up. The ground floor flat where the old
woman used to live is empty. True, the ground slopes
away a bit at the back, but if he'd fallen off that ground
floor balcony, the drop wouldn't have been sufficient to
kill him; to break a limb perhaps, but no more.

'Directly above him were the McIntyres. They say
the first they heard of something amiss was when Maggie and Oliver knocked on their door to see if they knew
where the caretaker might be. They say they did not go
out on to their balcony at any time that afternoon. I believe them.

'Above them is Carmela, who had a client with her
all afternoon. Knocking on her door failed to rouse her.
She only came to the door, fully dressed and immacu-
late, when her client was ready to leave. They alibi one
another.'

CJ was amused. He steepled his fingers and looked
at her over them. 'You really think she needs an alibi?'

Ignore that. 'Above Carmela is the Muslim family. The
father did come to the door eventually. He said they'd
been in all afternoon. They'd been scared when they
heard all the shouting but hadn't dared to look out and
hadn't seen anything. See no evil, hear no evil. The police believed him. I'm not sure I did. To me, he looked
like a man determined to avoid trouble.'

CJ raised one eyebrow. 'Perhaps, if you'd been through
what they've suffered, wherever they've come from,
*you'd* be frightened when a policeman knocked on your
door.'

Bea grimaced. 'I know. I'm being uncharitable. Take no notice. I'll feel better tomorrow. Now, directly above the Muslims is the empty flat once occupied by Tariq. I understand he left the place in a mess and, from my own observation, he'd dumped a pile of cardboard and other packing materials out on his balcony before he disappeared. The caretaker had told Oliver that he had some work to do after he left Harvey. I think he went into Tariq's messy, unoccupied flat, let himself out on to the balcony from the kitchen and started to throw all the rubbish down into the yard, so that he could dispose of it in one of the wheelie bins. The police agree with me that this was what must have happened.'

'Was there any packaging in the yard?'

'Yes. He was lying on some. Everyone believes he fell from Tariq's balcony.'

He laid his hand on her knee and pressed it. 'Good girl. That's today's problem solved.'

She removed his hand. 'It explains where the caretaker might have been, but it doesn't explain why he fell.'

CJ made a gesture as if drinking from a glass. 'He'd drink taken?'

Bea shook her head. 'According to Oliver and Harvey, he was sober enough when he locked the latter into his flat and took the keys away. I'm told that on a Saturday afternoon he took time off work to watch the football on his television. It was his custom to turn the volume up so high that everyone in the flats could hear it, but no one heard it today. So it's reasonable to assume that he died before the game started. I suppose he thought he had time enough to clear the rubbish from outside Tariq's flat before he turned the telly on. And fell. I repeat; why did he fall?'

A shrug. 'He probably had a bottle of whisky in his

pocket. Perhaps he found some drink in Tariq's flat on his way through and helped himself? Perhaps he was startled by a bird or an aeroplane flying low, turned to look up at it, and lost his balance.'

'They have to have a post-mortem in cases of accidental death, don't they? That should show if he'd alcohol in his body.'

The waiter served the entrée. It looked pretty. Mushrooms and something. The wine waiter proffered an appropriate bottle. Bea asked for water. She looked around. Low lighting, polished tables, spindly seating. The tables were set too close together for comfort. Were they expecting a full house?

CJ said, 'I assume you managed to release friend Harvey from his prison?'

'Mm. I suggested that the caretaker must have a duplicate set of keys hanging up in his office in the basement. Lucy Emerson helped me look. We found them, properly labelled, and took them upstairs to let Harvey out. He's enjoying the notoriety; Harvey, I mean. He's as gay as all get out and takes pictures of young men for fun...or so he tells me. I sincerely hope that's all he does take them for. He writes teenage pulp fiction and reviews films for one of the tabloids. Hence his fantasies about being the new James Bond. He also eats and drinks horror films. He's going to let me have a list of his favourites. Mostly about vampires, I gather.'

She tasted the starter. Pleasant enough.

CJ attacked his mushrooms with enthusiasm. 'So he's none the worse for wear and all's well that ends well.'

'Except for Helen. I thought she'd pass out on us after she spotted the caretaker on the ground. She was white as a sheet. Eliot and Carrie Kempton got her down to their flat and, after she'd had a little lie-down, I helped her with her make-up and saw her off to their important function on her husband's arm. And that's another thing.' She sighed. 'I thought Eliot was a bullying bastard, but he turns out to be an over-anxious and caring husband, desperately worried about his wife's health. I couldn't have been more wrong about him.'

CJ was amused. 'So you jumped to the wrong conclusion again?'

Bea gritted her teeth, but had to agree that she had done just that. 'I suppose.'

'Never mind.' He patted her hand.

She'd calmed down enough by now not to slap his hand away, but she did remove it from his grasp. 'I'm sorry, CJ. I'm no sort of company for you tonight. Too much going on. Maggie in distress. She's staying over at her mother's again tonight.'

'They don't call you Mother Hen for nothing.'

She tried to smile. 'Oliver is another problem. You'll say that I'm worrying unnecessarily but I don't like the way he's been drawn into acting—not exactly outside the law—but… No, let's call a spade a spade. He did act unlawfully by helping the caretaker to lock Harvey into his flat.'

'With the best of intentions, surely.'

'Doing evil that good may come of it? That's fudging the boundaries, and it makes me uncomfortable.'

'Ah, but that's just you, Bea. You're frighteningly sure that you know what's right and what's wrong. You see the world in terms of black and white, but really it's all shades of grey.'

She blinked. 'I know the difference between right and wrong, and so do you.'

A tinge of red came into his cheeks.

At that moment Bea realized how deeply offended

she'd been by Sir Lucas's manoeuvres. Too black and white, was she? Well, perhaps she was and a little flexibility might be in order. But there was something deep down within her that jumped up and down and screamed when she met up with a careless assumption that it was all right to transgress because, hey, didn't everybody do it?

Some of her other problems flitted through her mind. She could see now that they could all be resolved by taking the primrose path. Going along with what other people wanted might make for a quiet life…but wouldn't she be left feeling she'd acted against her better instincts?

For instance; Max wanted a nominal directorship which meant paying him director's fees, which would have to come out of the agency's profits and hardly reduce her workload. It would mean a cut in the amount set aside for her pension, and the maintenance of the building, etcetera. Taking Max on board might be pleasant for both of them in some ways, but if it meant unbalancing the books, surely it was wrong to do so?

On the other hand, if it advanced his career, ought she not to do it?

Risk-taking. People said you stopped being fully alive if you never took a risk, but Bea was not of their way of thinking. Risk-taking meant hazarding everything she owned. Risk-taking meant putting the livelihood of everyone at the agency in jeopardy. And for what? So that Max—who already earned a decent living in the Commons—might gain a little kudos here and a director's fee there?

Which led her on to thinking about Holland and Butcher. She didn't particularly want to think about them, but she could see that it was no good putting the matter off.

Here was a different problem. The head of the company had employed a rotten apple as his managing director once. What was to prevent him doing so again? She did not feel happy about working with a firm whose CEO lacked judgement.

On the other hand, as Max had said, a merger between the two companies would be to the advantage of both. And yes, she supposed she might even raise the money to buy them out, if she put her house up as collateral for the loan. She winced; that house was her shell, her protection against the world.

She shook her head. She was not that ambitious for fame and fortune. Surely she was better off as she was... Except that if she did push the agency into the big time and it worked, then she could easily afford to pay Max a director's fee.

What was best to be done?

She really didn't know. And it was time to pay attention to her host, instead of drifting off into daydreams.

CJ was giving his approval of the Sauvignon Blanc which the wine waiter was offering to him. Their entrée arrived, looking—and tasting—delicious. CJ was becoming nicely relaxed. 'Well, as you say; that's all water under the bridge, and no great harm done.'

She couldn't let that pass. 'And no good done, either. Oliver wasn't able to get through to Sir Lucas until after the caretaker's body had been removed because our favourite tycoon was in meetings and not to be disturbed. When he did manage to speak to His Lordship, he was informed that the traitor in the Vicori camp had been exposed, had sworn he'd acted alone, and had been dealt with. So there was no need for Oliver to go on looking for an accomplice at the flats. Thank you for your efforts, dear boy, and goodbye.'

'Poor Oliver.' A gentle smile. 'But Sir Lucas will no

doubt remember him when he needs another clever lad. It was a happy accident that threw Oliver into Sir Lucas's way.'

Bea wasn't so sure. Oliver was beginning to realize that he'd been led up the garden path, encouraged to wade through a pile of manure and been dumped when no longer of use. Oliver was feeling guilty, wounded, and angry; and didn't know who to blame for it. Perhaps he'd flee the commercial world, return to university and bury himself in academia. Bea didn't know what to say to him, and so had said nothing—which had probably been a mistake. He'd refused to go back home with her after the debacle at the flats.

*Please, Lord. Look after Oliver for me.*

She couldn't agree with CJ that there'd been no harm done. It seemed to her that a great deal of harm had been done not only on that day, but on previous days. The future didn't look all that happy, either.

'Cheers,' said CJ.

'Cheers.' She sipped and put her glass down again.

CJ said, 'Well, now you've cleared up that little problem, you can get back to normal. How is your son Max getting on these days?'

That touched another raw nerve. How much did CJ know of Max's latest plans? Perhaps nothing. Perhaps a lot. Once she would have been happy to ask his advice, but not today. She dismissed his query with a smile. 'Very well, thank you.'

She cleared her plate. There hadn't been much of the venison in a fruit sauce, but it had been sufficient. 'Delightful,' she said. 'Unexpected. This place should do well.'

'Dessert? Or just coffee?'

'De-caff coffee? Excuse me.' Her phone was shuddering in her evening bag.

She recognized Piers's number. 'Piers? What is it? Can I ring you back?'

'Where are you? Can you come over? I've got Oliver here, beating himself up. Too much teenage angst for one of my mature years. I've told him to make it up with you, but he's convinced you won't want anything more to do with him.'

'Ridiculous.'

'That's what I said. He says he's been walking around for hours, has tried CJ, but there's no reply. He wants to stay the night here and go back to university tomorrow morning. He says his life is over, etcetera. Any more of this, and I'll take to drink.'

'I'll be right over.' She snapped off the phone. 'Sorry, CJ. Oliver's in a state and I've got to go and rescue him. Has he been trying to get through to you on your phone?'

He looked startled, got out his iPhone and checked. 'I don't normally turn it off, but… Yes, it looks as if… I'll come with you, shall I?'

'I think I'll have to do this on my own. He'll be in touch with you again soon, I'm sure.'

'Nonsense.' He signed to the waiter for the bill. 'I expect he is a little downhearted with the way things have turned out, but it's all good experience as I shall tell him. I'll get us a taxi.'

Bea seethed, but it was true that CJ had the ability to conjure up taxis even in the heart of London and it was undeniably the quickest way to get around.

'Top floor,' said Bea, when they arrived at Piers's address. 'He never stays long in one place. He's moving again soon, but I'm not sure where.' She wondered which of them might have to take a breather before they got to the top, but though they both slowed down on the last flight of stairs, they arrived without too much puffing and panting.

'Welcome.' Piers opened the door with a glass of wine in one hand. He jerked his head sideways. 'I told him you were coming over, so first he wanted to run away and now he's locked himself in the bathroom.'

'He's making a mountain out of a molehill,' said CJ. 'Let me talk to him.'

'Be my guest.' Piers indicated where the bathroom lay and helped Bea take off her coat. 'I'm getting too old for this. First Max, and then Oliver.'

'Max?'

He shrugged. 'Wanted me to persuade you to let him take over the agency, or something. I'm afraid I couldn't follow all his arguments.'

'And what do you think?'

'It doesn't matter what I think. You'll do exactly as you please.'

'CJ tells me I'm too inflexible.'

'If he means you see things more clearly than most, then he's right. Have a glass of something? This is quite a decent red.'

She shook her head, took a seat and, like Piers, listened to CJ trying to coax Oliver out of the bathroom.

On a scale of ten, CJ's tactics didn't merit more than a three. 'It's not the end of the world. I'll have a word with Sir Lucas in the morning, and I'm sure he won't hold it against you that your first job for him went awry. You did your best, but circumstances were against you. I'm going to suggest that he finds you an intern position at Head Office, where you can really show what you're capable of...'

Bea switched off. If Oliver responded to this sort of blarney, then so be it.

She said to Piers, 'The phone call you had this afternoon. Did you manage to tie your prospective sitter down to a date?'

'Silly woman. She thinks Botox and face lifts will give her back her youth. She was a stunner in her day, I'll give you that; but now her face is so stiff she looks as if she's wearing a mask.'

'So will you paint her now?'

'I could paint her as an old crone, looking into the mirror and seeing her beautiful younger self. But I won't. Let her keep her illusions. I really must get round to painting you one day, Bea.'

'You say that every six months or so.'

'I mean it. But she did come up with one piece of gossip which might amuse you; a friend of hers has just sold his multimillion pound mansion in Chelsea to Sir Lucas.'

'Ah. Makes sense.'

They both turned to see CJ, his cheeks flying red flags of disappointment and anger. 'The stupid boy won't listen to me. Bea, you have a go.'

Bea sighed, stretched, and made her way to the bathroom door. 'Oliver, the sooner you come out, the sooner we can start putting things right. Have you had any supper? Because if not, perhaps we can pick up a pizza on the way home.'

Silence. She waited. The door cracked open, and Oliver appeared. Blotchy-faced. His voice cracked. 'I messed up.'

Bea nodded. 'We all do, at times. You can do penance tomorrow.'

He tried to smile. 'We frightened Harvey to death. No, I don't mean "to death", of course I don't. But I keep seeing his face when he fell back over the settee. I ought to have stopped things right there.'

'Uh-huh. You should. But he'll forgive you if you spend some time listening to his stories tomorrow. You can call it your community service. I'd advise spreading it over several days or you'll never get anything else done.'

CJ was not amused. 'What are you talking about? What penance?'

Oliver winced, but faced him. 'I'm sorry, CJ. I let you down. I let you both down. I was so taken up by the thought of Sir Lucas wanting me to work for him that I got carried away. Mother Hen did warn me. Maggie told me I was overstepping the mark, too. But all I could see was…' He wiped his face with his hands. 'All I could see was…'

'A ladder to the stars,' said Bea. 'You were so preoccupied with your task for Sir Lucas that you overlooked what else was happening at the flats.'

CJ stared. 'Sir Lucas has found the traitor at Vicori House. So what else is there to worry about?'

'Well,' said Bea, 'I suppose we can put the keying of Sir Lucas's car down to Tariq in revenge for the confiscation of his music equipment, but what about the rest of the odd happenings there? For starters; who poisoned Lady Ossett's supper; who arranged the tripwire which caused Sir Lucas to fall down the stairs; and above all, who pushed the caretaker over the edge?'

'What!'

'Then,' said Bea, warming to the task, 'there's the small matter of the call-girl cards; which is not such a small matter really, since it led to that nasty fight in the foyer. Come to think of it, I wouldn't mind knowing more about the death of the old lady on the ground floor, as that seems to be the first of the unhappy events which hit the building. So, shall we get a pizza on the way, or shall I make you an omelette when we get back home?'

# THIRTEEN

*Sunday morning*

BEA WOKE EARLY and lay in bed, allowing the events of the last few days to filter through into her consciousness.

Maggie was sleeping over at her mother's.

Oliver was asleep upstairs in his own bed.

Sir Lucas had unmasked the traitor in his camp but had not returned to his wife's side.

Lady Ossett continued to be on good terms with the Professor. Long might that last.

Bea decided that she would have a leisurely breakfast and go to church for a spiritual refill. She'd heard that going to church wasn't supposed to be like filling up a car with petrol but that's how it appeared to her. She liked to hear God's word interpreted and to join in songs of praise. She cherished the time of peace and quiet in which to worship God away from the stress of her busy life.

She didn't think she was a particularly good Christian. Her dear dead husband had encouraged her to believe that if she talked to God, He would listen and respond. Well, she did find it a comfort to talk to Him and tell Him all her troubles, but she was the first to admit she wasn't particularly good at listening to His replies.

Except…just occasionally it seemed that God did tell her things. A thought would pop into her mind from somewhere, she wasn't sure where, and it would lead to her taking such and such an action. Or into holding her tongue about…whatever. She'd spoken to the minister at church about it one day, and he'd said she must be sure that these thoughts chimed with Jesus's instructions for living.

She sighed. It wasn't always easy to know what did or didn't, was it? Except that just lately He'd been banging on at her not to have any dealings with the devil…

She giggled. She didn't think Sir Lucas would normally be considered a devil. Or, would he?

She dressed and, as she'd plenty of time before the service, took a cup of coffee downstairs to make sure that nothing alarming had been left for her to deal with when the agency closed at lunchtime the previous day.

Oliver found her there, an hour later, looking ragged.

She put down the phone with a long sigh. 'Lucky I caught that. Someone left a message on the answerphone yesterday, saying they'd been taken ill and couldn't run a dinner party at one of the Consulates this evening. I must have tried everyone but the chef at Claridges, but I've finally managed to track down someone who could fill in. What a morning.'

'We used to switch the phone upstairs when the agency closed at weekends.'

Bea lifted her empty cup, grimaced, put it down again. 'We've got a recorded message which says that if the matter is urgent, to ring my mobile phone number. My phone got smashed at the flats, remember? I've re-recorded the message so they can contact me on my old phone, but in future I think we'd better have someone else taking back-up calls over the weekend. One of the office girls might be happy to do it for a consideration.'

She yawned and stretched. Shot upright. 'Look at the time. I was going to go to church this morning.'

'You've got other work to do.' Oliver was steady-eyed. Serious.

She put her hands in her lap and swivelled her chair to look out of the window, across the paved garden and up through the bare branches of the sycamore tree to the spire of the church beyond. The words 'important' and 'urgent' came into her mind. Was it more important to go to church, or to deal with the problems at the flats? She could argue both ways.

Oliver said, 'People don't say "sorry" much nowadays, do they? But I need to get it out of my system. I'm sorry. You were right and I was wrong about Sir Lucas. I did know I was stepping over the line yesterday, but I got caught up in the excitement and… No excuses. I knew I was doing wrong. Then he dropped me, just like that. You'll say, "What did you expect?"' He tried to smile. 'I've been naive, haven't I?'

'Don't beat yourself up too much. Sir Lucas saw a bright young mind and made use of you for a while. No great harm done. Now, suppose we pool what we've both learned. For a start, can you fill me in on why you thought Harvey was scheming to kill Sir Lucas?'

He washed his face with his hands. 'Looking back, I can't think how I came to be so stupid. I got caught up in the excitement of the chase. I started at the top of the building and—'

'Wait a minute. Did you start in the penthouse?'

'Well, no. There's no point suspecting Lady Ossett, was there?'

Bea gave him a grim smile. 'Possibly not. I'll fill you in on that complication later. Right; so you started with the Professor—'

'Maggie had said his cat was missing, so I used that as an excuse to call on him. You know about his cat?'

'Of course. You were amused by the Professor's apps and decided he wasn't the person you were looking for. Then you went down to see Tariq? He said he was poorly and you let him off the hook. What you didn't know was that he'd already tried to leave that day, been fielded by the caretaker and knocked out for his pains. No wonder he was feeling off colour.'

'I wasn't to know that, was I?'

Bea refrained, just, from saying that if he'd listened to her, he'd have known all about it. 'So next on your list was—'

'Mrs Kempton. Carrie. Fluffy bunny. I made the excuse about looking for the cat, and I think she was glad to have someone to talk to and invited me in. I spotted her computer, an old one, not much cop, and she let me play with it because she said it was acting up and I discovered that somehow or other she'd got all the formatting marks to show, would you believe? So I put that right for her, and she was duly grateful. I whizzed through her files and there was nothing there which shouldn't be, so I crossed her off the list. She said it was a bit late by then to be calling on other people so I stopped for the night.'

'Then this morning you went back to Tariq's flat.'

'He opened the door in his pyjamas. He said he was feeling better but hadn't seen the cat. He suggested that if I went and had a talk to the caretaker, in private, before he started on his usual work, he might take me around and help me look for the cat. I'd been thinking it would be a good idea to have the man at my side, anyway, so I took the lift down to where the caretaker was working in the foyer, and I asked if we could have a word in private and we went down to his flat which is in the sub-basement and—'

'And Tariq slipped down the stairs and out of the

building while you talked to the caretaker. Tariq used you as a decoy.'

Oliver flushed. 'Well, I wasn't to know, was I? I told the caretaker what I was doing, that I was acting on Sir Lucas's orders, and he said we should go straight up and talk to Tariq about it. So we went up and, as you say, Tariq had gone. The caretaker threw a total strop. The mess in the flat, you wouldn't believe! There were the remains of takeaway meals, discarded clothes, surfaces scratched, a curtain torn. It was only natural the caretaker was angry. He said Sir Lucas would have to get some contract cleaners in to clear the place out and redecorate. He went out on to the balcony, and there was another pile of junk there. He said he'd try to deal with it later. Which I suppose is what he was doing when he fell over the edge. He said Tariq had a laptop and a PC. There was no laptop—he must have taken it with him. I looked at the PC but there was nothing incriminating on it.'

Bea nodded, non-committal. 'Then… Lucy Emerson?'

'Fluffy bunny with a steel core. The caretaker didn't bother to accompany me when I knocked on her door, but as luck would have it Carrie Kempton came down the stairs just at that moment—apparently they always have coffee together in the mornings—so she introduced me to Lucy. Carrie said how clever I'd been, putting her computer right, and we had a nice cuppa and a chat. Lucy Emerson does have a laptop but doesn't use it much. She let me see it and there wasn't anything on it which shouldn't have been there. I can't see her plotting with a vice-chairman of Vicori to bring Sir Lucas down, can you?'

'No, I can't. So, what about the Muslim family opposite her?'

'No surprise, they wouldn't open the door. The caretaker said they didn't talk to anyone in the flats and didn't know Sir Lucas, so it wouldn't be them. We didn't bother with Carmela either because, well, Sir Lucas said it wasn't necessary. So we got to Harvey.'

Oliver sighed. 'He opened the door wearing silk pyjamas—it was well into the afternoon by that time. I thought he looked like a petulant cockatoo. He said he was just about to go out so we couldn't come in. The caretaker asked if he'd seen the cat Momi, and the dear man shrieked and clapped his hands to his cheeks, defying any cat to enter his territory. We asked if we might look for ourselves, and he didn't want to let us in, saying we'd disturb all his "Top Secret" papers, but we insisted that we had to look and there wasn't any cat, of course. But his second bedroom is set up as an office, with a computer and printer and fax machine, and some rather nifty cameras.

'Also, pinned up on a notice board were photos of various young men which he seems to have taken with a long-range lens. All young, some of them in school uniform. He said he was taking the pictures for a story he was writing, which I didn't believe for one minute. His computer was on a screen saver. He tried to stop me, but I wanted to see what he'd got there and I found folders on a whole lot of people. I saw there was one marked "Camellia", which I thought might be his way of disguising "Carmela", and I was right. He'd snapped her as she'd let a number of different men out of her flat. Very clear photos of the men concerned. And one of them was—'

'Sir Lucas. Of course. Anyone else you recognized?'

'There's a photo montage of executives on the wall in the foyer at Vicori House. I recognized one of Carmela's visitors from that, though I can't recall his name. The closest I can get to it is that he's a vice president of one of the Vicori companies, third row down on the left on the board.'

'So, on the basis of a photograph showing this man outside Carmela's door, you assumed he was the traitor Sir Lucas was looking for? That he was using Harvey as a go-between, or perhaps trying to obtain information from Sir Lucas through Carmela? There might be another explanation, you know.'

'Why else would he be taking those photographs?'

Bea sighed. Oliver had not just jumped, but leaped to the wrong conclusion.

Oliver said, 'Harvey was burbling away about Carmela being a naughty girl, inviting me to laugh with him. I said I thought he'd been rather naughty, too, that I'd have to report him, and that he must know what the consequences were. He giggled and he said…' Oliver washed his face with his hands again. 'He said, "Oh yes, please!" and pinched my bottom.'

Bea tried not to laugh. 'Er, you've had advances made to you before now?'

'Well, yes; once or twice. But I hadn't seen this one coming. The caretaker was horrified, too. He started shouting at Harvey, saying he was a reptile and worse, and that Sir Lucas would deal with him and he was not to leave the apartment until further notice. Harvey took umbrage, said he didn't believe what he was hearing, that he had to go out on important government business and that MI5 would be watching. The caretaker lifted Harvey's keys which were on his hall table. Then he went into the kitchen and locked the back door, and took that bunch of keys, too. Apparently the bunch in the back door was Harvey's spare set. He became hysterical, shouting that he had claustrophobia and that we'd no right to lock him in.

'I wasn't thinking straight. I thought it served him right. He tried to rush the caretaker and got thrown back across the settee. I started to laugh. It wasn't till much later that I… Harvey really was frightened, you know. He was perspiring, and…flapping about in a way which I thought at the time was funny. But it wasn't funny, really. Was it?'

'Did he tell you what he does for a living? He writes teenage pulp fiction. He showed me a whole shelf full of his books; written under a pseudonym, of course. He also writes film reviews for one of the seedier tabloids. I saw his book of cuttings. He was due at a film premiere last night. I hope he made it. Of course he's got a vivid imagination, and I'm told he slides in and out of reality, but that's partly what makes him a success in his own field. Yes, he does yearn after young men which is sad, but I don't think he goes any further than looking.'

'Or pinching bottoms?' Oliver flushed.

Bea patted his hand. 'I know. Unpleasant for you. Be happy you are young and handsome enough to attract attention.'

Oliver couldn't give up so easily. 'What about the photos of Carmela and her "clients", then? Was he going to blackmail them?'

'He wouldn't take pictures of older men for amusement, and blackmail is not his scene. I suspect Carmela asked him to take them.' She sighed. 'Listen, Oliver, there's a lot you don't know about the people in the flats. Some very odd things have been going on there for months, if not years. For instance, did you know that Carmela and the dark-haired girl on the ground floor have been subjected to some unpleasant experiences by someone living in the flats?'

'Flat two? Evonne, spelled with a capital E. I met her yesterday when we were looking for the caretaker.'

'Right. Evonne with an E. It started some weeks ago. At first it wasn't too bad. Some call-girl cards were printed up with Carmela and Evonne's landline telephone numbers on them and left in the tenants' letter boxes.'

'What?' Half laughing, and half scandalized.

'Later, those same cards were put into telephone boxes near the Underground Station. Both women received nuisance calls asking for Miss Whiplash or whatever. Both were ex-directory, by the way. Carmela dealt with this by taking out her landline and relying on her mobile. Evonne and her flatmate Connor didn't know what to do. Evonne didn't seem to understand the significance of the fact that their numbers were ex-directory, but I'm sure Carmela did. Her livelihood depends on her reputation for discretion. Did she complain of this harassment to Sir Lucas? No, I don't think so. He wouldn't want his relationship with her to become common knowledge. She needed protection, and across the hall from her was Harvey, a man who liked to peep and pry and take photos. Why not ask him to snap her clients as they came and went? She only works in the late afternoon and on certain days. She could give Harvey dates and times. If she had an unexpected or difficult caller, it would be helpful to have a photograph of him.

'As it turned out, she didn't need that insurance, for the troublemaker stepped up his campaign by putting out a call-girl card with Evonne's address on it. Not her telephone number; her *address*. A punter duly called on her on Friday and was, of course, rebuffed. There was a ruckus which Carmela and I witnessed; the punter got the best of it and left. Carmela explained to me what had been happening over a cup of coffee, but on our way back I noticed something was wrong with the lift. We investigated and—'

'You didn't really see a body in the lift, did you?' Half laughing. 'I mean…not really?'

'Yes, I did. It wasn't a corpse but the unconscious body of Tariq on his earlier attempt to flee the nest. The caretaker was afraid that he had killed Tariq which was why he put the lift out of action, attacked me and destroyed my mobile. He wanted to make sure I didn't ring the police till he'd alerted Sir Lucas to what had happened. Fortunately for him Tariq was only unconscious for a while and came to himself while I was being ministered to in Evonne's flat. The caretaker took Tariq back up to his own place, Carmela kept her own counsel and the others hadn't seen anything, so it was convenient for everyone to believe I'd been, well, mistaken.'

'Which is where I came in,' said Oliver, wincing, 'and misread the situation.'

'Easy to do.' Bea was magnanimous.

'Wait a minute.' Oliver frowned. 'You said the first call-girl cards gave ex-directory telephone numbers, which means that someone knew them well enough to get access to their phone numbers? Someone in the flats?'

'Who else? I've been looking for someone who might have had a grudge against those two women. Playing around with the idea, it seemed to me that if a man wasn't getting enough sex, he might have tried it on with the other women in the flats. If he'd been rebuffed, he might have taken umbrage and got his own back by leaving call-girl type cards around with their telephone number or address on. Now you'll laugh, but at first I thought Eliot McIntyre fitted the bill because his wife is probably too frail to have sex at the moment.'

'That sounds right.'

'Yes, but I honestly don't think Eliot has eyes for anyone but his wife. Also, one of the *Big Issue* lads saw a businessman with ginger hair putting the call-girl cards into a local telephone box. Eliot is a businessman, but not a redhead. So, Oliver; have you come across a red-headed businessman in the flats?'

He got out his notebook, and went through it, page by page. 'Not the Professor, nor Tariq, not the Muslim. One of Carmela's clients?'

He looked at Bea, and they both shook their heads. 'No.'

Bea said sweetly, 'I'm sure she gives every satisfaction.'

Oliver returned to his notes. 'Not Eliot. Not Connor because he's shaven-headed. What about flat number four, immediately above Evonne and Connor? Have you been in that one?'

Bea tried to remember what she'd been told. 'Yuppies? Three-piece suits, fold-up bicycles?'

'That's just the female of the species. She's a ball-breaker, that one. I saw her when I was trying to find the caretaker. Six foot, black hair, dominatrix. Works in the fashion industry. She said her name is "Cyn" with a C. Short for Cynthia. I didn't see her partner. Didn't see any need to at that time.'

Bea's hand went to her mobile, and she pressed buttons. 'Mrs Emerson? Lucy? So sorry to have troubled you, such a difficult weekend, I do hope you managed to sleep well after all the trouble we had yesterday… Yes, it was really upsetting, wasn't it? I was wondering how poor Harvey was this morning. I know you keep an eye on him, you and Carrie… Oh, good. I'm so glad to hear it. I thought he'd bob up again, but you never know, and it's always difficult getting a window repaired at the weekend. Has he been able to find someone who lives in the flats and who might be able to…'

The phone quacked, and Bea rolled her eyes. 'Yes, it must be difficult without a caretaker, and the Professor is hardly... No; I agree with you. And I'm not sure that young Connor... Exactly; not the handyman type. And Mr McIntyre is so preoccupied up with his wife's health. It doesn't sound as if there is anyone else who... You plan to ask the man in flat four? I don't think I've met him, have I? What's he called?' She scribbled down a name. 'Isn't he the big Welshman who... I've got him mixed up with someone else, have I? He's not a redhead is he, by any chance? He is?'

Her eyes met Oliver's, and she nodded, handing him the piece of paper on which she'd written a name. 'Splendid. In this cold weather you don't want to leave a window broken... I can see it's going to be a real problem, not having a caretaker on site, but I suppose Sir Lucas will see to that soonest. Yes, I'll probably be popping round later to see if Maggie's all right. Bye.'

She put the phone down. 'Donald. Redhead. Businessman. Cynthia's partner. Lucy is of the opinion that he lets her have her own way too much. He could be the man who's been playing tricks on Carmela and Evonne. I have samples of the call-girl cards which a red-headed businessman put in a phone booth near the flats. I took the precaution of putting the cards in a plastic sleeve, so unless he's been very careful indeed, we'll find his fingerprints on them.'

'That would be proof enough to hand the matter over to the police.'

'I don't think either of the women would want to prosecute even if we had proof positive that it was Donald who did it. It may be enough just to tell him that we know what he's been up to. We'll have a word with him about it this afternoon.'

'Right. Problem solved.'

'Other problems remain. I think I'd like another cosy afternoon chat with Carmela. I know what Carrie and Lucy think about the other tenants, but Carmela may have a different take on them.'

The landline phone rang. 'Who…? On a Sunday morning?'

A strange voice. A man, educated; a hint of a Polish accent? 'Mrs Abbot? I'm pleased to have caught you. I represent the managing agents for a block of flats which Sir Lucas owns. I emailed you last night giving the details, but you haven't seen fit to reply.'

Bea put the call on speaker and rapidly accessed her emails. 'Apologies. I was dealing with another urgent matter this morning, but…yes, I have your email up in front of me now.'

'Sir Lucas asked me to contact you on his behalf to—'

'I'd like to speak to him, yes.'

'I'm afraid that won't be possible as he's on his way to Frankfurt for a meeting, but he left a message for me to check with you. He understands you run a domestic agency, and he's in urgent need of a replacement caretaker. He suggests you may be able to provide someone for us to interview at short notice.'

Bea let silence develop as she thought about this development.

'Mrs Abbot? Are you there?'

Bea said, 'Yes, I'm here. I don't believe we've done any business with you before.'

'I believe not. Sir Lucas indicated that we would be happy to transfer more of his business to you in future if you are able to help us out in this instance.'

'You are aware of the circumstances under which the previous caretaker lost his life?'

'A tragic accident, I understand. Deplorable. We always impress upon our staff the necessity of observing health and safety regulations. I understand that someone is being sent down from Head Office to take over for the next few days but I am looking for a long-term and permanent replacement. May I suggest you let me have, say, three names and contact details of suitable candidates by Tuesday morning?'

End of phone call.

Bea took a deep breath. Crunch point. She knew which way she wanted to jump, but would Oliver follow her lead? How clearly did he now see the temptation to give in to Sir Lucas?

'Did you get all that, Oliver? Sir Lucas acts fast. Let me interpret; a member of his staff—one of his security guards, I imagine—is taking over the caretaker's duties as of now. The caretaker's death has been written off as negligence and my mouth is being shut by the promise of more work for the agency. The subtext is that I drop my investigations and nothing gets into the newspapers. And don't say, "That's the way of the world," or I'll have hysterics.'

'That *is* the way of the world, unfortunately.'

'Then I am not of this world.' There. She'd said it out loud.

He frowned. 'I don't understand why he thinks we could supply him with a caretaker. The Abbot Agency doesn't "do" caretakers.'

'If I were anxious to keep in with Sir Lucas I'd bustle around, contacting everyone I knew in other agencies, in order to fulfil his order and earn his smiles. He's counting on my doing so. But I'm not going to follow the script he's laid out for me.'

He stared at her and through her. When it came to the

point, would he opt out of the fight so as to keep his options open with Sir Lucas and all that he represented?

She said, 'If you want to dissociate yourself from me in this then so be it, but let me make it clear: I'm going to continue poking and prying till I've isolated and dealt with the evil that's wrecking the lives of everyone in that building.'

'But he's found the traitor in his camp.'

'I never thought the problems at the flats emanated from Vicori. It's something to do with the people there. Someone, or maybe more than one, has it in for the rest of them. The damage to Sir Lucas was, I think, collateral.'

'Meaning?'

'I agree with Lady Ossett that the original target was not Sir Lucas, but his wife. Which brings us back to Maggie and makes me wonder if she herself is now in danger. Let's get over there and see what we can do to sort things out…that is, if you're willing to enter the field of battle at my side?'

# FOURTEEN

*Sunday noon*

'Who do we ask to let us in?' Oliver huddled his jacket around him in the east wind.

Even Bea was feeling the cold, and she was wearing a padded, full-length coat and her second-best pair of high-heeled boots. Both clutched bottles of wine.

'Slippers,' said Bea, producing a beaded pair from her handbag. 'They belong to Evonne, the girl in the ground floor flat. She lent them to me when I was attacked, and we're now returning them to her, with a bottle of wine by way of thanks.' She rang the bell for Evonne's flat and was invited to enter.

It was warm inside the foyer. So at least the central heating was working, even if the caretaker had been removed.

'Who are you?' A large man in a tracksuit, with a pale, flat face and a shaved head. He had 'nightclub bouncer' written all over him. Or, if you wanted to be mealy-mouthed, you might call him 'Security'.

'Are you standing in for the caretaker?' said Bea. 'I was told Sir Lucas had arranged for someone to come in.'

He repeated in the same dead tones, 'Who are you?'

The door of Evonne's flat opened. 'She's visiting me, Gary. It's all right.'

'Can't be too careful.' Gary glowered at them before disappearing down the stairs.

'Come in.'

Evonne gestured to them to enter, but Oliver flourished his bottle of wine and said, 'If you don't mind, I'd like to go up and apologize to Harvey for what happened yesterday.'

'Good on you,' said the girl and, while Oliver summoned the lift, she ushered Bea into her flat.

The air still stank of cigarettes, but some attempt had been made to clean the place up, and it was now possible to sit on two of the easy chairs. An old war film was playing on the television with appropriate bangs, whizzes and crashes. Connor was lying on the settee with his feet up, a can of beer in one hand and a cigarette in the other.

The girl pushed his feet off the arm of the settee as she passed. 'Shove up, Connor. We have a visitor.' And to Bea, 'Take a seat. Want a coffee or something?'

Bea sat, hoping the stain on the upholstery was dry, and laid down the bottle of wine and the bag into which she'd put Evonne's slippers. 'Coffee would be great. It was very kind of you to lend me your slippers. I don't know how I'd have got home without them. I hope you like the wine.'

'Well, thanks. Did they find out who killed the cat?'

'I haven't heard.' Which was true. Bea wondered if Momi's body had been disposed of yet, and if the Professor had decided to have another cat or not. And, thinking of what she'd heard about the Professor, whether or not his daughter was in favour of his friendship with Lady O.

Connor turned the sound on the television up.

The girl backhanded him. 'Give it a rest.'

Connor protested, 'It's my television.'

'It's my flat.'

Bea said to the girl, 'I really would like a cup of coffee, if possible. I seem to have missed lunch.'

'Coming up.'

Bea followed the girl out to the kitchen. 'Evonne, I wanted a word in private. Did you think it was Connor who'd put your name on the call-girl cards? Ah, you did, didn't you? I couldn't think up any other reason why you didn't call the police.'

The girl switched on the kettle, her back to Bea. And didn't respond.

'It wasn't him,' said Bea.

The girl said, 'Biscuits? We might have some, if that slug outside hasn't scoffed the lot.'

'You thought he'd set it up to impress you, so that he could appear as your knight in shining armour and rescue you when prospective clients appeared? I noticed you weren't displeased when he got beaten up by your visitor on Friday.'

'I was beaten up as well.'

'I saw. And Connor tried to defend you. He really did try to defend you, without any ulterior motive. May I ask what's gone wrong between you two?'

'None of your business.'

'True. I believe someone else in this building made a pass at you. Right or wrong?'

A shrug. 'Well, yes; but it wasn't anything serious, you know.'

'Donald; from the flat immediately above you.'

A look of surprise. 'How did you know? Did you say you wanted tea or coffee?'

'Either. It was only ever likely to be someone in the flats because the person concerned had access to your landline number and your address. You hadn't been getting on with Connor, and therefore you suspected him. Now, I've been told that someone other than the usual pimps recently dropped some call-girl cards off in a local phone box. My informant rescued a couple of the cards and described the man to me. He's a red-headed businessman.'

Evonne handed Bea a mug of coffee. 'Donald? Are you sure? What a lark if... No, surely you're mistaken.'

'He might have thought it was just a joke.'

'Some joke! Inciting men to phone me at all hours of the night...and that man on Friday actually tried to rape me.'

'You agree that Donald has to be stopped?'

'If it is him, then yes; of course. But...what on earth will Cyn say?' Shocked laughter. 'I mean, she's something else!' The girl made herself a cup of coffee, too. 'Are you sure, though? I mean, men try it on all the time. It doesn't mean that they're going to turn into stalkers or anything.'

'Not a stalker. Worse.'

'I suppose you're right. What he did *was* much worse. It's difficult to get my head round this. I mean, someone I know! Carmela's phone number was on the cards, too. Which means that he also tried making a pass at her...' Evonne was still in shock, but this amused her. 'I'd like to have seen her face! She's a toughie. Ugh. I'm trying to think of the mentality of a man who sets punters on to women who've refused him. Not nice.'

'No, and he's got to be stopped. The first step is to confront him with it, but for that I need your help. Will you come upstairs with me and talk to him about it?'

'No police.'

'Donald needs psychiatric help or he'll find another woman to persecute. If he agrees to counselling, then we can leave the police out of it.'

'My dad would kill me if it got into the papers. It was bad enough when I got a caution, the rioting last year, you know? I was off my head on something Connor had given me, but… No, I won't shove all the blame on to him. I was as bad as him. Have a biscuit, and we'll beard the dragon in her den. I'm looking forward to seeing you deal with our Cynthia. She's a dragon, you know.'

'In which case, perhaps we're rescuing a victim from her clutches?'

Evonne started to laugh, spluttered into her coffee, coughed, sneezed, and used some kitchen towel to blow her nose. 'Oh, you!' she said. 'All right. What do we tell Connor?'

'Nothing, till we're sure of our ground. Let's leave Connor watching his war film while we tackle the man upstairs.'

CYNTHIA OPENED THE door to them. Dressed all in black, six foot plus. Black hair, severely cut. High cheekbones. A frown. 'Yes?'

Evonne said, 'May we come in?'

Cyn transferred her frown to Bea. 'Is this the busy-body who's been turning everyone upside down?'

'Indeed,' said Bea, 'and more to come, I'm afraid. We really came to speak to your partner but—'

'What's he done now?' Fierce, but not defensive.

'Perhaps nothing,' said Bea. 'It may be a case of mistaken identity.'

Cyn didn't move to let them in. 'What's he supposed to have done, then?'

Bea produced the cards in their plastic wallet and held them up for Cynthia to see. 'These call-girl cards were left in a public phone box nearby. One of them gives the phone numbers for Evonne and Carmela. In consequence, they've had to deal with a number of unpleasant calls.'

'What? This is the first I've heard of it. What's it got to do with me?'

'Nothing. Carmela dealt with the problem by getting rid of her landline. Evonne and Connor dithered; did nothing about it. On Friday a new card was put in the phone box, giving Evonne's address. Not her phone number; her actual address, here in this building. A punter saw the card and called on Evonne, demanding her services. When he was refused, he tried to rape her. She and Connor had much ado to beat him off.'

Cynthia reached for the cards but Bea held them high, out of reach. 'There are fingerprints on them, made by the man who was seen to put them in the phone box. We have a description, and the description matches Donald.'

'Ridiculous!' She shouted back into the flat. 'Don! Come here!'

A man appeared behind her. Tall, slightly built, with ginger hair beginning to recede and nervously fluttering eyelids. He wore a blue and white sweater with a pattern of reindeer on it, over jeans. Office manager in casual attire.

Cynthia said, 'You heard? Tell them she's mistaken.' And to Bea, 'He's not much cop in bed, of course, but he wouldn't…' She turned back to him and gaped, because if anyone looked guilty, it was him.

Donald flushed. 'I… I…'

Cynthia said, in tones of disbelief, 'You can't mean that you…?'

He stammered. 'I-I-m s-sorry. It wasn't m-meant to be—'

'You bastard!' Cynthia caught him a backhander across his chin. He reeled back into the flat, ending up on his back like an insect, hands in the air, knees working to push himself along the carpet and away from her.

The door of the flat slammed in Bea's face.

Silence.

Evonne said, 'Ought we to do something?'

Bea chewed her lower lip. 'Mm. What would you advise?'

They stared at the closed door.

Heavy steps mounted the stairs behind them. The new caretaker. 'What's going on?'

The door to Cynthia's flat opened again. Bea and Evonne stepped back in haste as the wretched Donald was thrown out and across the landing. He ended up against the door of the McIntyres' flat opposite. An overcoat followed. The door slammed. Donald put his hand to his cheek, which was reddening.

The door opened. A laptop whizzed out, followed by an armful of clothing.

'What's all this, then?' The new caretaker, out of his depth.

The door of the McIntyres' flat opened and Eliot's head appeared. 'What's going on?'

More clothing. A suitcase, lid jumping open. Some books.

'Has someone declared World War Three?' Carmela, exquisitely dressed, descended the stairs, ready for her afternoon constitutional.

Cynthia reappeared, to toss out a gym bag and some shoes. She noticed Carmela and said, 'That worm gave your phone number out as a call girl.'

'Makes sense,' said Carmela. 'I wondered if it might be him.' She wore stiletto-heeled boots. 'No police.' As she walked across the landing, she accidentally or otherwise trod on one of Donald's hands.

He screamed.

Bea yearned for killer heels like that. So stylish. So deadly.

Carmela shook her heel out of Donald's hand and proceeded down the stairs without even turning her head.

Donald whimpered, holding his hand high in the air. 'Help me, someone!' Blood welled.

The caretaker said, 'Stop that racket!'

'Shouldn't we do something?' Eliot wanted to help, but didn't know how. 'He ought to have a bandage on that.'

Cynthia dumped another armful outside her door. 'I'll put the rest out for the dustmen tomorrow morning.' She went back into her flat and shut the door behind her.

Helen McIntyre peered over her husband's shoulder. 'What happened? Oh, Donald, that looks nasty!'

Eliot turned to Bea as the person who seemed likeliest to enlighten him. 'Shouldn't we get him to a doctor's or something?'

Donald was crying with pain. 'My hand's broken! Someone, help me!'

'He needs a doctor, all right,' said Evonne, addressing the McIntyres and the caretaker. 'He needs a psychiatrist. Don't you dare help him! It was he who put the call-girl cards in a phone booth with our phone numbers on them, just because I told him to take his hands off me. He doesn't deserve our pity.' And to Donald, 'Take a cab, and take your belongings with you.'

He whined, 'I can't. How can I? Someone lend me a handkerchief to put round my hand!'

Helen said, 'I'll fetch my first-aid box,' and disappeared.

Eliot, with distaste in his voice, said, 'I suppose we could store his things in our flat till tomorrow.'

The caretaker made up his mind to help. 'Don't you

worry. I'll see him off the premises, him and all his belongings. Your keys to this building, sir. If you please.'

'She's crippled me for life!'

Helen reappeared with a metal first-aid box, saying, 'No, no. It's not as bad as that.' She produced a large plaster and stuck it over the back of Donald's hand.

'Your keys, sir,' repeated the caretaker.

Donald was in tears, but fumbled a bunch of keys out of his jeans pocket, and handed them over.

'What's happening?' The lift doors opened to reveal Carrie and Lucy, fresh from their afternoon nap, and all agog.

Evonne, hands on hips, explained. 'This is the rat who put me and Carmela in danger. Not to worry; he's leaving.'

Donald, still crying and holding up his damaged hand, struggled to get into his overcoat. 'It was only a joke. You can't throw me out. Where am I supposed to go?'

'A hotel,' said Evonne. 'If they'll have you. Be grateful we're not calling the police. But listen to me! You'd better get your GP to refer you to a specialist counsellor, because if you don't I'll be ringing your line manager at work and telling him exactly what you've been up to. And yes, I do know where you work, because you told me how well you were doing, and how worthwhile it would be for me to be nice to you.'

The caretaker scooped up some of Donald's belongings. 'Let me help you with your things. Sir.' The door of the flat opened, and a heavy black plastic bag flew out, narrowly missing Donald. The door slammed shut again.

Helen dived back into her flat to produce a second black plastic bag, and together with Bea, they picked up everything of Donald's which wouldn't go into the suitcase and gym bag.

'Thank you, miss,' said the caretaker. 'I'll take care of this gentleman now. I'll get him a taxi and put him and everything he owns into it.'

Cynthia's door opened again, and a flutter of credit cards dropped to the floor, followed by an empty leather wallet. The cards had been neatly cut up. Oh. That was going to make life difficult for Donald, wasn't it?

Bea's estimation of Cynthia rose. A formidable woman, indeed. Now, what about his mobile phone, or did he have an iPad?

No sooner thought about than they, too, were thrown out on to the landing. It looked as if Cynthia had taken a hammer to both.

Donald, tears straggling down his reddened face, picked up what he could of the remains of his life and shuffled off down the stairs, followed by the caretaker humping his luggage.

Evonne brushed one hand off against the other. 'May his love life never improve.'

Lucy's and Carrie's eyes were round, their cheeks flushed with pleasure. 'What a scandal! Do you mean he really…? Oh, who would have thought it?'

Bea followed Donald and the caretaker down the stairs and out into the street. A nasty cold wind was blowing and Donald shivered as he stood, surrounded by luggage, waiting for a taxi.

Bea, uncharitably, hoped one wouldn't come along for quite a while.

She turned up the street and made for the local café, which she trusted would be open on a Sunday. It was indeed, and as crowded as usual.

She managed to get a table for two and ordered soup and a piece of pie, with some coffee to follow. While waiting for her food, she rang Oliver on her mobile.

'How are you doing, Oliver? Donald has been disposed of. Where are you now?'

'I've just finished up at Harvey's; I dare say I ought to feel sorry for him, but I don't. He's a regular peeping Tom, has pictures of everyone in the flats and has even taken some of people living in the building opposite. He says he uses them as the basis for characters in his stories, and all I can say is that he's lucky not to have been sued by someone before now. He's presented me with a signed copy of one of his little tales, which I do *not* intend to read.

'Anyway, I'm on my way up to see Maggie now because she's all on her own. Her mother's gone out, and Maggie doesn't know when she'll be back, but supper has to be on the table for…whenever. I asked her to come out with me, get a breath of fresh air, but she won't. How did you dispose of Donald?'

'With ease and the help of his ex-girlfriend. I'm shutting my phone off now to have some lunch, but I'll get back to you later.'

'You're coming back to the flats?'

'I think so, yes. I've someone to see first.' She clicked off the phone. She hoped she'd read the situation aright.

Yes, she had. For here came Carmela, standing in the doorway of the café and looking around for somewhere to sit. Bea indicated the chair opposite. 'I kept a place for you.'

'I thought you might.'

'Love your boots.'

'I do trust the blood can be washed off. A pity about the ones you wore on Friday. Are they repairable?'

'I'm afraid not.'

Civilities dealt with and food ordered, the two women got down to business.

Carmela said, 'My thanks to you for dealing with Donald. I thought it might be him, but I had no proof.'

'My proof came via a seller of the *Big Issue*, whose stand is by the public phone boxes opposite the tube station. He observes everything that goes on; sees the pimps putting the call-girl cards into the phone boxes, is amused by those who remove them. He spotted Donald putting some cards into the boxes, noted that he was not one of the usual run of pimps, and thought there might be a fiver or two in it for him if he collected some evidence. Which he did. I gave the lad fifty pounds, which I think was well worth it. I couldn't be sure Donald's fingerprints were on the cards, but the description I got did in fact lead straight to the culprit.'

'Money well spent. I'll repay you, of course.'

'I think I can understand what made him approach other women. Cynthia was too much of a good thing for him, so he tried his luck elsewhere and when that didn't work—'

'Yes, but when he'd been told there was nothing doing, he shouldn't have tried to embarrass us.'

'I rather think it caused more than embarrassment in Evonne's case. She suspected Connor was at the back of it, and it's ruined their relationship.'

'Poor Connor. He used to be such a handsome, go-getting lad. Comes from a good family. Both sets of parents were pleased when they hitched up, but then they went a bit wild, started to drink heavily, got mixed up in the riots last year. They didn't do any great damage or steal anything of value but they spent a night in custody and were heavily fined. She reacted by pretending not to care about anything. He shaved his head and became devoted to daytime television. Night time, too, I shouldn't wonder.'

Bea was curious. 'How do you know so much about the other tenants of the flats? I mean, usually in London you don't even know your neighbour's name, never mind their background. Ah,' she answered her own question. 'The two biddies.'

'They run up and down the stairs, taking in parcels and making sure we all have food if we get flu or whatever. Dreadful gossips, both of them. I don't dislike it in a way. As one grows older, one likes to feel there would be some backup if anything went wrong.'

'Understood. Was Harvey acting as your backup when he took photos of men leaving your apartment?'

Carmela laughed. 'Harvey overheard an altercation with one of my visitors who'd had a drop too much to drink and came out to see what was happening. It was rather brave of him, don't you think? The man concerned was a regular client but he'd just heard some bad news… which is no excuse for bad behaviour, but there; it happens. I have a pepper spray for protection and such conduct doesn't normally trouble me, but on that occasion I was pleased to receive assistance from my neighbour.'

Her coffee and Bea's soup came, and they both attended to the inner woman.

Carmela said, 'My way of life can be lonely at times, and Harvey can be good company. We occasionally meet up for an evening at the theatre or a film.'

'Was it he who decided to take pictures of your visitors? Er, you do know about that, don't you?'

'Yes, and his pretty pictures of the young men he fancies…not that he ever takes it any further than that, you understand. It was his idea to take the pictures of my visitors as they left. He felt he was protecting me. I didn't see any particular harm in it.'

'He might have used the pictures for blackmail purposes.'

A bland smile. 'For visits to a therapist?'

Bea laughed. Of course. 'Oliver tells me Harvey snapped one of Vicori's executives leaving your flat. Does Sir Lucas approve of that?'

'You mean, was my visitor working on me to undermine Lucas's position?' Her eyebrows peaked. 'Forgive me; I can't discuss that.'

Bea pushed her empty soup plate aside. 'I assume you have a fair number of shares in Vicori?'

A tightening of the mouth. 'I can't discuss that, either.'

'It was you who got Lucas to send in another caretaker so quickly?'

'I may have mentioned the necessity for a replacement.'

'Then you have better access to him than I have. I was told he's on his way to Frankfurt for a meeting.'

'So I believe.'

'He's left Lady Ossett for good, hasn't he?'

'I have no idea.' A bland smile.

'Do you attend her bridge parties?'

A nod. A glance at a pretty gold watch. 'Is that the time? I really must go.'

'Are you acquainted with the next Lady Ossett?'

'Who?' Carmela beckoned to the waitress for her bill.

'Another "who?". Who pushed the caretaker over the edge?'

'What!' That caused her to flush. 'You think…? No, really; that's not… Surely not!'

'Think about it,' said Bea, accepting her pie with an eye that glistened. 'My, this looks good enough to eat.'

Carmela got to her feet. No more smiles. Bea's question had shaken her. 'I cannot conceive there is any—'

'Who poisoned Lady Ossett's supper?'

'What!' This was news to Carmela.

'And I'm not all that happy about the death of the elderly woman on the ground floor, are you?'

'Oh, now you are being absurd.' But Carmela was flustered enough to drop her purse.

Bea handed it back to her.

Carmela said, 'Thanks,' and hurried out of the café, leaving the bill for her coffee on the table.

'Now she owes me much more than fifty pounds,' said Bea to herself. 'And I'm going to make sure I collect it.'

# FIFTEEN

*Sunday afternoon*

BEA NOTICED THE first few flakes of snow in the air as she returned to the flats. They rarely had significant falls in Central London. She couldn't remember what the weather forecast had been. She huddled into her coat and was reaching for the bell for the penthouse when a large, angry-looking man—someone Bea hadn't seen before—opened the front door while shouting back into the hall that this was his last word on the subject. He turned to leave but, on observing the change in the weather, stopped to fasten his car coat and search in his pockets for his gloves. He was so angry that his eyes passed over Bea without seeing her.

Bea waited because he was blocking the entrance.

The dark-haired girl, Evonne, appeared behind the man and pulled on his sleeve. She looked as angry as he. Father and daughter? A strong likeness.

Now, what did Bea know about him? Some sort of tycoon, not as influential as Sir Lucas but in that bracket. He rented the ground floor flat for his daughter and had offered her a job on the floor of one of his dress shops. The girl had declined.

'You can't!' Evonne was red in the face with anger—or distress.

He threw her hand off. 'Trust me. I can, and I will.' He pulled his coat collar up and thrust past Bea on his way down the steps.

Bea caught the front door before it could close, and entered. 'Trouble?'

The door to Evonne's flat was open, and young Connor was lounging against it. Smoking. He hadn't shaved for a couple of days so he was sporting designer stubble and the beginnings of a reasonable thatch of hair. It suited him. His clothes were as unkempt as usual. And that didn't suit him.

Evonne threw up her hands. 'Come in, why don't you, Mrs Abbot? It's visiting time at the zoo.' She pushed Connor into the flat before her. 'You, you've slept in your clothes again. Go and have a shower, clean yourself up. Think about where you're going to move to.'

'Moving out?' said Bea.

The girl picked up some newspapers and tried to shove them into an already overflowing bin. 'He's given us one week to move out. He's gone all heavy Victorian, doesn't want his name sullied by being dragged through the newspapers again. He doesn't know anything about Donald, and don't you dare tell him! He's got himself into a state about the caretaker's death though I can't for the life of me think why. As I told him, it had nothing to do with us. We didn't even know he was missing till Oliver came asking for him, and it was an accident anyway.'

Connor hadn't obeyed her order to have a shower and was still hanging around. 'I bet it was that tart from number seven who grassed on us.'

'What?' The girl picked a cushion up off the floor. 'What do you mean?' She changed colour as understanding dawned. 'You mean she told him about the call-girl cards and our visitor the other day? But...!'

Bea kept very still. Surely the pair must have known that Evonne's daddy was one of Carmela's clients? Well, perhaps not. These two were not in the habit of monitoring who came and went in the building.

Evonne pummelled the cushion in her hands. 'No, she wouldn't tell, surely. She was just as much of a victim as I was. And Donald's out of it now.' Another thought struck her. 'You don't think Donald would go to the papers about it, do you? No. Why would he? It would only show him up for the scumbag that he is.'

No, it wasn't Donald's dirty tricks which might put them in the newspapers, but it might be the caretaker's death. Carmela hadn't wanted to believe there was anything untoward about it, but Bea's interest might have made her rethink. Her loyalty to Sir Lucas was well established. She knew he needed to avoid a bad press.

Cynthia was not likely to talk, and the troublesome Tariq had departed, but there on the ground floor were a couple who had already been in the papers for their part in the riots. No jobs, no means of support. What else might they get up to? Yes, it was worth while Carmela tipping off Evonne's father—who was probably at his wits' end what to do about his daughter anyway—and who had in consequence overreacted by ordering the girl out of his flat.

Evonne threw the cushion at Connor. 'You stupid, good-for-nothing berk! None of this would have happened if you hadn't lost your job and become such a slob. I can't bear to look at you! Get out of my sight!' She was quivering with rage. When he didn't move, she screamed at him; 'Get out! Now!'

He shrugged and sloped off to the kitchen.

The girl's shoulders heaved. She put her hands over her face. 'Sorry! I shouldn't let him get to me.'

Bea put her arm about Evonne and led her to the settee. 'You really do care for him, don't you? Or you wouldn't be so upset. Would it be such a bad idea for you to get out of this place, make a fresh start? Have you anyone you can stay with?'

'A school friend, I suppose. Sleeping on her sofa. That it should come to this! I had such plans when I left university and set up with Connor. And now what! No job, no flat, no future.'

'What did you study at university?'

'Oh, the usual. Business studies. Along with a thousand others.'

'Are you computer literate?'

'Of course. Who isn't! Where will Connor go? He doesn't have any family in London.'

'What skills does he have?'

'A degree in literature. A fat lot of use that is. He refused to do teacher training, and he'd have been no good at it, anyway.'

'If he had some training, could he wait at tables?'

'Mm? I suppose so. He's presentable enough when he scrubs up. But he wouldn't want to do that, would he?'

'Faced with the prospect of no bed and breakfast, or taking a low-paid but worthwhile job; which would he choose? Is he so self-destructive that he'll lose you and start sleeping on the streets rather than work for his living?'

Evonne twisted her hands, didn't reply.

Connor had come in behind them. 'What sort of job are you offering?'

'I run a domestic employment agency. Here is my card. If you present yourselves there tomorrow morning, appropriately dressed and in your right minds, I'll see if one of my operatives can find something for you both.'

They stared at her. Evonne bit her lip, frowning.

Bea rethought her offer. 'Make it Wednesday morning.

You may need to shop for suitable clothes. And Connor;
let your hair grow.'

Connor said, 'Why would you want to help us?'

'The easy answer is: because I can.'

'You think we're worth it?' The girl was doubtful.

'I think,' said Bea, trying to sort her thoughts out,
'that you'd be better off out of here.'

'If we get ourselves jobs, it's odds on that Daddy will
let us stay.'

'If you get yourselves jobs, you can find your own accommodation and be independent.'

'But we like it here.' Even to her own ears, the girl
sounded doubtful. She looked at Connor. 'We were fine
here at first, weren't we? We had friends round and could
go out and enjoy ourselves. Our first home together. It
was great.'

'Can you pinpoint what went wrong?'

'Well… Lavinia, the old biddy across the hall, used
to get on my nerves, shouting at us every time we came
in and out—'

'Wanting us to run errands for her. I didn't mind at
first, though she did smell rather ripe—'

'She used to catch me by my arm with her stick, nearly
had me over a couple of times, so I started sneaking out
the back way until the caretaker caught me and…between
the two of them—'

'We laughed about it at first—'

'And then we didn't.' The girl's mouth turned down.
'And those dreadful old women upstairs kept knocking on
the door and telling us we should be happy to help someone in need, and that if we weren't working, we could
at least spend time with Lavinia, and I said she wasn't
our problem and then I got the full lecture about young
people being totally selfish and not caring about others

and I expected them to bring out some tract at any minute and tell me that I must be born again, or something.'

Connor grinned. 'They're quite something, those two. Reminded me of my great aunt, rest her soul. But it was too much for babble-mouth here, and she didn't half let fly with the Anglo-Saxon.'

The girl tried not to smile. Didn't quite succeed. 'Oh you!' She hit his arm, and he hunkered down on the settee beside her.

'And then,' said Bea, 'she died. Were you there?'

'We were down in Devon, weren't we? A long weekend with some friends. It was a relief, really. That sounds awful, but you know what I mean? We heard when we got back. It was strange at first, seeing her door closed whenever we went out. Then her grandson—was it her grandson or her nephew? Can't remember. Anyway, he arrived and the door was open and he was taking stuff out and putting it in a rental van, so we looked inside and said "Hello", as one does, and he bit our noses off, saying it was no use our scavenging around as Lavinia had left everything to him, and he wasn't into the business of letting us have keepsakes.'

'Which was a laugh,' said Connor, 'because who'd have wanted anything Lavinia had?'

The girl nudged him. 'Carrie Kempton did, didn't she? Don't you remember how cross she was about it? She said that after all they'd done for Lavinia, the least he could do was let them have some keepsakes. I think she had her eye on a Derby tea set the old dear had in a cabinet on the wall. Anyway, the house clearance people came and took the rest and now the place is empty. Waiting for probate, I suppose. I don't know how many years she'd got left on her lease. Not many. I suppose Sir Lucas will buy the rest of the lease off the nephew, do the flat up, and put it on the market again.'

Bea's phone rang. Oliver, wondering where she was.

'I'll be right up,' she said. She left a card for each of the two youngsters, thanked them for their time, and left them to argue about looking for a job or trying to change Daddy's mind about turning them out.

Bea took the lift to the sixth floor. The building was very quiet. Was everyone having an afternoon nap or dozing after Sunday lunch?

The decorators were not at work today, and there was no sound from Professor's flat as Bea climbed the stairs to the penthouse.

Normal life resumed when Oliver let Bea into Lady Ossett's flat. From the kitchen came the sound of a television competing with Maggie shouting something out on her mobile phone, while a kettle shrilled.

The television was also on in the sitting room, but muted. The view from the windows today was of lowering clouds and the promise of rain. No, of snow. As Bea watched, a few more flakes drifted across her vision. Followed by a few more. She shivered, though it was warm enough inside the flat.

Oliver said, 'Lady Ossett phoned a moment ago. She's still out with the Professor, having tea somewhere in Richmond, but she said she'd like Maggie to prepare something light for supper on their return. Maggie complains, but obeys.'

Bea nodded. 'Can you use Lady O's computer?'

'I suppose so. What do you want?'

'I'd like you to look up Carmela's credentials. Is she entitled to call herself a therapist, for instance?'

'I see what you mean. I think anyone can set up as a therapist.' He set about his task with enthusiasm.

Bea homed in on the wall where the Lucian Freud portrait had once hung. A Kashmiri rug had been tacked up there instead. It looked good. Of course, it wasn't worth as much as the portrait.

She drifted over to the window, to look out over the terraced garden. It seemed increasingly unlikely to her that someone had come up the fire escape on the afternoon of the bridge party in order to poison Lady O. It had been an 'inside' job.

Bea wasn't sure what it had been meant to achieve. Not Lady O's death, surely? No, not even Sir Lucas seemed to desire that.

To frighten Lady O? Y-yes. But why?

To kill the cat? Y-yes. But why choose that method?

Oliver lifted his head from the screen. 'Carmela's got some letters after her name but I don't think they're those of a reputable institution. Ah. Yes. College degrees provided by two American universities, possibly bought over the Internet. Hm. No, neither of them are what you might call trustworthy. She's a fraud.'

'Not a fraud. She doesn't pretend to be anything but what she is—and I'm sure she does provide therapy, of a kind. If Donald had gone to her for help I suspect she might have sorted him out. Can you look up Harvey for me?'

Oliver tapped keys. 'What for? He writes books. They're on his bookshelf. He gave me one. He's the film critic for one of the tabloids. He showed me a book of his cuttings.'

'I like to check everything. Harvey tells us he's written books and is a film critic, but is he really? He's a fantasist by profession. He keeps cuttings of reviews *someone* has written and of books *someone* has had published but is that someone really Harvey?'

'Oh, come on, now.' A pause while he tapped away. 'Yes, he has a website, and yes, his books are all here.'

'Who is his publisher? Is he self-published, or is he with a reputable royalty-paying publisher?'

'Who's got a nasty mind, then? Yes, here it is. A reputable publisher. Wait a mo and I'll access their website. Yes, specializing in his field. Both his website and the publisher give the name we know him by. He's genuine enough.'

'Back to his website. What does it say about the film reviews?'

Tap, tap. 'That's all OK, too. He has a blog. Hold on... I'll get on to that. Yes, yes. His blog covers what he's seen and what he's written about. Oh yes, and he's on Facebook and Twitter as well. You're barking up the wrong tree.'

'No porn on his website?'

'Give us a break. No. Definitely not. Yes, he's interested in young men, but I can't see that he's doing anything about it.'

'Apart from pinching your bottom.'

Maggie came flapping into the room in her flip-flops. 'Is that Harvey you're talking about? A scream, isn't he? I think he's completely and utterly sexless, but tries to make out he's gay. It's probably something to do with his mother denying him a cuddle when he was growing up, or taking away his teddy bear, or something.' She flung open a window, letting a cold wind in. 'I'm knackered, slaving over a hot stove. I'm cooking enough for five; us three, my mother, and the Professor, if he decides to join us for supper. Want a cuppa? Carrie Kempton brought us up some home-made chocolate biscuits which look yummy.'

'A cuppa would be good. I won't stay for supper, but

thanks. Maggie, are you coming home tonight?' Bea already knew what the answer would be.

Maggie pulled a face. 'Oh, baby; it's cold outside.' She shut the window again. 'You know I can't leave her.'

'She's got the Professor now,' said Oliver, still bent over the computer.

Bea said, 'I'll find someone to move in with her tomorrow. Oliver, see what else you can find on the other people in the flats, will you?'

Maggie shook her head. 'My mother needs someone she can trust. I can put off some of my jobs and do the others in the afternoon, perhaps, when she's busy with other things. Tea or coffee, everyone?'

Bea wandered around, looking at everything; looking at nothing. She didn't like it, but she did think Maggie was right in choosing to stay with her mother. There was still something nasty going on at the flats, and until it was identified and dealt with, Lady Ossett did need someone at her back.

Oliver looked up. 'Our Cynthia. She is one terrifying babe! She started from scratch in the lingerie business and is now worth several million. Floated on the Stock Exchange last year. Donald was on to a good thing. A pity he messed up.'

Maggie brought in a tray of mugs of coffee and a plate of delicious looking biscuits. She handed them round, collapsed on to a settee, flicking off her flip-flops, and ran her fingers up through her spiky red-at-the-moment hair. 'Cynthia terrifies me. And she always comes out on top at the bridge parties. What's that about Donald messing up?'

Bea told her. 'He tried it on with Evonne and Carmela, and when they didn't want to know, he had some call-girl cards printed up with their details on. Cynthia's just thrown him out.'

'Wow! Really?'

'Really. Did you say she comes to your mother's bridge parties?'

'Mm. I think Lucas asked her to. He put up some money to help her get started, you know.'

Bea stared at Maggie. 'What else do you know about the people who live here?'

Maggie counted them off on her fingers. 'Nothing much to say about the McIntyres. She's a wimp and he's overprotective.'

'Start from the top. The Professor.'

'He's OK. I suspect he's looking for someone to take care of him in his old age. Dunno if my mother is quite the right person, but as a stopgap he's useful to her. He's got a daughter who'd dearly love to shove him into an old people's home, but he's not ready for that yet.'

Oliver, tapping keys, said, 'He's OK. The genuine article. I doubt if he's good husband material, though. Married and widowed twice. Been single for some time.'

Bea handed the biscuits around. 'He's hungry for company, so he might be all right. What about the people opposite him, the ones who are in France at the moment?'

Maggie took a biscuit. 'Um. Yum. Strong chocolate flavour. And something else? Orange peel? The people opposite the Professor are a retired businessman and his wife. She's got heart trouble. They like it in France because their daughter lives there with her husband and their three grandchildren. I did wonder if they were doing the flat up to sell.'

'That makes sense. Maggie; for someone who doesn't live here now, you know a lot about the natives. I assume from Carrie and Lucy?'

'Aren't they sweet? They take an interest in everyone and everything, not like some old people who grumble about everything and never move from their armchairs. The next down is Tariq; well, he's gone and I gather he's left something of a mess behind him. He was warned about the music, you know. But you can't tell some people anything. Then there's Harvey...' Maggie's face cracked into a grin. 'Oh, poor Harvey. Getting locked in, and then getting stuck half way in and half way out of his window. Wish I'd seen it. But he's all right, really.'

Bea took a second biscuit. 'Is Carmela "all right, really"?'

A quick frown. 'I don't know. I've never understood exactly what she does for a living. Carrie says Carmela lets men talk to her and that that's all they do, but Lucy says that if I believe that, I need my head examining. I really don't know.'

Bea nodded. 'Agreed. So if we skip Cynthia and the McIntyres, that leaves us with the dark-haired Daddy's girl, Evonne, and her partner, Connor.'

'I hardly know them,' said Maggie. 'They have their own friends, not exactly my style. Carrie says they've been rather naughty and that they've let the side down. I used to think Connor was quite dishy, but he's shaved off all his hair and I don't think it suits him.'

'Which leaves Lavinia.'

'The old lady on the ground floor. She was here for ever, since before my mother came, and that must be seven or eight years ago now. Not that Mother was in the penthouse then. She only moved up here when she married Lucas.'

'Where was she before?'

'Where the Muslim family is now. Have you seen them yet? Poor things; the women jump if a car backfires, and the men look at me as if I were toast.'

'Nice toast, or something to gobble up?'

'Like, "I would if I could, but someone's watching."'

'Not nice. Do they speak English?'

'Well enough. The women let me into their flat once when they needed to know how to work the oven and they didn't trust the caretaker, which you can understand in a way. They wear those black cloak things whenever they go out, and when they have visitors apart from the family.'

Oliver took another biscuit, spraying crumbs as he accessed another website. Laughing. 'Harvey's blog! I must say, he writes amusingly. I can see why he's got a following.'

'Getting back to Lavinia,' said Bea.

'She used to frighten the life out of me,' said Maggie. 'She was ancient. Enormous. A big woman with a hairy chin, none too clean. She couldn't walk without a stick, and she breathed heavily all the time. She used to stand in the doorway of her flat and call out to everyone who came in or went out, wanting them to pick things up off the floor for her, or to go and buy her something from the shops. If I was in a hurry I used to rush through the foyer with my head down and pretend I hadn't heard her.'

'I thought she had a carer.'

'A succession of carers. I don't know how many she got through, but Carrie said she never liked any of them. She and Lucy used to pop in to see her at least once a day to make sure she was all right. The caretaker used to have terrible rows with her, but she used to shout back at him and… I don't know. I suppose she was lonely. My mother said she ought to have gone to an old people's day centre, but when she mentioned it, meaning nothing but kindness, Lavinia refused, saying she was all right as she was, and how dare my mother interfere. She wasn't a very nice person, but perhaps I wouldn't be very nice if I got to be old and my legs all swelled up and my family never came near me.'

'How did she die?'

'Heart attack. She was coming up to her ninetieth birthday. I don't even know exactly when it happened. One day when I came to visit my mother her door was closed and I thought "good", because she wouldn't be jumping out at me, and then my mother told me she'd died in the week. And I thought—which was awful of me, but there it is—that they'd probably had a lot of difficulty taking her body away because she was so big, you know. I wondered if they'd put her in a chair, or on a trolley, or what. It's odd how quickly you forget. I used to worry about meeting her in the foyer every time I came, and now I don't even think about her.'

Oliver was still at the computer. 'At least she wasn't on Facebook.'

Bea said, 'So, who else is?'

'The Lord High Executioner, Sir Lucas Ossett, pops up everywhere. At the Mansion House for a dinner, at a reception at one of the Middle Eastern embassies, at the opera with a cute little dolly bird on his arm—'

'Let me see!' cried Maggie and bent over him. 'Oh, wow! He's got a different woman with him every time.' She straightened up, losing her smile. 'But not my mother.'

Silence. No, not her mother.

Bea sighed. 'Best be prepared, Maggie. I really do think he's moved on.'

Maggie was near tears. 'Isn't marriage supposed to be for life?'

Silence. Yes, it was. But some people didn't see it that way, did they?

Bea still missed her own dear husband, every day of her life. Every now and then she'd turn round to ask him something only to find he wasn't there any more. She shook herself back to the present. 'I think I'll pop down to have a word with Harvey. There's time before supper, isn't there? I'd like a look at his portfolio of pictures.'

Oliver grinned, still tapping away at the computer. 'He'll keep you for hours if you're not careful. He likes an audience.'

Bea looked at her watch. 'Maggie, suppose you come and fetch me in, say, half an hour or so? I'd really like a word with the Muslim family, if possible, and you could introduce me.'

'What for?'

'I don't know,' said Bea. 'There's something I've been told, somewhere along the line. I keep feeling that something else is about to happen, and that if I don't stop it, there's going to be... No, I'm being silly.'

'Another death?' Oliver stared at her.

'Two deaths so far; Lavinia and the caretaker. Two disappearances; Tariq and Donald. I keep telling myself they're not linked in any way. And gut reaction is telling me that they are. Anyone want to argue with me about this? I'm ready to be convinced I'm wrong.'

'No,' said Oliver. 'I, too, think there's something seriously off beam here. Shall I accompany you to Harvey's?'

'No, thanks. He won't want to pinch my bottom, and if he does, he'll get my handbag across his face.'

She took the stairs down. It was only two flights.

Harvey let her into his flat with a: 'Hallo there! Come to visit the invalid?' His bonhomie was catching. 'I'm well on the way to recovery, thank you.' He held up his hand, to show he still had a plaster on it.

'I wanted to be sure you'd suffered no ill effects. I also

wondered if you'd let me have a look at your photographs of the neighbours. Oliver tells me you have a real talent in that direction.' She looked around, but there were no pictures of young men to be seen.

'By all means, dear lady. Come in, come in. Isn't this weather glorious? I shall be out with my camera early tomorrow. It doesn't happen very often that we get snow here, does it? And, alas, it goes so soon.'

'Do you go out into the parks to take your shots?'

'That's not my scene. Let me show you the ones I took last time we had snow.' He led the way to the second bedroom which, as Oliver had reported, was set up as a workroom with shelves reaching up to the ceiling and wide work surfaces at different heights below. There was the usual array of modern computers and printers which a serious photographer would need but also a collection of old cameras and even—she had to gasp at this—two ancient old typewriters on a high shelf.

No pictures of young men. Harvey approached a row of blue photograph albums, each one labelled with a date. 'I keep them in chronological order.' He ran his finger along the ranks, selected an album, turned pages and laid the volume flat on a work surface for Bea to inspect.

He had shot the fire escape, each stair rimmed with snow, from the ground level upwards. The balconies and railings danced up and up in a dizzying, hypnotic manner. She could hardly believe her eyes. The pulp fiction which he wrote, and his airy-fairy manner, had been misleading. 'Harvey, you are a true artist!'

## SIXTEEN

HARVEY BEAMED. 'That picture won a prize... I'll show you the newspaper cutting in a minute.'

Bea turned pages. More stunning photographs, all black and white; the backs of buildings, a stack of wheelie bins, the first track of a vehicle in the snow...

Harvey was pulling out more albums and pushing them back again. 'Now where is it? I had it out to show Oliver only yesterday.'

She continued to turn pages. Ah. A full length portrait of a large, angry woman leaning on a stick. Was this Lavinia? Yes, it must be. She was wearing a shapeless cardigan over a T-shirt and ancient trousers. Ankles overlapped soft shoes with Velcro fastenings. There were rings embedded in fat fingers, and she was leaning on a stout, man's stick decorated with metal badges. Bea's father had had a stick like that. Holidaying in the Alps, he'd bought a badge from each of the towns he'd visited and put it on his walking stick. In the Middle Ages pilgrims stuck metal badges on their hats or cloaks. Nowadays young people stuck similar fabric badges on their rucksacks.

Harvey was riffling through his albums, getting annoyed with himself. 'Where is it? Has someone been moving my albums around?'

Bea held up the album she was holding. 'Is this Lavinia?'

'Mm? Oh. Yes. Horrible woman, but one of my best

likenesses. I entered that in a competition at the National Portrait Gallery. It got a Commended.'

Bea turned pages and smiled, recognizing Carmela, looking stylish but thunderous. Next came a shot of two women in head to foot burkas, even their eyes concealed by masks. Harvey had caught them in the act of getting out of the lift, and they were frozen for all time in surprise. Bea laughed again.

He giggled. 'Silly creatures. I assume they're both hideous underneath all that mummery!'

Bea shook her head at him and turned more pages. Dark-haired Evonne led her partner Connor across the hall. He was almost unrecognizable with a full head of hair. 'Any comment on these two?'

'Pretty boy turns into street rat. The girl should wave her magic wand and turn him back.'

An elderly lady laden with a heavy tray. 'Oh, here's Lucy Emerson. What on earth is she carrying?'

He peeked over her shoulder. 'A tray of cakes. Taking food to those who can perfectly well manage by themselves. "*Timeo Danaos et dona ferentes.*"'

Bea's hands stilled on the book. Her Latin was rusty, almost non-existent. Did he really mean that you should beware of people bringing you gifts? 'Dear me,' she said, as lightly as she could. Speculation ran wildly through her head.

He closed the book she'd been holding and put it back on the shelf. 'Lucy and Carrie were most solicitous when I had flu last winter. Brought me hot chicken soup every day. I never had the courage to tell them it disagreed with me. Care for a cuppa?'

Bea said, 'Thank you. Have you got a good photo of Maggie?'

He selected a different album for her. 'Have a look while I put the kettle on.'

He went off to the kitchen and Bea turned pages. Pictures of autumn in London. Piles of leaves blowing in the air. Atmospheric clouds. Pigeons in flight. Carrie Kempton struggling with her umbrella in the wind. Lady Ossett—oh, what a laugh!—failing to hold on to a couple of large bags from a designer dress shop while reaching for the bell for the lift. Lucy Emerson in a jerkin and squashy hat, attending to her flower pots on the balcony, her backside prominent, a stout stick leaning against the wall.

The caretaker—not the current one but the one who'd fallen from the balcony—hunched over a cigarette, sitting in the yard, his broom beside him. Maggie…ah, Maggie touching up her lipstick as she waited for the lift in the foyer. Not one of Harvey's best.

Bea put the album down and went to the window to look out. Snowflakes drifted past, but they didn't seem to be in much of a hurry. There wasn't going to be a white-out.

Harvey came back with a mug of tea for her. 'I seem to remember that it's not a particularly good shot of Maggie.'

'Would you take one for me some time? I'd really like that. I'll pay for it, naturally.'

'Can do. No need to pay, after all you've done for us.'

He had a pair of very bright eyes. Were they guileless, or filled with guile? You could read him either way. Bea decided his eyes were filled with knowledge. Wise old eyes. The eyes of an outsider who saw most of the game, but refused to make judgements…although he might drop hints.

'I do my best,' said Bea, meaning it. 'Your tea is excellent. Thank you.'

'I'll find you that cutting about my prize-winning picture in a minute.'

'Not to worry. I'm sure you've won many prizes in your time.'

'That's the only one of the fire escape under snow. A neglected beauty, don't you think?'

Now what did he mean by that? She thought she'd picked up most of his hints… '*timeo Danaos*', etcetera. What was so important about the fire escape?

The doorbell rang. Maggie; arriving on time to rescue her. Bea thanked her host for a most interesting time and for the tea. And made her escape.

As they were going up the stairs Maggie said, 'Mother always calls him "that appalling creature" but I rather like him even if he does go on a bit. Have you seen his portraits? He took one of Lucas which ended up in the Vicori company brochure.'

'Yes,' said Bea. 'I mean, no. I've asked him to take one of you, Maggie. I'd really like it. You remember we wanted to put the photos of the founding members of the agency up on the wall? I want yours and Oliver's there as well.'

Maggie laughed. 'Did you see him take your photo, too? He's got this titchy little camera that he carries round with him so that he can get what he calls "true" snaps. He's probably got a couple of Oliver, already.' She came to a halt outside the Muslim family's door. 'Now you will be gentle with them, won't you? No sudden movements or shouting, or they'll jump out of their skins.'

'Would I know, if they're wearing burkas?'

Maggie rang the doorbell and waited; frowning, fidgeting, uncomfortable about this visit.

A thickset, olive-skinned man of a certain age opened the door. His eyes darted from Maggie to Bea and back again, and he made no move to welcome them into the flat. 'Yes?' He wore European dress, and there was a solid gold watch and bracelet on his left wrist.

Maggie said, 'This is Mrs Abbot, who has been so kind to me and to my mother. As I told you earlier, she's been talking to all the people who live here, trying to find out who has been playing such cruel tricks on them. You said she might call and talk to you, too?' There was definitely a question mark at the end of that sentence. Maggie wasn't at all sure the man was going to let them in.

Bea spoke in her softest voice. 'I appreciate this is an intrusion, but if you could let us in for a few minutes…?'

Maggie was eager to help. 'She's sorted out the nasty phone calls people have been having and—'

Bea said, 'You didn't have any of those, did you, Mr…er?'

Dark eyes travelled from one to the other. He shook his head.

Maggie pressed on. 'She also found out who damaged Sir Lucas's car.'

Something moved behind the dark eyes. He knew about that.

Bea said, 'You knew who that was, didn't you? It must have been horrible for you, living directly under all that loud music.'

'Tariq was not a good Muslim.'

Well, no. Not if he preferred men to women. His brand of rap music was hardly likely to appeal to this man, either. The man swung his door open and beckoned them inside. Once they were in the hall he closed his front door, locked it, and put the chain on. He led them into a big, airy room which overlooked the street. A conventionally furnished room with a huge television set and a marked absence of women. A slender, dark-haired young man rose to his feet as they entered.

'My son. Will you sit?' He gestured to one of two long, black, leather settees, each of which could have seated six people without any difficulty. 'Some tea?'

Bea was awash with tea and coffee, but accepted with a bright smile. 'That would be lovely.' She took a seat beside Maggie.

Through the door came a rotund figure in a burka, mask and all, bearing a tray on which a fine china tea set was perched. Another, slighter figure, also in a burka, followed with a teapot and stand. They must have been on standby, waiting to hear if their lord and master was going to let Bea in or not. Tea had been prepared in advance, just in case.

'My wife. My daughter. My name is Kamran. I have a jeweller's shop in the High Street nearby. Perhaps you have seen it?'

'I'm afraid not. I live some distance away. I imagine this is a good area for your business.'

'It is well enough. My son and my nephews work behind the counter.'

'Splendid,' said Bea, wishing she could see the two women's faces. She assumed that the roly-poly figure would be that of the mother, and the slim one would be the daughter? 'We are honoured to be invited into your home.'

'The honour is all ours.' He gave a little bow to prove it. The women poured tea for the visitors and retired to sit on upright chairs at the back of the room.

Their host and his son seated themselves on the opposite settee. 'Miss Maggie here has been telling us about your care for her, and of how you have been able to help the police with their enquiries in other cases. We do not concern ourselves with the comings and goings of the people who live in these flats. Some have been inquisitive beyond the bounds of politeness. Some have even been abusive.'

'Of course,' murmured Bea, trying to think who might have probed, and who might have been rude to these people. The two biddies would have been inquisitive, yes. Rudeness... Connor? Donald? Ah, the caretaker; that's who!

'We found the behaviour of the old woman on the ground floor and the attentions of the man called Harvey exceptionally difficult. For that reason my son and I usually come and go by the fire escape. I use my mobile phone at the end of the working day to advise my wife when she is to go down the stairs to let us back into the building. This avoids unwelcome encounters.'

Bea nodded. Of course. Which explained why Harvey hadn't any photos of this man...although the women had been caught leaving the lift? Presumably, they had to come and go by the front door when the man was out, or they couldn't get back into the building again. Did the man not appreciate that? She tried to catch their eyes, but could read nothing behind the masks they wore. She sipped tea, smiled, and remained attentive.

'In our culture, women do not put themselves forward and offer advice to the police. Nor is it considered appropriate for them to interest themselves in such matters.'

Was he getting at her? Probably. She would rise above it. 'I understand,' she said, wondering how many generations it took for women from such families to become emancipated.

'A woman's testimony is worth only half as much a man's. But we have discussed the matter, and I have agreed that my daughter will tell you what she knows of the death of the caretaker.'

Bea set her teacup down with care and turned to the silent pair sitting at the back. 'You saw it happen?'

The two shrouded heads turned not to Bea, but to

Kamran, who said, 'My daughter suffers from a woman's complaint if she doesn't get enough exercise. It is out of the question for her to attend a gym, of course, and my son escorts her to and from the college where she is training to be a dietitian, but she cannot walk in the park by herself for fear of being accosted…'

*You think she'd be accosted, wearing a burka?* Bea tried to keep her face straight.

'So I have bought her a cycling machine which she keeps on the balcony. Naturally, I have placed screens around the machine so that she cannot be observed while she is using it. I am a very modern father, you understand.'

'Indeed,' said Bea. 'No one can see her, but she can see everything that happens outside.'

He was offended. 'That was not the intention, naturally.'

'Naturally. But nevertheless, if something chanced to catch her eye…?'

'I do not listen to gossip. My wife and daughter… Chitter chatter, chitter chatter, all day long.'

*But not when you're around.* Bea inclined her head and continued to smile.

'However, as a man concerned with the well-being of my family, certain matters have been brought to my attention. I was seriously considering whether or not we should move. I do not know if, as a woman, you can understand this, but the terms of our contract would make that difficult. Let me explain; we could sublet, but—'

'I understand perfectly,' said Bea, through her teeth. 'What exactly was it that upset you?'

'I was not upset. I was…concerned.'

Bea inclined her head. 'Perhaps your daughter might tell me, in her own words?'

'I was coming to that.' He was not to be diverted. 'She observed the businessmen leaving the whore's flat in the evenings by the back staircase...'

Carmela letting someone out who didn't want to risk being seen? Sir Lucas? Evonne's father?

'She saw the cat come and go by the staircase. I do not care for cats so she did not let him in, or feed him...'

Bea suppressed a grin. Perhaps the daughter had, and perhaps not.

'She saw Tariq inviting a man into his flat, night after night. Not one of us, but a West Indian boy, who we later heard was to be his partner...'

The word 'partner' was delivered with distaste.

'She saw the two old women scurrying up and down the stairs on their errands of mercy...if you can call them that. At their age they should be looking after their grand-children at home...'

The two biddies. So they used the fire escape a lot, did they? Well, why ever not?

'She heard the breaking of glass, and the man Harvey screaming for attention, and she came to tell me of the problem...as if it was any business of ours, which it was not. My wife asked if she should go out to help him, but naturally that was out of the question. As I told them, the two old ladies would want to thrust their noses in without our having to be involved; which they did.'

Lucy and Carrie to the rescue. Of course.

'Scurry, hurry. Up and down the stairs they went, shouting out to one another and asking where the care-taker might be, and we saw... Yes, I, my son, my wife and daughter all went to stand outside on the balcony and right above our heads we saw the caretaker come out on to the balcony from Tariq's flat directly above us, in such a rage, using such language... I came back indoors, and I ordered my wife and my children to come in, too, but my daughter defied me! She stayed out there, listening to the words he was spitting out. As I told her, it was most unseemly.'

Bea shot a look at the two women. One had her head bent, the other stared straight ahead. Or so it seemed. How difficult it was to judge people's reactions when you couldn't see their faces!

'She heard one of the old women go clattering up the staircase to interrupt the caretaker as he was sorting out the rubbish which Tariq, that man of no principle, had left behind, and—' He turned to his daughter. 'Tell her what you saw.'

The woman who'd held her head low, lifted it up and would have spoken, but her father intervened.

'She could see everything, right above her head as she stood there in the doorway, where she was not supposed to be, as I have told her many times since. Right above her head there was the caretaker, ripping up a big cardboard box with his little knife, and the old woman was shouting, shouting at him to give her the keys, and he told her to…to go away, pardon my language, and she lashed out at him with her stick. Such violence! Oh, then at last my daughter understood that I was right, and that she should never have witnessed such an exhibition.'

'She didn't see him go over?'

'No, indeed. That would have made her a witness to a crime, and Allah alone knows where that would have ended, with court appearances and a total disruption of family life, not to mention having her name appear in the papers, which would not improve her chances of marriage. As it is, I can only hope that this brush with violence will have taught her a lesson.'

Bea looked from him to the son, who was sitting at

his side, nodding like a Chinese Mandarin figure. The son worked for his father and would inherit the shop one day. The son was not likely to make waves. Bea wondered if the girl would be better off in an arranged marriage. Who could tell?

Maggie was very quiet. Bea wondered what she was making of this.

Back to the murder. 'What actually did your daughter see?'

'See? She saw nothing. Have I not made that clear? Nothing, I tell you.'

Bea looked at the woman she supposed to be the daughter. 'You really did not see anything?'

Her father intervened. 'Have I not said? She was frightened, as a woman would be. She ran back inside, and she did not see the man fall from the balcony.'

Bea kept her eyes on the girl. 'Did he call out as he fell?'

She thought the girl dipped her head, but it was her father, predictably, who replied. 'Yes, indeed. He was yelling at the old woman in a most horrible manner. And then there was silence. My wife was much agitated, but I told her the quarrel was over, and in any case, it was not our business to be poking our nose into their affairs. But my wife has a tender heart…'

Here he gave his wife a look which was far from tender. 'And my daughter has too much curiosity and so, against my express wishes, the two of them went out on to the balcony, and I went after them, naturally, to warn them that this was not a good idea. By that time there was no sign of anyone on the landing above, and the caretaker was, unhappily, lying on the ground below, deceased.'

'Did you go down to help him?'

'Of course not. I brought my wife and daughter back indoors and told my son to lock all the doors.'

'You couldn't be sure the caretaker was dead. He might have been badly hurt but not dead. With a doctor's help he might have survived.'

'I know dead when I see it. The man was dead.'

Bea tried to get the daughter to speak. 'It must have been either Carrie Kempton or Lucy Emerson. Carrie lives one floor above you, and Lucy on the same level.'

'I do not know. I did not see, myself. My daughter said it was the one with the stick.'

Bea hadn't seen either women walking with a stick. The only person she knew who'd used a stick was Lavinia on the ground floor, and she was long since dead and gone. She stood up. 'Would your daughter be kind enough to show me where she was standing when the caretaker disappeared from view?'

The man stood. Not the daughter. He said, 'I myself will show you. I have forbidden my daughter to go out on to the balcony any more.' He led the way across the hall and into a neat kitchen, where a large pot was simmering on the stove.

Producing a bunch of keys, he unlocked the back door. One key opened the lock in the centre, and another attended to locks at the top and bottom of the door.

'See; this is where my daughter was taking her exercise.' Bamboo screens had been wired into place, completely enclosing their side of the balcony from all viewpoints except for that directly above. Inside this cage-like structure was an exercise bike under a waterproof cover. There was a light powdering of snow on the cover, proving that the daughter had indeed not been using it since the snow began.

Bea stepped out on to the balcony, annoyed because that day she'd worn another pair of high-heeled boots. This open ironwork was a death trap to anyone wearing heels. To her left was Lucy Emerson's section of the balcony, with her neat row of flower pots. An inch of snow showed that someone had recently come out of her back door, walked along the balcony and taken the stairs down. And then returned. Lucy? Or someone visiting her, perhaps. Carrie? The snow was still falling, lightly, filling in the telltale footsteps.

'We stood here, in the doorway. We looked up; so.' He looked up himself, as did Bea.

Up and up. It was quite true. Someone standing there would be perfectly able to see what was happening on the next floor up. Yes, their vision would be obscured by the grating above to some extent, but not that much.

'The police can organize a reconstruction,' said Bea.

'No police,' he said. 'My daughter saw nothing, you understand?'

Nobody else in the building would want the police brought in, either. It was a puzzle. A man had died, and no one was prepared to do anything about it. It sounded as if the caretaker's death had probably been more of an accident than a deliberate attempt at murder, anyway.

So why should Bea bother her head about it? She said, 'You personally did not see who was talking to the caretaker?'

'As I said, I saw nothing.'

'Your daughter heard him yell as he went over, and after that, there was complete silence? No other sound at all?'

'That is correct.' A frown. 'She said; a door closing. But of that she cannot be sure.'

If he stuck to his story and his daughter refused to speak out, there was no way to prove who had done it.

She sighed. 'Thank you. You have been very kind.'

She collected Maggie, thanked their host yet again and left the flat.

'Phew!' Maggie ran her fingers up through her spiky hair. 'He lied, didn't he? His daughter saw the whole thing, but he won't let her speak.'

'Mm. He made it clear who'd done it, though. You noticed?'

'What?'

'Harvey knows, too. Sticks,' said Bea, 'and Greeks bearing gifts.'

'What are you talking about?'

'I rather think we'd better call on Harvey. One floor down, isn't it?'

Maggie looked at her watch. 'This won't take long, will it? I've got to keep an eye on the supper.'

Bea rang Harvey's bell. And waited. She had an uneasy feeling that... But surely, why would anyone want to harm him...? Unless of course...

'Maggie, I don't want to be alarmist, but would you take the lift down to the basement and ask the caretaker if he'd let us into Harvey's flat?'

Maggie opened her mouth to object, changed her mind, and disappeared into the lift.

Bea waited. And waited. She rang the bell again. She knocked on the door.

No response.

The whine of the lift heralded Maggie's return, alone. 'He's gone out. There's a note on the door of his flat giving a mobile phone number, saying he'll be back tomorrow morning. I rang the number. He's in a pub somewhere, says he doesn't work on Sundays. So now what do we do?'

# SEVENTEEN

*Sunday evening*

BEA LOOKED DOWN at her boots, and then at the door. It was a very solid door. 'I don't think I could kick it in. Do you think Oliver could manage it?'

'But why? He's working on the computer.' Maggie fidgeted. 'Look, I need to put the vegetables on. If you're so desperate to speak to Harvey, I'll go up to the penthouse and down the fire escape and tap on his window.'

'Don't do that. It would destroy any footprints there are in the snow. Well, there's only one thing for it.' She crossed the foyer, put her finger on Carmela's bell and kept it there.

Carmela came to the door at last, looking not quite as soignée as usual. 'Is the building on fire?'

'I think something's happened to Harvey. May I go along your balcony…?'

'What?'

Bea flattened Carmela against the door in her haste to get to the kitchen. All the ingredients for a supper for two were neatly laid out on the counter, waiting to be cooked. Bea wondered in passing who Carmela was planning to share her supper with, but had no time to speculate.

The key was in the lock. She wrestled the door open and stepped out on to the balcony. It was getting colder by the minute. The powdering of snow on the balcony had become thicker. Bea caught her heel in the grating

and had to tug it free as she hurried along. Bother! Another pair of boots ruined.

Harvey's kitchen window. Newly replaced glass. Put
in by the replacement caretaker? Nobody to be seen inside. A frozen meal for one lay thawing on a wooden
chopping board.

Carmela was right behind her. 'What is it?'

'Harvey. Don't know. I hope…'

She pointed along the balcony to where some footprints were rapidly being obliterated as more snow fell.

Carmela tried the kitchen door. It opened. 'Harvey?'

Silence. A dripping tap somewhere?

Maggie loomed up behind them. 'Brrr. What gives?'

'Don't come in,' said Bea, following Carmela into the
flat. 'He was in his study. Which door is it?' She'd lost
her sense of direction.

'Here.' Carmela threw the door open and froze with
her arm held out, barring Bea's way in. Thus for a long
moment. Then she turned her head to look at Bea. 'How
did you know?'

Bea looked. Squinched her eyes shut, and opened them
again. Took a deep breath. 'I didn't. I think he tried to
warn me, but I wasn't quick enough to understand him.
But then, the footsteps in the snow…'

Maggie looked over their shoulders and yelped. 'Eeek!
Oh no! He can't really be dead, can he?'

Bea suppressed an impulse to snap Maggie's head
off by saying that he couldn't very well be still alive
with half his head missing, could he? He was dead. Deceased. Passed away. Had left us for a better place. Pick
your platitude. She felt the start of a cold, hard rage in
her stomach. She'd liked Harvey.

Maggie retched and ran back to the kitchen.

Carmela still didn't move. She was very pale. Her eyelids flickered. 'This one can't be written off as an accident. Or can it?'

'No!' Bea guessed what was coming.

Carmela passed her tongue over her lips. 'It could, you know. He was looking for something in his albums—'

'I see what you're getting at. If you wanted to twist things, you could tell the police that he'd promised to look out some cutting or other for me to see. He was annoyed with himself, said he'd misplaced it somewhere.'

'Well?' Carmela watched Bea for her reaction. 'He was reaching for something from that high shelf and pulled an old typewriter down on top of himself. Misadventure.'

Bea felt acid burn in her throat. 'You really think this can be brushed under the carpet? Of course Sir Lucas would prefer it. He doesn't want any bad press. But does his patronage mean so much to you that you'd write off Harvey's death as an accident?'

'I could ask you the same question; how much does it mean to you?'

Bea stiffened. 'I've passed the point of no return. I wouldn't give Sir Lucas the time of day.'

Carmela's mouth distorted into an attempt at a smile. She looked down at the remains of Harvey lying on his back on the floor. One blue eye stared back at her. The other had gone. 'I liked Harvey. He amused me. But if push comes to shove… I don't know… I really don't.'

Bea turned away. 'Have you got a mobile phone on you? I could use mine, but the call will come better from you, as you're a tenant and I'm only a visitor. '

'I'll phone for an ambulance from my flat. Coming?'

Bea rubbed her forehead, trying to think straight. 'I think it's best if you do it by yourself. We can't use the balcony because we need to preserve the evidence of the footprints as much as we can. I'm afraid the snow is continuing to erase them, but it would be best if no one else uses the fire escape till the police have seen everything that is to be seen. Suppose you go out by Harvey's front door, touching as little as you can on the way? We'll send Maggie back upstairs; no need for her to stay. You can let the ambulance men into the building when they arrive, and I'll stay here to make sure no one else disturbs what's left of him.'

'Poor Harvey,' said Carmela. 'What a wretched business.'

'She's got to be stopped.'

Carmela winced, and then recovered. 'I don't know what you mean. It was a tragic accident.'

*Sunday evening*

BEA DRAGGED HERSELF up the steps to her front door and inserted her key into the lock. All she could think about was throwing off her coat, sinking into the settee with a cup of something hot, and going to bed. She was feeling a mite queasy. Perhaps a cup of hot water or an indigestion tablet might be a good idea.

It was going to take some time for her to erase the image of Harvey's body from her memory. The ambulance men had come quickly enough. The doctor. A policeman. Carmela had been suave and persuasive. Maggie hadn't had anything to say. Bea had tried to raise doubts about the manner of Harvey's death. And failed.

Harvey's death was to be tidied away. Cut and dried. Misadventure. The building would probably be rechristened Accident Alley.

Bea was tired to her very bones.

The hall light was on. Odd. It was dark by the time

she'd left the flats. Oliver and Maggie were staying over-night with Lady Ossett, so who…?

'Where have you been? I've been waiting for ages.'

Her beloved son, Max. 'Sorry, Max. A tiring day.'

The cat Winston stalked the hall, weaving backwards and forwards, yowling. He was hungry. Max wouldn't have thought of feeding him, of course.

'Just a minute, Max. Let me feed the cat and then I'll attend to you. Phew! What a day.'

'I suppose you've been out enjoying yourself, as usual.' He followed her into the kitchen, looking at his watch. 'You've got ten minutes before the cab comes. We mustn't be late. Our reservation is for eight, and they won't keep the table.'

She scooped some food into a dish for Winston and let herself down on to a stool, still wearing her coat. She lifted one foot to inspect the heel of her boot. Yes, ru-ined, as she'd thought. 'Dear Max, I haven't the slightest idea what you're talking about.'

'Don't you ever listen to your phone messages?'

'I've been out all day, and my new mobile got smashed. You want to take me out to supper, is that it?'

He exhaled. 'Not just "take you to supper". This is important, Mother. I've booked us into the very latest restaurant. Our guests are Benton, the new managing di-rector of Holland & Butcher, and his wife, whose name I forget. This will cement our relationship in the best possible way, but you turn up looking like… Forgive me, Mother, but you are not exactly looking your best at the moment.'

She stared at him and through him. The image of Harvey's ruined face flashed across her eyes and disap-peared. She said, 'Benton. Yes, I remember. He's the man who's going to replace their Mr Butcher, who turned out to be both inefficient and a scumbag. You'd think they'd drop his name from the firm, wouldn't you?'

'Mother, will you listen to yourself? Of course they're dropping his name. Benton has been appointed managing director in his place, and tonight we're going to meet up with him and his wife and get better acquainted. This is important.' He smiled. Fatly.

Bea thought about throwing a tantrum. She thought about saying she had palpitations and needed to be whisked off to the hospital. She seriously considered knocking him out with something…

There didn't seem to be an ancient typewriter to hand for her to use as a weapon. Oh, poor Harvey…

Max looked at his watch. 'This evening has taken quite some arranging, synchronizing our diaries and all that. Now, I want you to pay extra attention to his wife. She's a director and has shares in the company. Not that she attends meetings or even goes out much, but Benton insisted that he bring her along because she's the only daughter of the old man, of Mr Holland himself. It's obviously a good idea for you to get to know her, put her at her ease. You can do that, can't you?'

A director. Shares in the company. Doesn't attend meetings. Daughter of that Grand Old Man, Mr Butcher, who was generally considered to be well past his sell-by date. What was going on here?

Her brain simply wasn't responding to the usual stimuli. Too tired. And her stomach was more than a little queasy.

Max had gone to a lot of trouble to arrange this evening, and she didn't like to disappoint him, but…she wasn't sure she could even rise from the stool, never mind get herself ready to go out and be sociable.

On the other hand, she'd been shilly-shallying about

making some kind of arrangement with Holland and Butcher for ages, and it was only right that she gave them her decision sooner rather than later. She hadn't been able to come up with any valid reason to refuse a closer arrangement with them apart from a ripple of unease about the way in which old man Holland ran the firm, and surely safeguards could be built in to prevent any repetition of what had happened before? Possibly she was being overcautious.

She told herself that Max had put in a lot of work on this project, so she should at least find out exactly how everyone saw the matter proceeding. He was right, and there was a good case to be made out for a meeting. If she found Benton to be sensible and trustworthy, she'd feel better about the whole thing.

She managed to get herself off the stool. Good girl! See, you can do it if you put your mind to it! To shower or not to shower? That is the question. What should she wear…the new black with the jet embroidery on the shoulders?

She had to take off the remains of the day. No, that wasn't right. She had to take off the *remains of the day's make-up*, applied that morning, so long ago. A decade ago. Before Harvey. Before defeat.

'Fifteen minutes,' she said, and made her way towards the stairs.

BEA RECOGNIZED THE RESTAURANT. She might have known it. CJ had brought her here…when? Surely it wasn't just last night, was it?

Max looked around, rubbing his hands. 'The latest thing. Had the dickens of a job to get a table. Ah, there's Benton and his wife, waiting for us. So sorry we're late,

Benton. My mother likes to take her time getting her public face on.'

Bea fixed a smile on her face. 'Delighted,' she said, air-kissing Benton's wife, whose name, it appeared, was Dilys.

'Dilys has the same problem,' said Benton, with a loud laugh.

Bea knew that it wasn't logical to dislike a man because of the way he laughed, but there it was; a factor in the equation. If Max knew what she was thinking, he'd lift his eyes to the heavens and say it was just like a woman to think such things important. What he didn't realize was that if you didn't enjoy the company of a man, you'd be foolish to get into bed with him. Sorry; she meant 'into a relationship with him'.

Dilys was younger than her husband, puffy around the face, wearing a ruffled black dress which must have cost a penny or two but which did nothing for her plump figure. She was stiff with shyness. A nice girl, thought Bea. Perhaps a little intimidated by her husband and the surroundings?

'Champagne all round?' said Max, signalling to the waiter.

Bea's stomach rebelled. 'Not for me.' She pushed back her fatigue and set herself to put the girl at her ease.

Max and Benton got on like anything, dropping their voices to communicate with one another, and then roaring with laughter. Telling naughty jokes? No, talking about a PR firm they liked the look of, which they might approach to redesign the logo for their merged business. Excluding her, who'd been deputed to amuse the child-wife? Hm.

Small talk. 'Tell me, Dilys; how many children do you have?'

Dilys spoke about her young family in a soft, breathy voice. Bea encouraged her to do so. It meant she hadn't to make too much of an effort herself. Her stomach was still acting up.

They transferred to a table in the dining room, where the seating was arranged by Max. He and Benton sat side by side: 'So that our two lovely women can get to know one another.'

Bea told herself she'd feel better when she had some food inside her. There were breadsticks on the table.

Sticks. Sticks and stones may break my bones. Kamran's daughter had seen the caretaker pushed over the edge by a stick. Lavinia had had a stick. Who else?

'My dear Mama!' Max, pseudo solicitous. 'I'll choose for you, shall I?'

'Anything but lobster. I like it, but it doesn't like me. Something light, and perhaps some sparkling mineral water.'

'No, no. The champagne will buck you up nicely. Waiter! Another bottle of champagne!' He beckoned the wine waiter. 'On this auspicious occasion...'

Max and Benton laughed, leaning towards one another. Enjoying themselves. We two, we happy band of brothers...sharing out the spoils they anticipated would come from the merger.

Fatigue kept Bea quiet.

Kamran's family were in the world, but protected from it. Hidden, almost. And wanted to remain that way. They weren't going to rock the boat by screaming 'murder'.

Dilys was talking about her youngest son's chickenpox, which...

Bea tuned Dilys out, watching Max and Benton decide together on what they should eat and drink. More champagne came. She sipped some and felt marginally better.

Max was in charge, of course. He would be paying the bill. He was in his element as the host, the fixer, the influential director.

She accepted a plateful of a fishy dish whose ingredients she didn't immediately recognize. Not lobster, obviously. The sauce was divine.

'Dilys, my husband says you're a director of Holland and Butcher?'

'Why, yes.' She dimpled. She must have been an attractive girl in her late teens, though now, sadly, was beginning to look middle-aged before her time. 'Pa is the chair—Mr Holland, you know?—and I always meant to go into the firm when I finished at college. I used to help out in the office in the holidays sometimes, and he made me a director when I turned twenty. Only then I got married and started having babies so I don't really have time for all that any more.'

'You attend the meetings?'

'No, but I give Benton my proxy vote, of course.'

'You still draw a director's salary?'

A nod. 'It's a great help with the children's school fees.' Not even a blush when she made the admission.

Bea sighed to herself. Yes, that was how it worked. The board of directors of some companies still had non-working directors who drew a salary. Max would be in good company if this merger came about.

The fishy dishes were removed, to be replaced with lamb noisettes. At least, that's what they looked like, though they tasted of... She wasn't quite sure what they tasted of, and she wasn't sure she liked it.

A long shot. 'Tell me, Dilys; are you any relation to Sir Lucas Ossett?'

'He's my godfather. Didn't you know?'

She was beginning to understand how Sir Lucas had

gained information about a possible merger. Bea said, lightly, 'He crops up everywhere. He married into the family of my protégée, Maggie, and has been talking about giving my adopted son a place in his organization. I'm told he can be a very generous patron.'

'Oh, yes.' Eagerly. 'He gave me a block of shares in Vicori when I was twenty-one, and when I got married he put a whole heap of money into Holland and Butcher.'

He did, did he? Put a good face on it. 'Splendid. So one day in the future we might be connected twice over.'

Dilys sparkled with pleasure. 'Benton says that Max is all for it.'

'I know he's very keen on it,' said Bea. 'But it takes two to tango, or words to that effect.' The champagne was making her feel light-headed.

Dilys wasn't stupid. She got the message, frowned and sent an appealing glance towards her husband, who refused to see it.

Bea picked at the lamb dish and pushed the rest aside. The two men were deep in discussion about finding premises for new offices. New offices for whom? Ah, for the joint company which would be called—wait for it!—Holland and Abbot. Over her dead body.

She wondered if Evonne and Connor would turn up on Wednesday, looking for jobs. Fifty fifty, she thought.

Benton had been imbibing champagne at quite a rate. His colour had risen. 'Well, are you two girls enjoying yourselves?'

Dilys sent an agonized look to him. 'Don't you think we should change places so that you can talk to Mrs Abbot?'

Good for Dilys, thought Bea. You're not as silly as your husband tries to make out. 'Oh, that's all right,' said Bea out loud. 'After all, we're not here to talk business tonight, are we, Benton? Some time soon, perhaps in the New Year, once we've all recovered from the festivities and my solicitor is back from his holidays, I shall have time to look at the paperwork you've sent me. Did I tell you he's off on a cruise? My solicitor, I mean. I can hardly believe it. He always said he could get seasick in a punt on the river.'

Silence. The men looked at her in shock.

'Oh, but surely...' That was Benton.

Max's colour had risen, too. 'Mother!'

She didn't want to show him up before his guests, but this had to stop. 'Don't you "Mother" me,' said Bea. 'I am not in my dotage, and I'm perfectly capable of choosing what I want to eat for dessert. Did I see some meringues on the dessert trolley? I love meringue but don't often indulge. I like almost anything but sago pudding.' She could hear her voice rising. Too much champagne, too much death. She was feeling rather peculiar. She really ought not to have come out this evening.

Dilys tried to follow Bea's example. Her voice cracked, but she managed to say, 'I'd love some pavlova, if they've got any. It's something I never have at home.'

'Nor me,' said Bea. She wondered who would deal with the defrosting meal for one which Harvey had left out on his kitchen worktop. She also wondered who Carmela had invited to join her for supper.

She said, 'I'm glad it's stopped snowing. I've ruined two perfectly good pairs of boots over the last few days. Perhaps I shall have to resort to wellington boots if I go out tomorrow.' The next time she went up that fire escape it would be in the clunkiest of her shoes with the thickest of heels. If ever.

Dilys tried to smile. 'My youngest has got some wellies with pink flowers on them. She wants an umbrella with ladybirds on, too. I'm afraid her taste is for the brightly coloured.'

'My dear, I warm to her. The sooner she goes to school, the sooner you can get back to work with Holland and Butcher, right?'

'Yes, but… I don't think…' She looked to Benton for help.

'Oh, I'm sure you'd be a voice for common-sense,' said Bea, aware that Benton was looking horrified. 'It's sadly lacking in many boardrooms today, don't you think?'

Max had turned puce. 'Mother!'

The dear boy had bitten off more than he could chew, hadn't he? 'Dear Max, you'd better not have a dessert. So fattening, and you know your dear wife worries about you putting on weight.'

Did Dilys giggle? It was a very small giggle, but it was definitely there. Benton looked daggers at his wife. Benton didn't understand what was happening. He was out of his depth. Good. No need to say anything else. No need for a row in public. Max had understood what she'd said. Now perhaps they could all go home and get some sleep.

Bea felt most strange but couldn't think why. She'd only had one glass of champagne, and two courses, of fish and meat. Not lobster. No, no. Pray there hadn't been lobster in the sauce! But she recognized the symptoms only too well.

'Time to go beddy-byes,' said Bea, helping herself to her feet by leaning on the table. 'Waiter, was there lobster in the first course?'

'I don't think so, madam. Shall I enquire?'

'Mother, we haven't had our coffee, yet.'

She shook her head at him. 'Sorry, everyone. Got to make my excuses.' Where was the ladies' room? Ah. Yes. There. Across the room. Could she make it in time?

She let the door slam to behind her and dived for the nearest loo. Up it came. Ugh. And again.

Another slam of the door. Dilys had followed her. 'Can I help? The waiter admits there was some lobster in the sauce! Oh dear.'

Bea retched again. And again. She wanted to tell the girl to go away, but hadn't enough energy to do so. Dilys hovered. Bea slipped down to the floor, and stayed there, waiting for the next upheaval.

The door banged again as another diner entered. And banged again when she left. Dilys disappeared. Bang.

Which reminded her. Dimly. Kamran said his daughter hadn't heard anything after the caretaker took a dive down into the yard, except—and he wasn't entirely sure about that—she might have heard a door closing.

Which meant that she could guess—as he had—who'd killed the caretaker.

And he'd passed that information on to Bea, who was quite unable to do anything about it.

'You poor thing,' said Dilys, reappearing with a bottle of mineral water in her hand and a box of tissues. 'Max has told the maître d', who's told the cook, and they're taking that dish off the menu and of course there'll be no charge for the meal, but oh dear! Poor you! Could you drink some water? Here, I've got some tissues. If I wet them, I can get you cleaned up. And then we'll take you home.'

Bea croaked, 'Water. Thanks.'

Dilys ministered to her. Good for Dilys. Nice child. Deserved a better partner in life than Benton.

At last Bea got to her feet, swaying, stomach empty. Dilys fetched Bea's coat; Max had a cab waiting, and she was transported home. She saw that the answerphone light was blinking in the hall, but she ignored it. She'd be all right tomorrow. Hopefully.

# EIGHTEEN

*Sunday night to Monday morning*

A DISTURBED NIGHT. Bea went on retching at intervals. The floor rose up to meet her when she got off the bed. Luckily, her bedroom was en suite.

She dozed and woke. It was morning.

What day of the week? Monday? Probably. She felt dreadful.

She tottered down the stairs to feed the cat and collect some bottled water to drink. She mustn't get dehydrated or she'd be seriously ill. She used the internal phone to advise the manageress at the agency that she'd been incapacitated, found her mobile phone and went back to bed. She was alone in the house but didn't want company, thank you very much.

She dozed awhile. Her symptoms were subsiding. Or were they? No, they weren't. She made it back to the toilet just in time. And dozed off.

In the evening she fed the cat and began to worry about Maggie and Oliver. She rang Maggie, who never ever turned her mobile phone off. It was turned off this time, though.

She rang Oliver, who did answer eventually. 'Oliver, are you both all right?'

Oliver sounded subdued. 'Sorry not to have rung you. Maggie and I had a rough night. Stomach upset. Something we ate. But we're all right now, more or less.'

So they'd had a reaction to the lobster, too? No, no. Think straight, Bea. They didn't have lobster for supper and…they must have eaten something else. But they were all right now, which was more than she could say for herself. She envied the ability of youth to throw things off.

'What happened?' said Bea, trying to think clearly. 'Is Lady Ossett all right?'

'Sure. They didn't eat with us last night. Stayed out till late.'

'Oh. Good. I think. I've had a stomach upset, too. Speak tomorrow.'

She went back to bed.

*Tuesday*

SHE GOT UP, feeling swimmy in the head. She knew she ought to eat something, but couldn't face it. It was odd that Maggie and Oliver had also had a stomach upset. She had a horrid feeling she was missing something important. Her head was muzzy. She couldn't think.

She rang Oliver again.

He sounded tired. 'Yes, we had another late night. I don't know how you oldies cope! Lady O quarrelled with the Professor about something obscure in a crossword puzzle, would you believe? Then, just as we were about to go to bed she decided to change all the furniture round and we were up till two o'clock doing that. She had me on the Internet looking for new lamps to buy. Yes, you might well laugh…'

Bea really was laughing. She hadn't thought she could, but she did. 'Has Maggie been able to go off to work today?'

'Looking like death, but yes; she has gone. I promised not to leave Her Ladyship alone, which is fine because she isn't out of bed yet and I gather she has appointments with the beauticians this afternoon. She's got them coming here, rather than her going to them. I thought I might be able to get away, but she's paranoid about being left alone.'

Maybe she was right to be paranoid. 'It's all right, Oliver. You look after her. I'm OK. Or soon will be.'

'The Professor knocked on the door a while back with a bunch of flowers for Her Highness, so I imagine all will soon be fine in that department again.'

'You think it's a match made in heaven?'

'What has heaven got to do with it?' Oliver was unusually terse.

'Well, I've been off colour for a while, too, so I'm taking it easy today. I should be back on form again tomorrow. Keep in touch, right?'

She made herself some toast and decided she didn't want it. Ate half a banana. Fed the cat. Drank a lot of water. Checked with the agency that all was well. Was asked what she wanted to do about a request for a caretaker that had come in over the weekend. Bea remembered this was Sir Lucas's attempt to involve her further in his network. She told her manageress to say that the Abbot Agency didn't provide caretakers and that they would pass the enquiry on to someone who did.

Bea was not, definitely not going to be drawn into Sir Lucas's orbit. The manageress was considerate enough to ask how Bea was feeling, and to recommend that she drank flat Coca-Cola to replace the salts she'd been losing. Bea didn't have any in the house. 'I'll send one of the girls out for some for you.'

A large bottle of Coca-Cola duly appeared. Bea was instructed to drop a few grains of sugar into the liquid, to reduce the bubbles before she drank any. With some misgivings she followed the instructions and, slightly to her surprise, it did help.

She dozed on the settee. Tried to think. The others hadn't eaten the lobster, so…what did that mean?

After a while she got up to hunt for a telephone number which she hadn't used for some time.

The detective inspector was not available at the moment. What had she expected? That he rush to her side with handcuffs ready to take someone into custody? That wasn't likely to happen, was it?

The odds were against anybody doing anything.

She might as well let the matter drop, forget all about the people in the flats, and concentrate on minding her own business.

*Wednesday morning*

She woke with a slight headache, after a quiet night, but otherwise feeling she was on the mend. She drank some more water, managed to make her way into the shower and out again. She looked in the mirror and blenched. She looked as if she'd aged ten years. Would make-up help? No. She wasn't ready for that yet.

She knew she had to get some food inside her, but the thought of cooking made her feel faint. Perhaps some dry biscuits?

If only Maggie or Oliver could return… But they were looking after Maggie's mother, and it was right that they should do so, or Lady Ossett might meet with an 'accidental' death, too.

How to prevent it? Well, she wasn't capable of preventing a fly from settling on her arm at the moment, so she must put them out of her mind until she felt better.

She didn't feel up to getting dressed. She brushed out

her hair, put on some lipstick, a housecoat, and her bedroom slippers. Very gently she let herself down one flight
of the stairs to the kitchen.

Tea. Not too hot. A plain biscuit, or even two? Another
half of a banana. They stayed down.

Winston required to be fed. She obliged. She scanned
the Business section of the morning papers, and yes, there
was a report about a forthcoming AGM at Vicori House
where ructions were expected, tra la. She wondered how
Sir Lucas's broken arm was getting on.

She could tell that her agency staff were at work, as
the phones were ringing down below. She accessed the
messages on her answerphone. Nothing drastic, but one
of them needed to be attended to. She took a note about
it downstairs, thanked her manageress for the Coca-Cola
and said she hoped to be back at work the following day.
She was told that at her age it would take time to recover.
Thanks very much. On her way out, she remembered
that young Evonne and Connor might call at some point
looking for a job, so she warned the manageress to look
out for them and help them if possible. But if not…tough!

Back upstairs she let a few tears fall. Then brushed
them away.

*Dear Lord, what am I supposed to do? Two deaths al-
ready. Possibly a third. A man's arm broken. He could
easily have made a fourth. And no one is being called to
account for it. I feel as if I'm shouting into a bank of mist.*

*I've asked all the right questions, I've tried to make
people see what's happening, and what do I get for it? A
bonk on the head and food poisoning.*

*Max ought to have made sure I didn't have any dish
with lobster in it, when he was ordering. Uh, oh. Not his
fault. I should have made sure of it myself.*

*I've tried to talk to CJ. He doesn't want to know.*

*Piers can't help. Not his scene.*

*Max...? Don't be daft. If I can prevent him from pinning his colours to the Holland and Butcher mast, that's as much as I can manage.*

She noticed that a heavy rain was falling outside. That would wash the remains of the snow away...together with the footprints on the fire escape.

Even the elements were conspiring against her.

She hauled herself upstairs, pulled on casual clothes and attempted some make-up. It made her feel better. Slightly. Winston the cat came up to keep her company. She made her bed, put aside for cleaning the dress she'd worn to the restaurant.

As she stood at the front window, looking out over the street, where the cars were going swish, swish as they passed by, she heard an inner voice say, *for evil to triumph, it is only necessary for good men to do nothing.*

Did that mean she had to try once more to get someone to interfere at the flats? Possibly. But she couldn't do it by herself. She'd tried that. She needed help.

She'd asked for help and nothing had happened.

*Don't give up.*

She went downstairs, found some paper and her notebook, and settled down to making a chart of who lived where at the flats, with appropriate comments. It took some time, but clarified her thoughts.

Her front doorbell rang, and someone let himself into the house. 'Mother?'

Max. Of course.

She didn't feel up to arguing with him. 'Dear Max; how thoughtful of you to call. Yes, I am feeling a little better this morning. Not quite my usual self, but getting there.'

'I suppose it could have been worse.' He was grumpy

this morning. 'I had to explain to Benton that you were not feeling the thing.'

'No, indeed. Dilys was sweet. A nice child.'

He wasn't interested in Dilys. 'I said we'd have to meet up again, as soon as you're back on your feet. What about tomorrow lunchtime?'

Why couldn't he take a hint that she was not interested in the projected merger? She decided to play the invalid card for all it was worth. She let herself down on to the settee and put her feet up. Winston leaped on to her lap, turned around three times, and deflated. She closed her eyes. 'I do hope I'm not going to be sick again.'

He blenched. 'Can't you get Maggie to look after you?'

'I would if she weren't guarding her mother's back. Oliver, too. I can't draw them away from the front line.'

'What front line?'

She didn't reply, but kept her eyes closed. She could hear him shuffling around, fiddling with his watch strap, unwilling to waste a minute but also unwilling to risk being there if she was going to be sick.

He touched her forehead. Clumsy boy. But tender-hearted. 'Hope you feel better soon.'

She didn't open her eyes, and heard him leave the house. Good. She snuggled down, one hand in Winston's fur. The cat was purring. She relaxed. Slept.

Awoke to a peal on the front doorbell. Was it afternoon, already?

Winston had departed. She stood up, feeling more like herself, and went to let her caller in. Detective Inspector Durrell. Intelligent, laid back, of mixed ancestry, with a growing family and a wicked sense of humour.

Maybe God had answered her prayers, after all. 'Am I glad to see you!' She almost kissed him.

'They pulled me off another case to deal with you.'

He looked yearningly towards the kitchen. 'You haven't any food or drink on the go, have you? I seem to have missed lunch. And breakfast.' He thought about it. 'I did have something to eat last night. I think.'

She led the way to the kitchen. 'I'm recovering from a bout of food poisoning which you won't want to know about but which... How many people have to get sick before health and safety close down a restaurant?'

'What?'

She sighed. 'No, I don't suppose one person being sick is enough. I asked if the fish dish had lobster in it and was told that it didn't. But it did. The restaurant apologized of course, but personally I don't think it was very helpful of them to say there wasn't any lobster in the dish when there was. So I've been knocked out for the last couple of days. Well, put that one down to experience and refuse to visit that particular restaurant again, right? I could do with something to eat now. What would you like?'

'Anything.' He stretched. Seated himself on a stool. Winston the cat immediately jumped up on to him and sat there, purring, confident that by this means he'd get to be fed.

She opened the fridge. She couldn't take fried food. There were some chicken fillets. She enquired of her stomach whether or not they would do and received an affirmative answer. 'Something with chicken and rice do you?'

'You're a wonder, Mrs Abbot. And a pain in the der-rière, of course.'

She tried to laugh. 'You've been told to silence me; is that right?'

'Not at all. I've been told you know where to find the villain in the case.'

She gaped. 'What! Who...?'

'Tariq. There's a warrant out for his arrest, and the word is that you will know where to find him.' He twisted round to look up at the cupboards behind him. 'Are there any biscuits in the tin? Or some of your home-made cake? I have the fondest memories of working with you before. Your cooking is out of this world.'

'I don't know whether to laugh or cry. I suppose this is Sir Lucas getting back at me because I refuse to bow down and worship at his shrine. I'm in shock. I haven't the slightest idea where Tariq may be. Anyway, what's he charged with?'

'Everything from spitting in the street to murder.'

'What nonsense.' She sent him a sharp look. 'I'll feed you, but in return you'll promise to listen to my side of the story, right? I suppose you've been told that nothing must rock Sir Lucas's boat, and that I'm a silly woman whose imagination has run away with her.'

'Serious doubts have been raised as to your sanity. I'm informed on the highest authority that as soon as you've told me where he's hiding you should take a holiday in the sun.' He found some peanuts and started to eat them.

Bea put a saucepan under the tap and dropped it. 'Sorry. Still rather tottery, I'm afraid.'

A firm hand took the pan off her. 'You're not fit. You sit down, and I'll cook.'

'You can cook?'

'I learned when my wife was tied up with three children under school age.' He set the water on to boil. 'Now; start from the beginning. Someone attempted to kill Sir Lucas—'

'Well, actually, I don't think they did. His fall was collateral damage.'

'You amaze me! And not for the first time. You keep

the onions in a stand by the back door, I seem to remember. Go on.'

'I have to set the scene first. Sir Lucas is a giant spider. He sits in the middle of a beautiful web, a structure with worldwide appeal which attracts lots of shiny, juicy flies. Once within his orbit, the flies find they're so entangled that they can't get free.'

'Ah. He gives out money and patronage, so no one wants to offend him? Carry on.'

'He likes to think that everything in sight belongs to him. When he moved into the block of flats in which he and his wife lived, he tried—and mostly he succeeded—to put all the other tenants on short-term contracts only. Yes, this is important, so you needn't look bored.'

'Was I? Where's the salt? Ah. Got it.'

'This meant he could control the tenants who lived in the flats. Three or four people who'd lived there before he owned the freehold resisted his charms, and kept their long-term contracts, but they were all senior citizens and he could afford to wait for them to die off. To encourage them to think about moving, however, he raised the service rents, which put pressure on those with a restricted income. You follow me?'

'He's a business man. Yes.'

'He issued new contracts to some tenants and put money into other tenants' businesses. Carmela was his "therapist"; don't ask me what that means because I don't know. He put money into the dominatrix Cynthia's business. A colleague took another flat which is currently occupied by his daughter. Then there was one leased out to a couple of Sir Lucas's employees, which was eventually sublet to Tariq.'

'Ah; now we're getting to it. He's the man I'm hunting, the man who set the trap which set Sir Lucas tumbling down the stairs.'

'No, it wasn't him. To get back to Sir Lucas. Men who run empires are always looking over their shoulders to see who wants to stab them in the back next. Consider his situation: he's facing a hostile takeover bid, and he suspects someone in the company is trying to oust him from power. In addition he's planning to divorce his current wife and take on a younger woman who has money of her own. When he trips and falls he assumes it's all part and parcel of a plot to get rid of him. He sets his security people to ferret out the mole at Vicori House and—realizing that if the wire across the stairs had been intended for him, his enemy must have an accomplice at the flats—he looks around for someone to blame there as well. He jumps to the conclusion that the villain must be Tariq, but even he needs a smidgeon of proof, so he brings in an outsider to investigate.'

'This is where you came in?'

'Not so fast. One of his problems was how to keep Lady Ossett calm at that crucial point in time. The last thing he wanted was for her to go yowling to the papers about their separation or a trip wire on the stairs. But his younger mistress was beckoning. So when the incident occurred, he seized on it as an excuse to walk out of the penthouse suite, telling Lady Ossett that this was a fake separation to keep her from harm while he identified the villain of the piece.'

The inspector suspended operations, wooden spoon in the air, 'She wasn't responsible for the tripwire, was she?'

'No, of course not, but she was sharp enough to realize that all was not well, to look very hard at his motives, and to wonder who the trap on the stairs was really meant for. She went along with his story in public but in private she was genuinely afraid for her own personal safety. Rightly so. She got into such a state that she ordered her daughter Maggie to return home to look after her.'

'What? But why would anyone want to kill her?'

'That indeed is the question. I'm not sure that the intention was to kill. It may have been just to frighten.'

'Why would Tariq want to frighten her?'

'He didn't. Look; Tariq is a red herring. He got up everyone's noses by playing music too loudly, too late and too often. Sir Lucas and/or Lady Ossett complained, and Tariq's music equipment was confiscated. It was an open secret that it was Tariq who keyed Sir Lucas's car and, either in response to that or because he wasn't any good at his job, he got the sack, which meant he fell behind with his rent. Naturally, Sir Lucas, being paranoid and imagining that everyone had it in for him, conceived that Tariq was the accomplice to whoever it was at head office who was plotting his demise.'

'And he wasn't?'

'No, it was all in his imagination but, being Lord High Everything and accustomed to having his slightest whim obeyed, Sir Lucas overreacted. He instructed the caretaker at the flats to confine Tariq to quarters until such time as he could be interrogated by his security men… which caused further complications.'

The inspector was using far too many saucepans. Men always did. She quailed at the thought of the washing up this might entail. Thank goodness they had a dishwasher.

'Are you saying Sir Lucas imagined the trap on the stairs?'

'Oh no. There was one, but I really don't think it was meant for him.'

'Is there any evidence that it existed, apart from Sir Lucas's story?'

'Yes, I took some photographs of the holes left by the nails or screws or whatever. They're on my computer at the moment. The holes were filled in later, by the way. In my opinion, Sir Lucas was lucky to get away as lightly as he did. If Lady Ossett had tripped, the result might well have been fatal.'

'I'm going mad here. Why would anyone want to kill her?'

'And I say again; I think the intention was more to frighten than to kill, as evinced by the second attempt on Lady Ossett's life. The steak which she'd left out for her supper was treated with poison, which resulted in the death of the cat Momi who lived in the building. Lady Ossett said she'd sent the evidence of the cat's poisoning to Sir Lucas, but I doubt if he did anything about it. His view is that Lady O stage-managed the death of the cat in order to persuade him to return to her.'

'But...who would want her dead—or frightened? Apart from Sir Lucas... I mean. It wasn't him, was it?'

'It wasn't him. The poisoning of Lady O's supper was done by someone who attended the bridge party. Take your pick. There's quite a number of suspects.'

The inspector looked grim. 'Let's get back to Tariq. I have a warrant for his arrest burning a hole in my pocket. Do you, or do you not know where he may be found?'

'No, I don't. What's more, I don't believe he's done anything to justify being hunted down like this.'

'Look at it from my point of view. He's been sacked from his job, was in arrears with his rent, attacked His Lordship's car and is accused of setting a potentially lethal trap for him. What's more, he flees before he can be handed over to the police and have his guilt or innocence established.'

'Can you blame him for trying to leave? Do you suppose he would have got a fair hearing if he'd sat back and waited to be arrested…for something which he hadn't done? He fled the building at his second attempt, yes. The first time the caretaker caught him trying to leave, knocked him out, and shoved him back into his flat with a warning not to try that again. Fortunately, he managed to escape the following day.'

She gave him chapter and verse while the inspector dished up a steaming pile of saffron rice mixed with chicken nuggets, onions and herbs. The scent of it rose to Bea's nostrils like incense. For a moment she wondered if her stomach would cooperate, but fortunately, it did. She reached for forks, gave one to the inspector, and set to work. They ate in silence. Bea told herself to take it slowly and only eat a little or she'd get indigestion or end up sitting by the loo all evening.

Slow and sure does it. She suspended operations when she'd eaten a third of what was on her plate.

The inspector burped and apologized.

She beamed at him. 'Any time you want to leave the police force, I'll find you a job as a chef.'

The inspector was nothing if not dogged. 'Could Tariq have killed the caretaker?'

'He was long gone by the time the caretaker toppled over the balcony.' She took another mouthful and disposed of it slowly. Gently does it. 'To continue with the tale of What Sir Lucas Did. He knew about the Abbot Agency, not only because Maggie now lives with me but also because some time back he'd put money into a firm which trains people for domestic service, and who are angling for closer relations with me. Sir Lucas has had a poor return on his investment with this other company because their management structure is weak. He saw that if a merger with the Abbot Agency were to go through,

I'd sort the other firm out, which would save his investment. So that's how he knew about me.

'Also, he'd heard from a mutual friend that I'd been
involved with sorting out one or two nasty situations in
the past, and he conceived the idea that I might be useful
to him by acting as nursemaid to his wife. And then his
eye alighted on young Oliver. "Ah-ha," he thinks. "This
brainy young man has the right skills to track down the
miscreant who has dared to dispute my right to rule over
all I survey." He thought he could kill several birds with
one stone by employing us both. I admire the man, in
a way.'

'How many birds and of what kind?'

'What sort of bird would you call Lady Ossett? How
about a Bird of Paradise? I didn't want Sir Lucas to co-
opt Oliver. I know how power corrupts. I was afraid Oliver might be induced to bend the truth in order to please
His Highness. I lost that one. He got Oliver involved with
the prospect of a good job in his organization if he would
track down and expose the traitor at the flats through
their computers.

'Oliver, being young and impulsive, took off like a
Roman candle. He thought he'd found the villain when
he came across a man called Harvey, a writer of pulp
fiction who liked to claim he was something in MI5.
Oliver swallowed the tale, he and the caretaker locked
Harvey into his flat to await retribution, Harvey roused
the neighbourhood with cries for help, the caretaker went
into Tariq's flat to start clearing out some rubbish, and…
was pushed over the balcony and down several storeys
into the yard below. Squashed flat. Dead. And the witness heard a door close straight after.'

'I'm informed it was an accident. You're not eating?
Coffee?'

She shook her head. 'No, no. I'm fine. Just taking it slowly. A witness told me someone pushed him. And no; I can't produce the witness, who'll deny everything rather than be dragged into court.'

He gave her an old-fashioned look. 'You'll tell me sooner or later. So who do you think killed the caretaker?'

'One of two people. I need to get into someone's flat to check, but I should be able to tell you who it was to-morrow.'

'Do I insist you tell me who it is now?' He switched the kettle on to make himself some coffee.

'Wouldn't do any good. But I'll tell you what to look for, if you can get a warrant to search the flats.'

'That'll take a bit of doing, seeing as how there's not supposed to have been any real crime committed. So far you've given me nothing to divert me from the search for Tariq. Misadventure. Accident. A stupid prank, tripping someone up as they went down the stairs.'

'What about Harvey's death? And the footprints in the snow?'

'What snow? It's long since gone. I'm reliably in-formed that Harvey's death is just another accident.'

She sighed. Closed her eyes. 'I can't get the picture of him out of my head. He didn't deserve to die like that. He was a comparatively young man, and talented. I main-tain he was murdered.'

'Convince me. Who murdered him, and why?'

'Well, not the McIntyres; she's sick, and he's devoted. They can only think of their own problems. Not Cynthia and Donald; ditto. Not the couple on the ground floor; ditto again. Not Carmela or the Professor, and not the Muslim family.'

'Which leaves—'

She took another mouthful of the chicken dish, said,

'I've made a chart which shows where everyone lives or lived. Don't you dare touch my plate while I fetch my notes. You can work it out from that.'

# NINETEEN

She found the chart, laid it before him, and returned to her food.

| | | | | | |
|---|---|---|---|---|---|
| 7th fl. | No 14 –Penthouse | Over the whole floor – Sir Lucas/Lady Ossett Wire stretched across stairs Lady O's supper poisoned. Cat died. | | | |
| 6th | No 12 | Away – decorators in. | | No 12a | Prof Jacobsen, cat Momi Crossword compiler. |
| 5th | No 10 | Mrs Carrie Kempton Divorcee. Do-gooder. | | No 11 | Tariq, loud music. Keyed Sir L's car. Caretaker killed from his balcony. |
| 4th | No 8 | Mrs Lucy Emerson Widow. Do-gooder. | | No 9 | Muslim family Witnessed caretaker's fall. |
| 3rd | No 6 | Harvey Middleton Fantasist. Murdered. | [lift] [&] [stairs] | No 7 | Carmela Lessbury Therapist, friend of Sir Lucas. |
| 2nd | No 4 | Cynthia and Donald Dominatrix & stalker. | | No 5 | Eliot/Helen McIntyre Devoted husband/wife ill. |
| 1st | No 2 | Evonne and Connor Daddy's girl/ shaven head. | | No 3 | Lavinia, heart attack? Died. Old/obese. Used a stick. |
| Semi-basement | No 1 | Caretaker | | | Boiler, air conditioning unit, laundry, cleaners' cupboard, maintenance. |
| Sub-basement | Garage | For residents | | | |

THE INSPECTOR PUT his finger on a name, moved his finger up, and then down. 'You think one of those two did it? Why on earth would they?'

A sigh. A shake of the head. Bea took another mouthful of the chicken dish, which was cold but still tasty. 'I think I know why, but as to which of them did it, I'm not sure.'

'Do you think they might have acted together?'

'There again, I don't know. They might have done.'

He threw his arms wide. 'Ridiculous! Why on earth would either one of them decide to go on a killing spree?'

'I don't suppose this person sees it that way at all. Consider; she's living on a restricted income, and although Lady Ossett invites her and her friend to the weekly bridge parties, the stakes are becoming uncomfortably high. Lady Ossett has money to burn and has been somewhat patronizing to two elderly ladies who don't have a man in tow. It's a situation which can breed envy and resentment. In addition, you remember that Sir Lucas has been trying to put them all on short-term contracts? Lucy and Carrie have lived there some years. One of them has a decent enough length of time left, but the other has only eighteen months. And where is she to go when that runs out? She can't afford to renew.'

'All right; that establishes envy. But from envy to manslaughter is a big leap.'

'From discontent and envy to being involved in the death of an old lady is a small step. Lavinia could be very tiresome, waylaying the other tenants on their way in and out of the building, demanding this or that favour. Then one day she died, natural causes, heart attack.

'I'm not claiming that one or both of the friends were responsible for bringing on Lavinia's fatal heart attack, but one or other of them must have been present at the time of her death, or the old lady's stick wouldn't have acquired a new owner. Harvey took photos of everyone, and he took one of Lavinia, leaning on her walking stick. It's an unusual one, decorated with metal travel mementoes. Lucy has one such stick in her hallstand, and also in a photo Harvey took of her. It wasn't given to her as a memento of the dear departed, you know. I checked.'

Bea took another mouthful of her chicken dish. It was good. And giving her some energy, too. 'So; a little bit of naughtiness, there. And she got away with it.'

'You think it was Lucy?'

'On balance, yes. She's the dominant one in the partnership, and she ended up with the stick. But they were not the only ones in the building who were going through a difficult time. I don't need to enumerate all the problems the tenants had, but let's look at them from the point of view of two elderly ladies with not enough to do and an interest in their neighbours' doings. What did they make of Tariq and his lifestyle? There was his new partner, noisy parties, the loss of his job and the keying of Sir Lucas's car. Naughty, naughty. But—giggle, giggle—it all made for an amusing bit of gossip.

'Then there were the rumours of Sir Lucas's double dealing with his wife. Lady Ossett was not popular, and they must have enjoyed the idea that she was being taken down a peg. And then, oh my dear! The delicious scandal of the call-girl cards!'

'What! What's that?'

'Didn't you know? No, I don't suppose Sir Lucas ever got to hear about that. The victims certainly didn't want it broadcast. Yes, there were men calling at all hours, demanding sex of Carmela and Evonne. Who'd have thought it! But of course, Carmela was asking for it, wasn't she? And as for those two young things on the ground floor, giving the place a bad name, getting caught up in the riots, taking drugs no doubt, what a disgrace! The sooner they were out of here the better!'

'What!' said the inspector again. 'You mean that—'

'All dealt with,' said Bea. 'But at the time it must have seemed to the two ladies that they were living in the middle of a seething cauldron of sex and sin. And none of it was down to them. So, giggle giggle, why not stir the pudding? They were always up and down the stairs, visiting the other tenants. You could say they were poking their noses into other people's business to enliven their own dull lives, or that they were genuinely interested in trying to help others less fortunate than themselves. One of them probably was being charitable. The other was not beyond making bad worse.

'She starts off by fixing a wire across the top stairs. She'd been a Girl Guide and had learned practical skills. The trap was intended for Lady Ossett, but in fact it catches Sir Lucas and is the final straw in his decision to leave. He thinks it was set up by someone working with an enemy of his at work. Lady O is not so sure. She wonders if perhaps she'd been the intended target.

'"Oh, goody, goody," thinks our killer. "Now Lady O is upset. More!" She attends the next bridge party and makes an excuse to go out to the kitchen. Momi the cat is prowling around, so she puts poison on the meat which had been intended for Lady O's supper and feeds it to the cat. It's a premeditated act. She'd brought the poison with her. Whether she'd actually intended to kill Lady O is another matter. I'm inclined to think not. The aim was to distress, not to kill.

'She might have stopped right there, but when Harvey is locked into his flat by the caretaker, she has a fit of righteous indignation. She knows Harvey wasn't responsible for the wire across the landing and has been wrongfully imprisoned, so in a fit of public duty she takes it on herself to confront the caretaker. He's gone out on to the balcony where he's dealing with the junk left by Tariq. She follows him by going out through her friend's kitchen door on to the balcony, and in the ensuing argument she uses her stick to poke at him—and he goes over the edge. What she didn't realize was that there was a witness to the caretaker's death.'

'What? Who?' He peered at the chart.

Bea made a tired gesture. 'She's no good to you. She won't testify. But I can tell you what she saw, which was a woman using a stick to push the caretaker off balance and over the edge of the balcony. And yes, it might be a different stick. For all I know, Carrie Kempton has a dozen such sticks in her flat.'

He snatched the chart up again. 'If your witness—who I assume lives opposite Mrs Emerson but directly under Tariq—heard a door close, then surely it was Mrs Kempton whom she heard returning to her own flat.'

'From what the witness said, I don't think there'd have been time enough for the killer to go down another flight of stairs before going back into the building and closing the door behind her, so yes; I think the killer went back into the building through Carrie Kempton's flat. But remember that Lucy is in and out of Carrie's flat all the time.'

'The witness is a member of the Muslim family?'

'Wild horses wouldn't get them into court to testify.'

The inspector threw up his arms. 'This is all hearsay. I can't act on hearsay.' He took a turn around the kitchen. 'What about Harvey's death? It's been put down as misadventure. You're not going to tell me that was murder, too? Why would one of the old dears want to kill him?'

'Harvey had worked out what she was doing, and he tried to warn me. He talked about fearing people who bring you gifts, and he showed me a picture of Lavinia leaning on her stick. He'd taken a photo of Lucy with what looks like the same stick. I don't think he'd have turned her in to the police, but I do think he warned her to be careful, and that made him a threat to her. I think she used her stick to pull the typewriter off the shelf above his head. It might not have killed him. It would certainly have frightened him, and maybe that's all she intended to do. Unfortunately, the typewriter hit him fair and square. Exit Harvey.'

'But…' The inspector shook his head. 'There's nothing to be done about…well, anything. Is there?'

Bea drooped. 'I suppose not. But it doesn't half go against the grain, and I'll be worried sick about Maggie and Oliver till I can get them back home.'

The inspector was the one to get roused now. 'If what you say is correct then, having got away with so many "incidents", I can't see why she would stop now. The moment someone crosses her, they'll be for the chop, too. She must think she's invincible.'

'If you tell her you've got your beady eye on her, perhaps she'll stop?'

Someone rang the doorbell. Hard.

The inspector sighed, consulted his watch. 'Well, I suppose I must be on my way.'

'Let's hope it's no one important. I'm not up to visitors.' Bea led the way to the hall and looked through the peephole in the front door.

Her breathing quickened, and she put her hand to her throat. 'It's Lucy Emerson.'

The inspector said, 'You're afraid of her?'

'She gives me the willies.'

The doorbell rang again. Impatiently.

Bea said, 'I don't want to let her in.'

'If I stay…?'

Bea braced herself. 'I'm being silly. What could she do to me in broad daylight?' She opened the door. 'Lucy? Do come in. My visitor is just leaving.'

Mrs Emerson beamed. She was carrying a covered basket and using a stick. *The* stick. 'Well, just for a moment, then. I heard you'd been poorly, and I thought you might welcome a visit. Also, I have something to tell you.'

'Do come in.' Bea opened the door wide and ushered Mrs Emerson in. 'The sitting room is the door on the left. And—' to the inspector—'nice of you to call. See you again sometime.'

He said, 'Thanks,' and took the door from her.

As she followed her guest along the hall, Bea heard the front door close behind her. She shivered. 'I'm feeling the cold today. May I take your coat? Go on through while I turn the central heating up in the hall.' She hung up the coat and adjusted the thermostat, pleased to hear the central heating respond. She'd leave the door open, to let the warm air circulate. 'Will there be a frost tonight, do you think?'

'What a lovely house.' Lucy twitched the cover off her basket and brought out a plastic container holding a huge chunk of chocolate cake, oozing with cherry jam. 'I hope you like chocolate cake.'

'Delicious. How kind of you. I'll save it for later, if you don't mind. I've had a nasty stomach upset and am not eating much at the moment. Do sit down.'

'Did you eat some of Carrie's biscuits? She's losing the plot, you know. I don't know what she put in the last lot she baked, but they gave me a most unpleasant night.'

Yes, of course. Carrie's biscuits. Bea had eaten two,

and she'd begun to feel queasy even before she got to
the restaurant and the lobster had done its work...and
that explained why Oliver and Maggie had had tummy
upsets, too.

Lucy sat, four-square. 'This is so difficult... I don't
know where to begin.'

Bea suppressed the impulse to tell the woman to begin
at the beginning.

Lucy fiddled with the silk scarf she was wearing. 'I
need to ask you for your understanding; not for me, you
understand, but... I thought that you of all people might
be able to help her. You see, we've been friends for so
many years, Carrie and I. I ought to have seen it coming, the paranoia or whatever they call it nowadays. But
I didn't. Perhaps I didn't want to see it? I've hardly slept
these last few nights... I couldn't make up my mind what
to do, and then it occurred to me, that dear girl Maggie told me you had a friend in the police force...? Am
I right?'

Bea nodded.

Lucy leaned forward. 'Then you'll know what's best to
be done. I can't do it. It would be a betrayal of everything
I hold dear, but she needs help, you see. Psychiatric attention, perhaps? I've heard of such things, but I've never,
most fortunately, had to... But if you can see to it, perhaps the doctors can save her from... You understand?'

'Not exactly, no.'

'I left her in tears. I keep telling her the courts will be
most understanding when she explains, a series of unfortunate accidents, no more, but...in the wrong hands, if
they decided to prosecute... They'd hardly want to send
her to prison at her age, would they? It would be such a
waste of taxpayers' money. However, something must
be done, I realize that, because there's no denying she is

very depressed. I thought that you might be able to put
her in touch with someone, get the doctors involved.'

'I don't understand.' And indeed, Bea did not understand. She'd thought Lucy was the guilty party. Was it
Carrie, after all?

'Such a silly girl she is.' Lucy produced a hankie, blew
her nose and wiped her eyes. 'We've known one another
for ever, you know. Since we were at school together,
although parted by fate for many years. But once we'd
met up again, on a visit to Kew Gardens it was, almost
fifteen years ago, how time flies... And my husband
was still alive then, but oh dear; it hardly bears thinking
about, does it?'

'No, no,' said Bea, her brain whirling, trying to consider two opposing theories at once. 'Take your time.'

Lucy gasped out a sigh. 'What you must think of
me, letting her carry on like that, but of course at first
I couldn't believe it. I mean, you wouldn't, would you?
Everyone knew what Lavinia was like, and really she'd
long outstayed her welcome, hadn't she?'

'Carrie Kempton killed Lavinia?'

'Oh, no! No, no, no! Of course not. Nothing like that.
It was all Lavinia's fault. She wanted someone to run to
the chemist for her there and then, and we were on our
way back from a long day out and were both very tired,
but did that stop her? Oh, no. She started shouting, and
then she lifted her stick to hit me, and dear Carrie got
hold of it and twisted and Lavinia lost her balance, you
see, and fell. And died right there, before our very eyes!'

'How awful.' Bea's eyes were on the stick Lucy had
kept at her side. It was a very stout, solid stick. It could
do a lot of damage if you were hit with it.

'We were ever so upset, as you can imagine. Carrie
was so pale, I thought she'd fainted, but luckily she came

round and I got her upstairs to her flat to have a little brandy and a lie down before I called the paramedics.'

'And you took the stick yourself?'

'Oh no, dear. She took the stick, feeling a bit tottery, you understand. She's been using it ever since, and very useful it is, too.'

'I thought I saw it in your hallstand.'

'Yes, of course. Sometimes she leaves it there for days on end. But she gets bouts of, what do you call it, labyrinthitis? When her head swims? And then she uses it. But her short-term memory is going, and she doesn't always remember…so I brought it with me, to give it to you. Out of harm's way.'

How clever the woman was. She would have an answer for everything, no doubt. So let's test her out. 'So it was Carrie who stretched the wire across the landing to trap Lady Ossett? Why did she do that?'

Lucy shifted uncomfortably. 'I'm afraid dear Lady Ossett hasn't always been the soul of tact. She has often treated us like poor relations, and we have our pride, you know. Also, she kept making remarks about how convenient it was that Carrie should have managed to acquire such a good stick when everyone knew that Lavinia's relations wouldn't let anyone have so much as a cup and saucer by way of a memento. Not tactful if you have such a thin skin as my dear Carrie.'

'You think Carrie wanted to get back at Lady Ossett by making her tumble down the stairs? Rather a dangerous prank, don't you think?'

'Yes, well; that's what I said to her, too. But it was Sir Lucas who fell, and when Carrie told me what she'd done, I went upstairs straight away and did away with the wire.'

'And filled in the tack holes later?'

'As you say. I thought that would be the end of it. I was

horrified when Carrie told me she'd given the caretaker a little push…' Lucy put her hankie to her mouth again.

Bea didn't know what to think. Was this woman really concerned for her friend or was she a monster, entirely without remorse for what she had done?

Lucy set aside her hankie and lifted a portion of cake out of the box, looking for somewhere to put it. 'You're looking rather pale, Mrs Abbot. Can't I coax you to try a piece? It'll do you good.'

'Yes, I'm sure it will. But not yet. Why do you think Harvey had to die?'

'What a silly boy! He told Carrie to keep away from him or he'd tell on her, so of course she had to kill him.'

'Not an accident, then?'

'No, no. She pulled the typewriter down on top of him with her stick! Now you can understand why I couldn't leave it with her, can't you? Is there a plate I can put this cake on for you? And perhaps find you a fork to eat it with?'

'Not at the moment, thank you.' Bea noticed it was getting dark outside. The nights were getting longer, and the days shorter…and she couldn't tell for the life of her whether Lucy was lying or not. She put on the side lamps and drew the curtains over the windows. 'So, you want me to phone the police for you?'

Lucy had returned the cake to its box in order to dab at her eyes with her hankie again. 'We've been such friends for so long, it makes me feel like a traitor, but I suppose you must. I tell myself that she would do the same for me, if things were different, but…she needs help, doesn't she? It didn't occur to me till I was on my way here, but she's been so depressed, I felt I had to do something, even if it was the wrong thing, before she… You understand?'

'Not exactly, no.'

'Her sleeping pills!' Lucy clapped her hand over her mouth and looked up at Bea with wide eyes.

Bea said, 'You think she might commit suicide?'

'Oh, don't say that! No, no!' The woman began to rock to and fro. 'Not suicide! Not my dear, dear friend!'

Bea stared at Lucy, and then reached for the landline phone.

'Who are you ringing? The police?' Mrs Emerson could move quickly when she wished. She was on her feet and at Bea's side in a trice. 'The doctor?'

Bea said, 'Oliver. He's nearest. He can check on her.'

Lucy laid a square hand over Bea's, preventing her from completing the number she was calling. She glanced at the clock. 'Not yet. Give her time to… Give her time.'

'Time to commit suicide? Hasn't she the right to speak for herself? Only after that can the doctors decide whether or not she's fit to stand trial.'

Lucy continued to hang on to Bea's hand. 'No, no. You mustn't!'

'You want her to die?'

'Isn't that the best thing that could happen? She wants to go out with dignity. We've got to give her time.'

Bea tried to move the woman's hand and failed. Curse her weakness! That lobster had a lot to answer for. 'Mrs Emerson, when you arrived, you asked me to use my influence with the police to get Carrie a proper hearing. Now you say you don't want her disturbed. What is it you really want?'

'I want the police to know why she's seen fit to end her life so that you can get them to close the case.'

'Nothing I can say would be of interest to the police. I have no first-hand knowledge of events, and I don't think they'd accept my word for it that it was Carrie who brought about three deaths.'

'You refuse to help me? And Carrie at death's door?'

'I see no reason for her to attempt suicide. What I do see is that you have a motive for silencing her. You want her to take the blame for bringing about all those deaths, whereas it was really you who was responsible. Am I right?'

'You think that I… Oh no! How could you!'

'If you're innocent, then prove it by letting me phone the police. Please, take your hand off me.'

Lucy clung on, glancing back at the clock. 'It's too soon. What good would it do to bring her back now, to face months of doctors and tests and spend the rest of her life in a locked ward, in a state of drug-induced dependency? That would be no act of friendship, would it?'

'On the other hand, she might revive enough to accuse you of being a three-times killer?'

'What nonsense! I thought I could rely on you—'

'To do what? Back up your story? Allow Carrie time to die? I'm not in the business of deciding who lives and who dies. Now, please take your hand away so that I can call the police.'

Mrs Emerson glared at the clock. 'You really are the most stupid woman I've ever met. Well, I've tried reason, and you've refused to listen, so you've brought it on yourself—'

Lucy hefted her stick, swinging it up and round as if she were on the golf course. Bea ducked and threw herself sideways…

# TWENTY

'GOTCHA!' THE INSPECTOR wrestled the stick out of Mrs Emerson's hand, even as it whistled past where Bea's head ought to have been.

The woman opened her mouth and screamed.

Bea, sweating, stumbled to the door and held on to it. That was a close call.

The inspector turned Lucy round and thrust her back on to the settee. She gulped and was silent, gazing at them with huge eyes.

He said to Bea, 'I didn't leave when she came.'

'No, I hoped you wouldn't.'

'You left the door open so that I could hear everything she said. And I did. I've already phoned the police to get round to the flats and check on Mrs Kempton.'

'Oliver might still be quickest.' Once more she reached for her landline and this time succeeded in pressing buttons. 'Pick up, Oliver!'

'Try Maggie?'

'No, no. She's out at work.'

Lucy recovered her nerve. She was even smiling. 'You'll be too late. She'll be gone by the time you get there, and I'll be the only one left to tell the tale.'

'Pick up, Oliver!'

Oliver picked up. 'Hello?'

'Oliver, this is an emergency. We're worried about Mrs Kempton. Can you—'

'What's going on? I've just been downstairs to let a

couple of policemen in, but they wouldn't say what for, except that they needed to speak to Mrs Kempton urgently. They can't get any answer at her flat, so I told them to come up here to the penthouse and go down the fire escape at the back. They seem to think something's happened to her. I thought Mrs Emerson might know, and I'm just about to go down to her place to see if she can help.'

Bea said, 'Lucy's here. Get hold of the caretaker. He's got keys to both their flats. Carrie could be in either—and hurry! I think she needs medical help!'

'Too late, too late!' sang Lucy.

The inspector was on his own mobile. 'Yes, break the door down if necessary. Oh, you're on the fire escape? Get in through the kitchen, then. Which floor are you on?… Ah. Good…' He caught Bea's eye. 'One on each floor.'

Lucy laughed. 'If you break down my door, I'll sue you!'

Bea was holding on to her phone. 'Oliver, are you there, still? You're on your way down the fire escape? Good. Lucy says Carrie may have taken some pills… Perhaps you can warn the police…? Ah, they're breaking into the flat now?… And…?' She listened for a while.

Let her phone arm drop.

Spoke to the inspector. 'They've found her. She's dead.'

Lucy laughed. There were tears on her cheeks. 'Oh, my precious little friend. Oh, oh! Now there's no one to tell the tale but me.'

'Oh yes, there is,' said Bea. 'I lied just then. They found her. She's unconscious but still alive. And the paramedics are on their way.'

*Thursday morning*

THE INSPECTOR RANG, EARLY. 'They pumped Mrs Kempton's stomach out. She's very weak, but they think she'll be all right. She wants to talk. I'm going in to see her now. Would you like to meet me there? You know what's been happening better than I and can pick it up if there are any inconsistencies in her statement.'

When Bea got to the hospital, she found that Carrie was in a private room with a policeman sitting outside her door. The inspector got clearance from the nursing staff that it was all right to talk to the old lady for a while and took Bea in with him. Carrie lay back on the bed, looking as frail as old lace—and about the same colour.

The inspector said, 'Mrs Kempton, do you feel well enough to tell us what happened?'

A nod. 'I'll try. Oh dear, how awful this all is.' There were tears in her eyes.

The inspector said, 'You've had a rough time. I'm not going to ask you to make a formal statement now, though I will take some notes. When you're better, you can come into the station and tell us everything.'

She nodded. 'I don't want to see her again. How could she!'

'Let's start at the beginning, with Lavinia's death. How did that come about?'

'I suppose it was my fault, really. Lavinia caught us as we came in. We were both very tired. Lucy went to call the lift but Lavinia got hold of my arm, wanting me to go straight out again and fetch her something from the chemist. I fear I was sharp with her. She threatened me with her stick, and I tried to step back out of reach but she caught me a blow on my shoulder. It hurt! Lucy got hold of the stick and twisted it out of her hand, and Lavinia sort of slid sideways on to the floor and died. There and then, in front of us. I was so shocked. Lucy helped me up to my flat and made me lie down. Then she phoned the police. I would have said something about the stick, but Lucy said not to because it wasn't anybody's fault. She told me to say we'd found her lying on the floor, dead. I agreed, but I wished Lucy hadn't kept Lavinia's stick… She gets dizzy spells, you know. She did have a stick she got from the hospital, but she preferred Lavinia's.'

'Labyrinthitis?'

'I don't know what the name is, but she gets some pills from the doctor for it.'

'That can be checked.'

The freckled hands plucked at the sheet. 'We've been friends for so long… We've had such good times together… I even said she should move in with me when her contract ran out.'

'You have keys to one another's flats?'

'Of course.'

'When did you first suspect Lucy had set the trap for Sir Lucas on the stairs?'

'It wasn't meant for him, but for Lady Ossett. Only, she went out for the evening and he was caught instead. I told Lucy that was very naughty of her, and she promised not to do it again.'

'It was she who poisoned the cat Momi?'

A half smile. 'That cat used to dig up the plants in Lucy's pots. He was a pest. I don't like cats much, either.'

'You must have realized Lady Ossett would be very frightened by the cat's death?'

'Well, yes. But as Lucy said, she deserved it, and there was no great harm done, was there?'

'Did she tell you she'd pushed the caretaker over the edge?'

'No, no. Surely she didn't! She couldn't! Oh, I can't think!' Tears. Real tears.

Bea said, 'Would you like some water, Carrie?' And held the cup while the old lady took a sip or two.

'You're doing so well,' said the inspector. 'Now, if you can just keep going a little longer... Tell us what happened when the caretaker died.'

'I really don't know. We were both up and down the stairs, in and out of the lift, trying to find someone to release poor Harvey. I think I must have been downstairs talking to the young couple on the ground floor when the caretaker fell, but of course we didn't find out about it till Mrs Abbot spotted him. He wasn't a very nice person, but... Oh dear.'

'You asked Lucy about it afterwards?'

Carrie's eyelids flickered. 'I'm sure it must have been an accident.' In other words, she'd suspected it hadn't been but had decided not to confront her friend about it.

'And Harvey's death?'

'Poor Harvey.' Tears welled up. 'He used to love my carrot cake. It was my turn to make a cake for tea, and we usually took some down to him, but that day it was snowing and I had a sore throat, so Lucy went down with a piece for him.'

Bea intervened. 'What did you put in the chocolate biscuits you brought down for us the other day?'

'They weren't mine, dear. They were Lucy's. I'd run out of cocoa powder, so she made them instead. She bakes lovely cakes.' Again tears welled.

'But these biscuits made us ill.'

'Really, dear? I wonder why. She did say they were rather special, but I didn't have any because I was eating up some of her Victoria sponge which she'd made the day before, which wasn't quite fresh but still very pleasant.'

'She warned you not to try the chocolate biscuits?'

'I don't remember. Maybe she did… Oh dear, this is all so terrible!'

The inspector pressed on. 'You must have discussed the matter with your friend and wondered where all these deaths would end.'

A nod. 'We agreed it was just too awful for words, and that it would probably end in tears, but I didn't imagine… Not really… She couldn't! But if she did… Poor Lucy. She seemed so normal, but she must have been suffering so much.'

'She says you tried to commit suicide.'

'Oh no, dear. I would never do that.'

'So why did you swallow all your sleeping pills?'

'I don't have any. Well, only some herbal tablets, but they're harmless. It's true I had been feeling a little run down, the anxiety you know, so many terrible things happening. Lucy brought me some hot chocolate and said I should drink it, and I did…and I never thought, not once, that she'd turn on me. Oh dear, oh dear…'

Carrie closed her eyes and turned her head away. No more questions.

The inspector and Bea left the ward together, leaving a police officer behind to take a formal statement from Mrs Kempton when she was sufficiently recovered.

The inspector said, 'Lucy blames Carrie. Carrie says she really didn't know anything. I have my notes, but even if Carrie recovers sufficiently to give us a proper statement, would it stand up in court? Would it be sufficient to convince the Director of Prosecutions to act? And if not, where's the proof that Lucy is a murderer and ought to be locked up?'

Bea shrugged. 'Lucy tried to kill Carrie with a hot drink laced with sleeping pills—which were not Carrie's.

I expect you can find the doctor's prescription for the
sleeping pills and the treatment for Lucy's labyrinthitis
in her flat. And she did attack me. Thank you for saving
my life, by the way.'

'Think nothing of it. We'll check with Lucy's doctor,
of course, and if he confirms the pills were for her, then
that will help. But, unless we get a confession, we'll have
to go with the attack she made on you, and you'll have to
testify in court. Are you prepared to do that?'

'Yes. But you've arrested Lucy and will keep her in
custody?'

'I have and I will—provided she doesn't produce a
tame solicitor with a silver tongue who can get her out
on bail.'

Bea grinned. 'Not if Sir Lucas is told who caused his
fall down the stairs. I'm sure a word from him might result in a failure of nerve on the part of most solicitors.
He's a powerful man; let's make use of him for once.'

'Hah! A good thought. I'll see that he is informed
straight away. You're looking much better today, Mrs
Abbot. Back to your usual form, I take it? May I give
you a lift back home?'

*Friday evening*

'MY MOTHER IS a cow!' Maggie wept. 'And I feel guilty,
even thinking that!'

Bea put on her most reasonable tone of voice. 'Your
mother is a past master—or mistress, if you prefer it—of
the art of making people feel guilty, but in this case I really
can't see she's got much to complain about. Sir Lucas is giving her the penthouse and a more than comfortable amount
to live on, she's got the Professor dangling after her, and
she's sure to pick up some more admirers on her cruise to

the West Indies in the New Year. Tell her you'll only hamper her style if she keeps asking you to accompany her.'

Maggie stifled a giggle. 'Do you think I dare?'

'Of course you can,' said Oliver, who was frowning over a list he was making. 'What's more important is who we invite to our end-of-year party. I've got Max's list; he keeps adding to it everyday—'

'Forget his list,' said Bea. 'I see no reason to hold a party just so that he can return favours to the important people he knows. Nor, may I add, do I see any point in inviting the directors of Holland and Butcher to celebrate a merger which I'm pretty sure I don't want. I am not, repeat not, going to give a party for business reasons.'

Maggie dried her eyes and blew her nose. 'Can't we have a party just for ourselves? I know we're not proper family, exactly—'

'We are more *proper* family than most I can think of. Our family has more to celebrate than most at this time of the year, so I thought we'd invite lots of people who are not in a position to give a party themselves. I was thinking about CJ, for instance; he's a widower, and lonely now his son has moved out; then there's Piers, my ex, who has no family to speak of unless it's me and Max. Next on the list is you, Oliver. How would you like to invite some of your university friends? Ones who have nowhere else to go in the holidays? They can bring sleeping bags and doss down upstairs in your quarters. Maggie; the same applies to you. Your boyfriend must come, of course. Then who would you like to invite? Old friends or new? Customers who have become friends?'

Maggie gulped. Her eyes were enormous. 'You'll scream, but…could I invite my mother and the Professor? I mean, they probably wouldn't want to come, and if they did come, they'd probably look down on everyone else but... I'd like to give them the chance.'

'Why not?' said Bea. 'I have a couple of old friends who are going to be on their own as well. Let's do the whole thing in slap-up style. There's always chefs and waiters on the agency books who want to work over the holidays; we'll have all the food and drink brought in and served for us, and cleaners to restore the place to normal afterwards. We won't even do the washing up ourselves. We'll have gifts for everyone who comes; nothing too expensive, possibly vouchers from Harrods food hall? We can invite as many people as we like, the only proviso being that we have enough chairs to seat them all. Any other suggestions?'

Oliver said, 'I think Carrie Kempton might find it too much—'

'She's going into sheltered accommodation, poor thing,' said Maggie.

Oliver gave Bea a wicked look. 'How about we invite Carmela Lessbury?'

Bea ironed out a smile. 'Hospitable I may be. Stupid I am not. She'd have Piers and CJ asking if they might call on her in five minutes flat.'

Oliver grinned. 'That's rather uncharitable of you, isn't it?'

'I've been taking lessons from a mistress in the art of being a cow. Carmela gets an invite over my dead body. Besides which, she owes me fifty quid for finding out who put her phone number on the call-girl cards, not to mention the fact that I ruined two perfectly good pairs of boots in the course of duty.'

Oliver's grin widened. 'Wasn't Sir Lucas happy to reimburse you?'

'He sent me a nice cheque by way of a thank you, and

I've seen just the pair of boots I want in Harvey Nicholls. With killer heels. And no, Maggie; he doesn't get an invite, either. And that, my dear ones, is my last word on the subject.'

Maggie giggled. 'Mother Hen is a cow!'

Oliver aimed a blow at her and missed. He was laughing, too.

'Enough!' said Bea, trying to look stern. 'Now, back to work!'

* * * * *